RAY COULDN'T SEE MUCH OF THE DOG ANYWAY, AS IT HAD TAKEN REFUGE IN THE CRAWLSPACE UNDERNEATH SOMEONE'S HOUSE.

He and Nick and the ACO beamed flashlights in at it, but the mutt had its front legs out before it, pinning down whatever it was gnawing on. When they spoke to it, it curled back its lips and growled, defending its prize.

"What's it got?" Nick asked.

"I can't see from this angle," Ray said. "I'm going to the other side, to try to see through that lattice-work."

"Okay."

Neighbors had gathered, and a couple of patrol officers worked on keeping them back. As Ray gingerly settled himself on his stomach and aimed the flashlight under the house, he heard a male voice raised in anxiety, or perhaps anger. "But I'm the one who called the cops in the first place!" Someone else answered in conciliatory tones. Ray couldn't make out the words, but he understood the man's response. "It was human, I'm telling you!"

The dog's ears perked at the shout, and it raised its muzzle. Ray could see just enough of its treasure, lying limply across the dog's right foreleg, to make it out. "It *is* human, Nick."

"Human what?"

"I can't be absolutely sure, but I believe it's a hand."

Original novels in the CSI series:

CSI: Crime Scene Investigation

Double Dealer
Sin City
Cold Burn
Body of Evidence
Grave Matters
Binding Ties
Killing Game
Snake Eyes
In Extremis
Nevada Rose
Headhunter
Brass in Pocket
The Killing Jar
Blood Quantum
Dark Sundays
Skin Deep
Shock Treatment
The Burning Season
Serial (graphic novel)

CSI: Miami

Florida Getaway
Heat Wave
Cult Following
Riptide
Harm for the Holidays: Misgivings
Harm for the Holidays: Heart Attack
Cut & Run
Right to Die

CSI: NY

Dead of Winter
Blood on the Sun
Deluge
Four Walls

CSI:

CRIME SCENE INVESTIGATION™

THE BURNING SEASON
a novel

Jeff Mariotte

Based on the hit CBS series CSI: Crime Scene
Investigation produced by CBS PRODUCTIONS,
a business unit of CBS Broadcasting Inc.

Executive Producers: Jerry Bruckheimer,
Carol Mendelsohn, Anthony E. Zuiker,
Ann Donahue, Naren Shankar, Cynthia Chvatal,
William Petersen, Jonathan Littman

Series created by: Anthony E. Zuiker

POCKET **STAR** BOOKS
New York   London   Toronto   Sydney

Pocket Star Books
A Division of Simon & Schuster, Inc.
1230 Avenue of the Americas
New York, NY 10020

First Pocket Star Books paperback edition July 2011

POCKET STAR BOOKS and colophon are registered trademarks of Simon & Schuster, Inc.

For information about special discounts for bulk purchases, please contact Simon & Schuster Special Sales at 1-866-506-1949 or business@simonandschuster.com.

The Simon & Schuster Speakers Bureau can bring authors to your live event. For more information or to book an event contact the Simon & Schuster Speakers Bureau at 1-866-248-3049 or visit our website at www.simonspeakers.com.

Cover design and illustration by David Stevenson

Manufactured in the United States of America

10 9 8 7 6 5 4 3 2 1

ISBN 978-1-4391-6087-9
ISBN 978-1-4391-6931-5 (ebook)

For Maryelizabeth, with love.
—JM

ACKNOWLEDGMENTS

My greatest thanks to former *CSI* connection Corinne, to current CBS connection Maryann, to web guru Dianne Larson, to editor Ed, and to agent Howard. As usual, anything authentic about the science in this book probably came from the Crime Lab Project or Dr. D. P. Lyle, and anything authentic about animal control from Anita Ridlehoover. Mistakes, if any, are mine alone.

1

"THE POOL!" CAPTAIN Marc Fontaine shouted. He jabbed his gloved index finger toward it, underscoring his point.

His crew understood his meaning, and responded with a minimum of delay. Chris, Jackie, Alonso, Cherie, and Vaughn—the Engine 42 crew—were professionals through and through, and watching them work always swelled his chest a little. Pride was supposed to be one of the deadly sins? He didn't go along with that. Pride was what got a day's work done, and when lives and property were on the line, there was not a thing wrong with it.

Cherie and Chris hauled the portable pump from the truck through the pool gate. The pump weighed almost two hundred pounds, and its twin-cylinder, 27-horsepower engine would push out 550 gallons a minute. The others were already laying hose, so it would be in place as soon as the engine cranked up.

The early autumn day had been hot, topping the

112 mark down in the city, Fontaine had heard. All that concrete and steel trapped the heat, radiating it out through the day and into the night and driving the readings up. Even here on Mt. Charleston, temperatures had reached the low nineties. The last rain had been more than a month ago, when summer's monsoon storms gave up the fight. And it had been a good year for the monsoon, which meant lots of fresh growth that had spent the last several weeks drying out. Optimal conditions for a big blaze, and now they had one. Thick, bitter smoke clogged the air.

There were eight other engines scattered throughout the mountain neighborhoods, and helicopters chattering overhead. Fontaine's crew would make its stand on a cul-de-sac, surrounded by expensive homes. Those homes didn't have big backyards, because they were on a ridge, and on three sides the drop-off was sudden, the ground falling away into pine-blanketed canyons. So far the fire was concentrated to the west, and their mission was to keep it there.

Fontaine wanted to light a backfire here, to deprive the main fire of fuel so it wouldn't run up the canyon, wouldn't jump to these houses. But between the time he had been assigned the task and when the truck had reached its destination—slowed in its progress by fallen trees and by the vehicles of the few residents who had been slow in obeying the evacuation order—the fire had already started up that flank. A backfire was out of the question now; they needed to focus on defending homes.

As long as it stayed to the west, they could handle it. If it ran around the northern rim and came at them from two sides, or three?

Then it would be time to retreat. And fast.

Trouble with a cul-de-sac was, there was only one way out.

Fontaine had been a wildland firefighter for most of the last two decades. He had seen it all; had seen the changes in the way people thought about fire, the way crews attacked it. He'd survived being trapped for three days in the midst of one of the west's biggest conflagrations, armed only with his Pulaski tool and pure dumb luck. He had seen more and more houses, even huge overpriced McMansions, raised in places like this: the wildland-urban interface. People built first, and only afterward thought about what they would do in the event of a fire. Most of them, if asked, would have said, "Let the fire department put it out." Words to that effect, anyway. Some swore they would defend their property with garden hoses.

Standard garden hoses, they would find, only moved about four to seven gallons a minute. And they melted. It didn't take long for even the most courageous of them to realize they had made a big mistake.

Fontaine had a house on the mountain, too, where he lived with his wife, Marla. But he kept his property clean and safe, surrounded by a hundred feet of defensible space, mostly bare earth and a few scattered, heavily watered plants. He had visited this neighborhood at least a dozen times, trying to persuade the owners of the danger, of the need for reasonable precautions. So many of them didn't want to spoil the view, they said. They had moved up here to be among the trees. That was fine, Fontaine thought, as long as you made sure those trees didn't ignite your shake roof.

There was a certain beauty to fire in wild places. Fontaine had watched it from a hillside during the night, in the brief time between when he had knocked off for the day and the few hours he'd slumbered uneasily under a tarp. Darkness consumed the mountain, as usual, but in that darkness were scattered pools of yellow-red flame throwing off silver smoke. From a distance, he could almost view them as Japanese lanterns shining through a dense fog, except he knew what they were doing to the forest and what they threatened to do to those who lived there.

But that was last night. Now, above the racket of the helicopters and the fire's own crackle and roar, Fontaine heard the rumble of the pump, the shouts of his crew. He allowed himself a smile. The fire was moving up the western slope, but it wasn't a crown fire. Not yet. It was moving at ground level, and that slowed it down a bit. They had made it here in time.

He was more intimate with fire than with any human being, with the possible exception of Marla. He had lived with it for thirty years, and with Marla for only twenty-four. He had refused to have children with her, because life with fire had taught him that death waited behind every closed door, on the far side of every wall. The only thing predictable about fire was its willfulness, its ability to thwart expectation.

You couldn't trust fire, and that was a larger life lesson he had taken to heart. He trusted Marla, and not a hell of a lot else.

It was instinct, he supposed, that told him when the prevailing breeze shifted. He couldn't feel the slight change in its direction, not in his bulky gear, with the fire below generating its own wind. But he knew it, just the same. The change wasn't dramatic, but it was enough. Vaughn shouted, and Fontaine saw a firebrand wafting past a house: a small section of shrub, flames tonguing the air around it, trailing sparks, brilliant reds and yellows against the smoky gray sky.

It came from the north.

Fontaine ran that way. The fire wasn't supposed to be there yet. They were supposed to stop it before it got there. That was the plan.

Subject to change.

Fire created its own air currents. A big fire generated powerful ones. This one had blown sparks, firebrands, or both, around the northern point while they had been en route, or while they'd been standing here preparing to attack the west. From the north, it had continued moving east.

Fontaine stood at the point—he was an island, and fire was the sea.

"Get out!" he screamed into the radio. "We're surrounded! Go! Go!"

His crew reacted at once, wasting not a second, not a breath.

They dropped hoses, scrambled for the truck. Alonso was at the driver's door when the fire hit, a wave of it, engulfing them. Fontaine could hear his anguished cry, though his earpiece and through the air. He was that close.

He lived just long enough to shed a tear for his crew members. That single tear sizzled, boiled, burned.

Marc Fontaine never felt it.

2

"Seriously? A dog?"

"That's what it says." Ray Langston was riding shotgun, Nick Stokes driving. They had come straight from another scene, a relatively straightforward domestic homicide, if that could ever be said about a situation in which a wife had opened three holes in her husband with a .22. On their way back to the Crime Lab, they had received text messages. Ray had read his out loud.

"We're going to meet a dog. A live dog?"

"It says an animal control officer will meet us there. So I'm assuming it's alive." Ray chuckled. "You know as much as I do, Nick."

Nick made a right at the next corner. They were closer to the scene—the dog scene—than they were to the lab, but not by much. "Yeah, but . . . a dog."

"Apparently the dog is a crime scene."

"That had better be one heck of a crime," Nick said. "Or one heck of a dog."

* * *

The dog, it turned out, was a mutt. Brown and white with splotches of black, maybe part shepherd, part Labrador, part something else. Ray couldn't see much of it anyway, as it had taken refuge in the crawlspace underneath someone's house. He and Nick and the ACO beamed flashlights in at it, but the mutt had its front legs out before it, pinning down whatever it was gnawing on. When they spoke to it, it curled back its lips and growled, defending its prize.

"What's it got?" Nick asked.

"I can't see from this angle," Ray said. "I'm going to the other side, to try to see through that lattice-work."

"Okay."

Neighbors had gathered, and a couple of patrol officers worked on keeping them back. As Ray gingerly settled himself on his stomach and aimed the flashlight under the house, he heard a male voice raised in anxiety, or perhaps anger. "But I'm the one who called the cops in the first place!" Someone else answered in conciliatory tones. Ray couldn't make out the words, but he understood the man's response. "It was human, I'm telling you!"

The dog's ears perked at the shout, and it raised its muzzle. Ray could see just enough of its treasure, lying limply across the dog's right foreleg, to make it out. "It *is* human, Nick."

"Human what?"

"I can't be absolutely sure, but I believe it's a hand."

"A hand?"

"That's how it looks from here."

"Okay," Nick said. "Who owns this dog?"

"Dog lives here," the ACO said. He jerked a thumb toward the gathered onlookers. "Owner's over there. That woman in the green."

Ray looked at the audience. "Officer, please bring the homeowner here."

"What about me?" a man called. "I'm the one who called you guys."

"And we appreciate that, sir. But please stay right where you are."

One of the officers, a slender young woman with a brown ponytail, led the homeowner under the hastily erected barrier of yellow tape. "That's your dog?" Ray asked her.

She nodded grimly. "That's Booger. Booger, you're a bad boy!"

"Do you know where he got that hand?"

"I have no earthly idea."

"Unless you can get him to come out, we're going to have to tranquilize him." Ray couldn't bring himself to use the dog's name.

"I was trying, before everybody got here. Then when the sirens came, and all the people, he went even farther back. He won't come."

"Do you want to try again, just in case?"

She bent down in front of the opening to the crawlspace. "Come here, Booger! Here, boy! Momma has a treat!"

Booger eyed her and snarled. Maybe he knew she didn't really have a treat.

"It's no use," the woman said. "He's never been very well trained."

Ray addressed the ACO. "Can you knock him out?"

"Of course."

"It won't hurt him, will it?"

"He might have a headache when he wakes up," the ACO said. "If dogs get headaches. Won't kill him is all I know."

"You might not want to watch," Ray suggested.

"My ex bought the damn dog in the first place," the woman said. "Then left him here when he moved in with some bimbo. You can do whatever you want to him."

"We don't want to hurt him."

She offered a slight shrug.

"Do it," Ray said.

"Coming up," the ACO said. He hustled over to his truck. When he returned, he was snapping the sections of a long pole into place. A needle gleamed on the end. "You know the old joke? Wouldn't touch him with a ten-foot pole?"

"I've heard it," Ray said.

The ACO brandished his fully extended pole. "I get paid to do that." He laughed at his own joke as he fitted a syringe into the pole's tip. "Ten-foot pole," he said, laughing again.

It wasn't that funny, but Ray didn't say anything. They needed the man, and his ten-foot pole.

The ACO went to where Ray had been, and extended the pole through the latticework. The dog snapped at the pole, but the man jabbed the needle into its haunch. Once the pole was withdrawn, Booger whimpered a little, then turned his attention back to his gnawing. A few minutes passed, and the dog relaxed, finally going limp. Ray could hear it snoring. "I'll bring him out," the ACO said. He was a hefty guy. Although the day's heat had lessened after the sun set, he had sweat running out of his hair and soaking his collar. Ray hoped he could fit in the crawlspace.

The man broke down his pole, then got onto his belly and slithered under the house. "So much for that scene," Nick said softly, standing beside Ray. "If he's dropped bits of tissue or blood under there . . ."

"You're right," Ray said. He watched the ACO close in on the dog. He couldn't get to his knees under there, couldn't lift the slumbering animal, so he settled for grabbing its collar and one upper leg and backing out the way he had gone in, dragging Booger behind him. Sweat rolled off the man's forehead.

They would still collect any bits of the hand they found under there, and soil samples, but he thought it was all too contaminated to be much good.

When the ACO came out, he tenderly lifted the dog and held it out toward the woman. "He'll be okay in a little while," he said.

She kept her hands by her sides. "Put it on the porch."

"Lady loves that dog," Nick whispered.

"No wonder the husband left." Ray lowered himself gingerly to one knee. "Guess I'll get the hand."

"I'll get it," Nick said quickly. He pointed toward Ray's cane with his chin, probably unconsciously. The whole team had been good about not reminding Ray of the stab wounds he had suffered at Nate Haskell's hands, the loss of a kidney, but he knew nonetheless that none of them had forgotten. The truth was, though he was mostly recovered, they did still hurt all the time. He had winced, getting down on his belly to look at the dog, and again getting up. He was glad to let Nick fetch the hand.

"Thanks," he said.

"No problem."

Nick took his field kit under the house with him, although it was awkward going. He was thinner and fitter than the ACO, but there still wasn't a lot of room. Ray, on hands and knees, tried to help by beaming his flashlight where Nick needed it.

Nick took forceps from his kit, and small evidence bags, and plucked what Ray could only guess were bits of shredded skin from the ground. Finally, he reached the hand, which he lifted with a piece of sterile paper and placed into a paper bag. Most people, Ray thought, would have put it in plastic—that had been his inclination, when he had started this job. But plastic trapped moisture, and a moist body part in an airtight bag was a perfect cauldron for growing all sorts of bacteria. Paper would breathe.

When Nick emerged, sweating and filthy, Ray changed places with him and went back under, though not nearly as far and wincing all the way, for some soil samples. As he had told Nick, he didn't believe this was the original scene—the dog had initially been spotted carrying the hand more than a block away. He had only brought it here because this was home, and he knew he could gnaw in peace under the house. They needed samples, regardless.

By the time Ray came out, pain lancing from his ribs and back, Nick had cleaned up as much as he could. He still held the bagged hand. "How does it look?" Ray asked.

"It's pretty much a mess. That mutt really mangled it. Of course, we don't know what shape it was in to begin with."

"True."

"So much epidermis is gone, I can't even make out the skin color."

"Can you tell if its separation was natural or forced?"

"You mean, did someone cut it off? Have to check that at the lab, I didn't take that close a look."

"Well, I didn't see any other body parts in there. It's going to be hard to get much off it, in the condition you describe. There might not even be any ridge impressions left."

"Didn't see any."

"And the way that dog was slavering all over it, any DNA we get from the tissue will be suspect. Maybe Doc Robbins will be able to come up with something for us to test."

"He'll love having a severed hand to work with."

"I'm sure."

"You know what's worse?" Nick asked.

"What?"

"He might be getting used to them."

That fact had slipped Ray's mind. The whole scenario, with the dog under the house, had driven it from his thoughts. And, in his defense, he'd had a lot on his mind recently.

But Nick was right. Over the past few months,

four other severed hands had shown up on the streets of Las Vegas. They weren't exactly becoming commonplace, but they were no longer as rare as Ray would have liked.

"Let's get out of here," Nick said. "If he doesn't want to deal with it, I'm sure someone will lend him a hand."

Ray gave him a groan. "That was awful, Nick. I'd never have fingered you for a punster."

Nick shook his head. "You win, Ray. Let's go. If you promise not to make any more hand jokes, I'll even let you drive."

3

SHUTTING DOWN A major thoroughfare was always a problem. There was pressure from the mayor and police leadership to do the job fast and reopen the road. Traffic snarled around the closure, while nearby roads got more use than they could accommodate.

The good thing about this instance was that it was after midnight. But Las Vegas was truly a city that never slept. Even when it came to automobile traffic, the time showing on the clock was not the only consideration, or even the primary one.

The fact was, a crime scene on a city street took far longer to process than one nicely confined inside four walls. And Catherine Willows wouldn't allow her people to be rushed. Rushing meant missing things, and the job of crime scene investigation required missing as little as humanly possible.

The street scene was a complicated one, made even more so by the nature of this particular crime.

Catherine was appreciative that there were some cops who understood that, and who made a point of siding with the Crime Lab against those who argued in favor of a quick resolution. One of those was Captain Jim Brass, whose resemblance to a bulldog had more to do with his persistence and demeanor than his physical appearance. Catherine found him standing with some other detectives, the mayor, and other city officials, and people she didn't recognize, outside the trailer the LVPD had set up as a command post for the scene.

"Talk to me, Jim," she said. "What've we got here? I mean, I know it's a disaster, that goes without saying."

"Glad you're here, Catherine," Brass said. He led her away from the clutch of people and toward the mess on the street. At each end, onlookers and media had been sealed out by yellow crime scene tape and rows of uniformed cops.

"I brought Sara and Greg. Earl's meeting us here. It's been a quiet night, so far."

"Good thing. We'll need everyone, especially Earl."

"That's what I figured." Earl was a longtime explosives tech. He was called crusty by his friends—antisocial by the less generously inclined—but he knew his way around a bombing site.

"Ray and Nick are on their way to the lab with evidence in a different case, but they'll join us if they can."

"We can use the extra help. Here's the scoop, Catherine. You know who Dennis Daniels is."

Who didn't? Daniels was one of Nevada's wealthiest media moguls, a man who had turned a string of regional newspapers into a mini-empire that included TV stations and DCN, a twenty-four-hour cable news organization—not one that threatened the big three, but one that had made its owner a very wealthy individual. "Of course. Daniels Cable News—he made sure his name comes first in the title. Is he one of the victims?"

Brass nodded. "Story is he's considering running for governor. He was returning to his office from what's been described as a fundraising event at a private home in Lake Las Vegas. More like pre-fundraising, getting face time with some of the local movers and shakers who might finance him, if he decides to jump in. His entourage was in two vehicles." Brass pointed to the two, both SUVs—except from here they looked like one oddly shaped mass, some sort of modern sculpture, asymmetric and resisting easy interpretation. "He's already got the skeleton of a campaign staff in place, has some of the top people in Nevada politics locked up. Daniels and his campaign manager, Connie Pruitt, were in the Escalade. She's the only political pro in this group—the others work for his media organization. The driver was a staffer named Bryan Donavan. Daniels has been traveling with a bodyguard, Garrett Kovash, and he was in front with Donavan."

"I've heard of Kovash," Catherine said.

"Bodyguard to the stars. The Escalade was in front, and Maureen Cunningham, his adminstrative assistant, followed in that Ford Escape hybrid, driven by DCN manager of operations, Eldon Wohl." Brass swept his arm around in the general direction of the freeway. "They exited I-15 at Charleston, then made the left on Las Vegas Boulevard, headed toward the downtown headquarters, where everyone but Donavan and Wohl had left their private cars.

"Just before they reached Gass Ave., a roadside bomb exploded."

"A roadside bomb? Is this Las Vegas, or Baghdad?" Catherine asked.

"Maybe a desert is a desert is a desert," Brass said. "Anyway, the blast picked the Escalade up and dropped it down on the driver's side, which happened to be the side Daniels was sitting on. Wohl tried to brake, but his Escape plowed into the Escalade."

With his description, Catherine got a better sense of how the two black SUVs lined up, or didn't. She saw the Escalade on its side. The Escape had slammed into it at an angle. Probably Wohl had stomped on the brake and the vehicle had fishtailed before hitting the Escalade. The impact had shoved both vehicles toward the far side of the road, where traffic flowed basically southwest.

The vehicles would be difficult to process, all twisted steel and broken glass, no doubt full of blood and other fluids. But they weren't the only problem, and maybe not the worst. The explosion had shattered the windows, and some of the street's pavement was mangled, debris had flown everywhere.

"Injuries?" she asked.

"Only Kovash walked away under his own power," Brass said. "But everybody's walking away."

"That's something."

"Yeah. Not going to make your job much easier, though. And paramedics had to use the Jaws of Life to open the Escalade."

"Getting the injured out always takes precedence." She believed that was the only way it could be. Employing the Jaws of Life, however, meant more debris, more contamination of the crime scene. As it was, paramedics would have been in a hurry to get to the victims, so they wouldn't have been worried about compromising the evidence. They could track blood from one place, where it had been spilled, into another, where it hadn't, throwing off the process of analysis. Same with other DNA evidence, even trace evidence, the dirt that got on their shoes, the plant material that clung to their pants legs. Analyzing a crime scene was like putting together a complex puzzle; every piece put into place affected those around it. When someone came through and scrambled the pieces, it got even more complicated.

Being a busy public street, Las Vegas Boulevard and the sidewalks flanking it were depositories of all manner of objects. Wads of gum, and gum wrappers. Cigarette butts, and wrappers. Candy wrappers. Beer and soda bottles. Plastic grocery bags. Plastic trash bags, empty and full. Used condoms. Oil stains. Bloodstains. Tire marks. Shredded tire. Torn newspaper. Various nails, screws, bolts, nuts, tacks. One half of a pair of pliers. The list was virtually endless.

And the investigators couldn't know, until they hauled it all in and checked it out, what was important and what wasn't. There was no way to know at a glance that this cigarette butt held the bomber's DNA, while that one had been tossed aside by a tourist from Tennessee without so much as an outstanding parking ticket. That lamppost might hold the bomber's fingerprints, or that newspaper box, or that piece of a Milky Way bar. It all had to be picked up, dusted, sprayed, and otherwise examined.

If an average crime scene was like a puzzle, then a scene like this was like putting together the world's hardest puzzle without a box. Only by figuring out how the pieces went together could you see the final picture.

"Is there CCTV?" she asked. Las Vegas had more closed-circuit video cameras per capita than any other city in the country.

"There's a camera at the pawn shop over there," Brass said. "There's one at the signal, on Gass. I haven't seen the footage yet, but I imagine we'll be able to see the bomb go off."

"With luck, we'll see the bomber."

"We'll need a lot of luck, so keep your rabbit's foot handy. I don't need to tell you, Catherine, there's a lot of heat on this already. Daniels is rich and powerful. And he's got a political agenda, which he makes sure DCN represents at every opportunity. If he runs, it'll be as an independent, which means he pisses off people on both sides. But he brings a lot of attention to Nevada, which means the governor and both senators are going to be paying attention, not to mention the mayor and every media organization in the state—much as they'd like to pretend he doesn't exist."

"I had to wade through them to get here."

"I know this is a tricky scene. I've got your back. You tell me what you need, what we can provide, and you'll get it, even if I have to wash the sheriff's car for a year."

"I'll try to make sure that doesn't happen, Jim," Catherine said. "And I appreciate the offer. You're right, it's going to be a big one. I hope Ray and Nick get here in a hurry. In the meantime, I think we'd better get started."

"Keep me in the loop," Brass said. He tossed her a smile and walked away, back toward the suits gathered around the command post. Catherine caught Sara Sidle's attention and nodded toward the job ahead of them.

"Here he is," the mayor said as Brass approached the group. He beckoned Brass over to the clutch of people around him, which included the Clark County sheriff, a slender young brunette wearing jeans and a worn WLVU sweatshirt, and an athletic blond man in a casual shirt and dark pants. Garrett Kovash stood slightly to the woman's left. He was tall and movie-star handsome, his teeth polished and capped to perfection, his dark brown hair tousled just so—must have been hard, Brass thought, to come out of the accident that way. His clothes were torn and stained but there might have been a Teflon shield on his skin, for all the effects he showed. He could have broken concrete blocks with his jaw. "Captain Jim Brass, this is Joanna Daniels, Dennis's wife."

"Pleased to meet you," Brass said, extending a

hand. She looked at it for a good ten seconds before she shook it. Her eyes were rimmed with red, her nose chapped. "I'm sorry for the circumstances."

"Me too, but they tell me he'll be okay. He's very strong."

"If he can survive the TV business, he must be."

"And this," the mayor said, waving Brass's attention toward the blond man, "is Brett Cunningham. His wife, Maureen, was in the car following Dennis."

The man thrust his hand forward aggressively. He was in his late thirties, Brass estimated, and although he had not been crying, he was tense; a vein in his jaw throbbed like a tiny snake swallowing its prey. "Daniels's administrative assistant," Brass said. "Although from what I've heard, she's much more than that . . . pretty much runs his life, according to the stories. Pleasure."

The man didn't speak, just gave Brass a quick shake and a quicker nod.

"You know Mr. Kovash, I think?"

"We've met." Brass held his hand out toward the big man, who took it in a merciless grip. "Garrett."

"Glad to see you on this, Jim. It's terrible."

"It is," Brass agreed. "What about the other victims? Can I get contact information from someone, so I can make the notifications?"

"Donavan, who was driving Daniels's vehicle, is single, as is Eldon Wohl," Kovash said. "Connie Pruitt is married, but she and her husband live in Maine. I'm sure I can get you his number."

"Good," Brass said. "Thanks, Garrett."

The mayor directed his attention toward Joanna Daniels. "Jim will be heading up the investigation.

You couldn't ask for better. He's a cop's cop, through and through."

"I'm not sure if that's a compliment or a curse," Brass said. "But trust me, we will spare no effort getting to the bottom of this. The crime scene folks are already on it, and they're the best we've got. They'll analyze the video, see if the perpetrator left behind any evidence, and—"

"There's video?" Brett Cunningham asked.

"There are a couple of locations on the block with cameras that are pointed toward the street. If he's on the video, that'll be a big help, but it's not absolutely necessary. Every criminal leaves traces of himself— or herself, as the case may be—at the scene."

"You mean like DNA?" Cunningham asked.

"DNA, fingerprints, footprints, tiny flakes of skin. It could be almost anything. We've convicted people on the basis of pollen trapped in a pants cuff."

"Didn't put O.J. away."

"That was more a matter of the trial than the evidence," Brass said. He didn't know which was worse—people who expected CSIs to be magicians, or those who assumed, mostly on the basis of that single case, that it was all an act, an illusion sold to feeble-minded juries but not scientifically sound.

The truth, he thought, was that it fell somewhere in the middle. Not every case could be closed with crime scene evidence, and sometimes the science was open to interpretation and debate. Other times, it was a lock, and no matter how defense attorneys tried to tear it down, it carried the day through the sheer accumulation of incontrovertible fact.

He turned toward Mrs. Daniels. "Can you think of

anyone who might want to attack your husband in this way? I know every wealthy man has enemies, and those who dabble in the political world pick up even more, but they usually aren't the kind who resort to violence. Has he received any threats?"

"All the time," she replied. "More lately."

"Are you kidding?" Brett Cunningham grabbed Brass's arm. The detective shook his hand off, casually, without seeming to acknowledge the action. "All those protesters outside his office every day? I've been worried about Maureen for weeks. And Dennis, of course."

"In our experience, the ones carrying picket signs aren't usually the ones who commit violent acts," Brass said. "If there have been threatening letters or e-mails to your home, Mrs. Daniels, I'd like to see them, please. And phone calls, if you've saved them."

"Yes, of course."

"Garrett, same thing for his office."

"You got it, Jim."

"Do you have any other ideas, Mrs. Daniels? Anyone you know of who has it in for your husband?"

"I wouldn't have any idea. I was able to talk to Dennis, while they were putting him in the ambulance. He was conscious, so I asked him if he knew who would do such a thing. He said he didn't."

"It's a terrible thing, for both of you, your families, and the other victims. Rest assured, we'll do everything we can to find the bomber, and fast."

"And you'll keep us posted on your progress?" Brett asked.

"To the extent that's reasonable. Our main consideration has to be what's best for the investigation, as I'm sure you understand. When it's practical to be in touch with you, without diverting resources from that effort, then of course we'll do so."

"That's the best we could hope for," Joanna said. "Thank you for your effort, Captain Brass."

"You can thank me," Brass said, "after we catch him."

4

GREG HAD ALWAYS liked working with Sara. In earlier days, he'd had an unabashed crush on her. That had faded as he got to know her better—not that he thought any less of her, but their friendship had deepened and matured in a different direction. He had been happy for her when she married Gil Grissom. He was also glad she had returned to Las Vegas to work with her comrades at the crime lab while Grissom taught in Paris.

She was on her hands and knees, wearing coveralls, booties and a surgical mask, marking the location of every object she found that might conceivably have some bearing on the case. Greg wore a similar outfit, but he was still involved with the preliminary task of photographing the overall scene: the street, place where the bomb had cratered street and buckled sidewalk, the SUVs joined together by the force of impact. He had already made a couple of preliminary sketches; his photos would fill in the details.

When he finished shooting the broader scene, he moved in closer on the items Sara was marking. Among the usual urban detritus were things that seemed more pertinent to their specific task—bits of twisted aluminum, short lengths of copper wire, a chunk of sharp-edged plastic. These might have been bomb components, and Greg moved in close with the digital camera, making sure to compose the shots with Sara's numbered cards in them, so they would fit into the overall picture he was creating of the scene. They also helped represent the scale of the objects.

"Whoa, Greg, careful," Sara said. He moved the camera away from his face and saw that he had almost stepped on her hand, as she placed a numbered card next to a scrap of shredded fabric.

"Sorry."

"You're shooting digital, right?"

"Yes."

"So I guess that whole issue with the admissibility of digital photos got resolved while I was away?"

"For the most part, yeah. It's still on a state-by-state basis, but most courts will allow them. There might have to be testimony stating that they accurately reflect conditions at the scene, but there's plenty of metadata associated with a digital photo that can show it hasn't been tampered with."

"And photographs on film can be retouched, as well," Sara said. "Makes sense to me."

"Especially on a scene like this, when we're under the gun to release it in a hurry so traffic can flow."

Sara had moved on to a chunk of rubber, probably from one of the vehicle tires. "It's a real quandary for them, isn't it?" She shifted her gaze to the command posts. "They want the street opened *now*, but they also want us to do our best work."

"Can't have both."

"And it bugs me that there's so much pressure on us to do everything right, when the victim is rich or politically connected. Like we don't always do our best, no matter who's involved."

Greg scribbled a note in his photography log, then tucked the notebook into his pocket and went to one knee to shoot the fabric scrap Sara had just marked. Every exposure had to be documented for later. "I guess that's why we do what we do, and they don't. In the media game you have to be concerned about how things look. We have to stay above all that."

"Above it, or under its boot heel," Sara said. "Hard to be sure which."

"There's no such thing as doing too good a job," Catherine said, joining them. "Or having too much documentary evidence. Keep that camera busy."

"I'm getting it all," Greg assured her.

"Good. Don't worry about the politics of this, either of you. Brass has our backs on this one. We'll have all the time we need."

"That's good to hear," Sara said.

Catherine pointed to the chunk of plastic. "Have you photographed this, Greg?"

"Yep."

She squatted beside it, picked it up, and turned it over in her gloved fingers. "Looks like it might be part of an electronic component. There's a tiny bit of a threaded hole here, where a screw fit in."

"Part of the bomb?" Greg asked. "That's what I thought when I saw it."

"Could be."

"Let me take a look," Earl said. He had been on hands and knees, picking up bits of detritus with tweezers and turning them this way and that, but when he'd heard the word bomb, his response was instantaneous. He gave a loud grunt as he heaved his considerable bulk to an upright position. He was wearing a blue Oxford shirt with his usual bow tie, this one adorned with multicolored polka dots. The tight curls of his once coppery hair had mostly gone silver, creating the impression that the wires that he dealt with in his professional life had somehow affected his physical appearance. "I think you're right, Cath," he said when he examined the object. "Most likely part of the detonator."

"You think it was detonated remotely?" Greg asked.

"Looks like an IED, an improvised explosive device. They're not everyday things here in Las Vegas, but in Iraq and Afghanistan they're the biggest threat coalition forces encounter. They use various methods to defeat them—jammers that block the detonating radio signals, heat sources on long poles to set off those that are heat sensitive before vehicles reach them, that sort of thing. But even with all that effort and technology, they're still damn destructive."

Jim Brass ambled up to the group, hands in his pockets. "Does this look like the same sort of thing to you, Earl?"

"I haven't found much of it yet, but at a glance, yeah."

Catherine took the bit of plastic from Earl and set it back down, being careful, Greg noted, to place it in exactly the same way it had been when she picked it up, even though it had already been recorded. "What are you saying, Jim, you think this is terrorism?"

"It's almost certainly terrorism, in the sense that terrorism is the use of violence to achieve a political end. I'm not saying I think it's foreign terrorism, though. It could just as easily be a veteran, back from one of those combat zones, who learned about IEDs there."

"I don't like to think about vets doing something like that," Greg said.

"I don't either. But at this point, our job is to consider every possibility. That's all I'm saying. There are veterans involved in those protests outside the DCN building. They're protesting Daniels's support for a funding bill they say will raise taxes. It's not the kind of issue that's likely to antagonize fundamentalist Islamic jihadists, but it riles a certain segment of our own population."

"I agree," Catherine said.

"You think those demonstrators are involved?" Earl asked.

Catherine was engrossed in studying what looked like a curved section of aluminum pipe. "Let's just say that given some of the things they were saying, I was afraid the situation might escalate."

"Like those signs showing Daniels in a hangman's noose?" Brass asked. "You think that's a giveaway?"

"I think it's not my job to guess," Catherine said.

"Fair enough."

Greg moved the camera away from his eyes. A uniformed cop had wandered over toward where they were working, and he was afraid the man might step on something important. They were taught not to, but in the moment they often forgot. "Excuse me, officer," Greg said. "You need to keep out of this area for now."

Brass turned to the new arrival, a pudgy man with a ruddy face and short coppery hair. His shirt-tails seemed to resist any attempt to keep them tucked, and he had a rumpled look about him that suggested it was his usual state. "Greg's right, Benny," Brass said. "Go keep those reporters on the far side of the yellow tape."

"Right, captain," Benny said. He halted in his tracks, turned, and wandered away.

When the cop was gone, Catherine faced her co-workers, chagrin evident on her face. "Do you think he heard us?"

"I wouldn't worry too much about it," Brass assured her. "Benny's not the world's greatest cop, but he's okay."

"I just don't like to be caught speculating about a crime. My job is to find the facts, not guess about them."

"I know that. Don't worry, Cath."

Catherine took Brass's advice, and tried not to worry. By the time she got a call from Undersheriff Conrad Ecklie, ordering her back to the lab, she had mostly forgotten the incident. Conrad was sketchy about why he wanted her, though, and that drew her concerns back to the surface. Nick and Ray had arrived and were pitching in at the scene, so she left the effort under Nick's command. Driving over, she tried to run through the conversation with Ecklie in her mind, hoping to anticipate his questions so she could provide the right answers. In the long run, though, she knew she had made a mistake, and whatever punishment was handed out to her, she would have to accept.

To her surprise, Ecklie didn't mention her comment. When she walked into his office, expecting a dressing down, he met her with a big smile and an expansive gesture, indicating another man in the room. She didn't recognize the visitor; he was a Latino with salt-and-pepper hair, a trim mustache, and a solid build. His suit and shoes probably cost as much as a small car.

"Catherine, this is Juan Castillo, from the Nevada AG's office. Juan, this is Catherine Willows, night shift supervisor at the Las Vegas Crime Lab."

Castillo rose from his chair and offered his hand. Catherine took it, and he gave her a firm, steady handshake. "It's an honor to meet you, Ms. Willows," he said.

"Thanks, I guess." She was taken aback. "It's a little late at night for the attorney general's office, isn't it? I thought you guys kept daytime hours."

"We work around the clock, just as you do," Castillo said. "And when Undersheriff Ecklie told me about your people, I knew I had to adjust my schedule to fit yours."

This was not at all what she'd been expecting, and so far her confusion hadn't been cleared up. "Conrad, can I ask what this is about?"

Ecklie sat behind his desk, templing his fingers. "Juan can fill you in."

"This is about a homicide investigation," Castillo said.

"That's kind of what we do."

"I'm aware of that, certainly. This particular one is a bit outside the norm, even for you, I'm afraid."

"In what way?"

"You might have heard about the fire on Mt. Charleston," Castillo said.

"A little. It's been all over the news for a couple of days."

"Yes. It's a big fire, a terrible tragedy. Seventeen homes have been lost so far, and more are in immediate peril. By the time it's controlled, property damage will be well into the millions. Double digits, I'm sure. That, however, is not the worst of it."

"You did mention homicide."

"Indeed. I'm afraid six firefighters perished when the wind shifted suddenly, surrounding them and their engine."

"So they were killed by the fire."

He handed her a manila folder. What she saw inside shocked her, and she wasn't easily shocked anymore. The folder contained photographs of the dead firefighters: their protective clothing scorched, several of their bodies curled in the pugilistic position, the boxer's pose, hands in front of their faces as if defensively, backs bent forward almost double, flesh blackened and blistered. The photos were awful, and she closed the file again after a quick study. "This tells me that they were burned, but not that they were alive before the fire. I'd have to know more."

"Of course we'll have full autopsies performed," Castillo said. "But the team was in radio contact until shortly before the incident. We have no reason to doubt that the fire was the cause of deaths. But the manner of death is what we're talking about here."

Distinguishing between cause and manner began to clue Catherine in. The mechanism of death involved what physiological changes in the body led a person from the state of being alive to the state of being dead. The cause of death was what the immediate precipitator of those changes was, in this case, the fire. But the manner of death took a longer view, involving why the fire started. "You think it was arson?"

"Our investigation is ongoing, obviously. The fire is only forty percent contained, at this point. But yes, the Forest Service's initial investigation points to the fire having been intentionally set."

"The Forest Service is involved. So it's a federal case?"

"Much of the fire has burned public lands. The place we believe the fire started, though, is on state land. Nevada wants to prosecute this case to the fullest extent of the law."

"Meaning what, exactly?"

"Meaning the attorney general wants to find out who started the fire, and to charge that individual with the homicides of the six firefighters. And I want to make sure the case is airtight, because making that case is going to involve a tough courtroom fight."

"No doubt. Has that been done before?"

"Several states are prosecuting these cases more rigorously than they used to, Catherine," Ecklie said.

"Undersheriff Ecklie is correct," Castillo added. "A California man was sentenced to death for starting a fire that killed firefighters. He's still appealing the sentence, but a judgment like that sends a clear signal that arson will not be tolerated. In the past, people who have set wildland fires have walked away with minor sentences, three years, seven years—even when those fires burned hundreds of thousands of acres, destroyed dozens or hundreds of homes, and even killed. We want people to understand the severity of this crime. It's not a small thing, starting a fire like that. And when people die, the person who set the fire should be punished accordingly."

"What Juan wants—what the attorney general has asked for, to be more precise," Ecklie said, "is for the best criminalists in the state to work this crime scene. The state has its own people, but they don't have a lot of experience with this sort of arson investigation. Your people, at least, have dealt with a forest fire scene before."

"That was a little different," Catherine said. "That was a case in which a killer tried to use an existing fire to hide a homicide."

"Nonetheless, your investigation involved studying the fire itself," Castillo said. "We have people, the Forest Service has people. But the LVPD has the best people, the best lab, and we want the best on this one."

"When do you want us to get started? We're kind of in the middle of something now."

"I told him about the Daniels incident," Ecklie said.

"I understand that your resources are limited," Castillo said. "By tomorrow afternoon we hope to have the fire fully contained. At that time, it should be safe for your people to go into the area where we believe the fire started. I'd prefer not to waste any more time than we have to."

Her team had been working most of a shift already, and the Daniels scene was far from finished. Mt. Charleston was only twenty minutes from the city limits, but investigating a forest fire was going to be another big, complicated job.

Ecklie and Castillo pinned her with their gazes, expecting a response. "Okay," she said. "I'll have a couple of people knock off what they're doing, and get some rest. They'll be there around noon, if that works for you?"

"Noon will be perfect," Castillo said. "You have the attorney general's thanks. And my own."

"We do what we're told," Catherine said.

"Still. This is somewhat above and beyond."

"Well, with any luck it'll also be over quickly, because I have a feeling I'm going to need all my people right here in town until this Daniels case is put to bed."

"I'll do anything I can to ease the gap, Catherine," Ecklie promised. "This really is important, what Juan's trying to do. And your people really are the best."

"Thanks for the vote of confidence, Conrad." A couple of days in the mountains? She was tempted to assign herself to the task. Everybody in her unit could use a break from the city, she knew. Not like it was a vacation, but it was still a change of scene, a promise of cooler weather, and maybe a little more restful than a typical shift.

She had at least twenty minutes to figure out who to send. No problem.

That was why she earned the big bucks, wasn't it?

5

CATHERINE WILLOWS HAD worked nights for most of her adult life. She had been an exotic dancer, then a medical student—not necessarily a nighttime pursuit, but people who could function on little sleep did better than those who couldn't—and finally, a lab technician, a mother, a CSI, and a shift supervisor. Sleeping during the day came as second nature.

This day, however, she had a hard time of it. Traffic sounds outside disturbed her, as did light leaking in around the edges of her curtains. When she finally fell asleep, she was restless, tossing around, winding herself up in the covers.

She had been at it for only a couple of hours when the phone rang. For a few moments she was determined to ignore it, but it didn't stop and she decided it was better to answer it. Sleep wasn't working out that well, anyway. She disentangled and grabbed it before voicemail picked up. "Willows," she said.

"Catherine Willows?" An unfamiliar voice, male.
"Yes?"

"This is Evan McCandless, with the Channel Nine news team."

The next word caught in her throat. "Yes?"

"I wonder if you'd like to comment on—"

"I'm sorry, Mr. McCandless. I don't comment on anything. If you want a comment, call the department's public information office."

"But you're the one—"

"I said I'm sorry. Off the record, I'm the one who worked all night and is trying to sleep. Good-bye."

She hung up the phone. She knew she should play the press better than that, but she was too tired for fine diplomatic maneuvers.

Her head had just hit the pillow when the phone rang again. She sat upright, grabbed the phone. "Look, Mr. McCandless—"

"No, this is Cynthia Sweeney, from the Press-Enterprise," a female voice said. "You've been talking to Evan McCandless?"

"Only to tell him I wouldn't talk to him. Or you, Ms. Sweeney. As I told him, if you want a comment from the PD, you need to talk to our public information office."

"You might want to change your mind about that. I'll give you a fair hearing, Supervisor Willows."

"Just what is it you're looking for a comment on? Never mind. I don't need a fair hearing, I need about eighteen hours of sleep." Catherine hung up again.

The next time the phone rang, she let voicemail take it. And the time after that.

Sleep, it appeared, would be a rare commodity today.

Giving up, she turned on the TV, scrolled through channels until she found a local news broadcast. The second thing she saw there, after a quick glimpse at a news anchor who—true to the job title—seemingly never moved away from her chair, was her own face. "Early this morning, Las Vegas Police Department Crime Lab supervisor Catherine Willows blamed the bombing that injured media kingpin Dennis Daniels on anti-tax protesters," the anchor said. "Officially, the department is saying there are no suspects yet, and the investigation is ongoing. But sources in the department say—"

Catherine punched the power button on the remote. Her phone was already ringing again. She ran her fingers through her hair, buried her face in her hands. This was not good, not good at all.

Sooo not good.

Voicemail took that call, and she started to let the next one go that way as well, when it occurred to her that all the calls might not be from the press. There might be one from Ecklie, or even from the sheriff, calling to upbraid her for her error. She decided to nip that in the bud and dialed the department's public information office herself. She had friends there, and they'd tell her how to play it.

After a couple of minutes and two transfers, she was on the line with an old hand and a longtime friend. "You really screwed the pooch this time, Cath," Charlie said. "We've been fielding calls all morning."

"Yeah, they have my home number, too. I did not talk to the press, Charlie, I swear to you."

"Somebody did."

That sloppy cop. Benny something. "Brass knows him, his name's Benny. He overheard me say something. Maybe I was out of line, but I definitely wasn't talking to anyone outside the department."

"We're trying to put a lid on it, Catherine, trust me."

"What I want to know is if the department can cover me."

"We'll do what we can. We've been trying to tell them that your statement isn't the real story, that it was an unofficial speculation meant to be kept among colleagues."

"That's true, but in a way, that makes it sound worse. More honestly my opinion. We toss around possible scenarios all the time, but they're not for public consumption."

"There's no way to put a happy face on it, Cath. We're trying to make deals, offering people exclusive bits and pieces if they'll bury that angle and play up the one we want played up."

"Which is?"

"Which is there was a horrific attack against a member of the media, an important man in this town, and his staff. That's a story. It happened, we're on top of it, and we won't sleep until we find those responsible."

"Literally," Catherine said, biting back a yawn.

"Sorry?"

"Nothing. So, is it working?"

"To a degree. I won't lie to you, Catherine.

You're going to be a story—not the only story, but a story—for a day. Maybe two, at the outside. One thing about the press, they've got the collective attention span of a gnat. Two, three days from now, you'll be forgotten."

"I can't wait."

"It'll blow over. I'm not wrong on this. I know those people. You going to be okay?"

"Always, Charlie," she said. "Always."

She did trust Charlie. He knew his stuff.

She just hoped he was right *this* time.

Nick and Sara made it up Mt. Charleston by noon, showing their IDs at multiple checkpoints to be allowed into the fire zone. The mountain still smoldered; tendrils of smoke joined earth and sky from what seemed to be dozens of different places. The sight made Nick think of the barred door of a prison cell, and he mentioned that to Sara.

"That's the goal here, right? To make sure someone ends up in a cell?"

"From what Catherine said, maybe the gas chamber. I try not to think about what sentences people might get. All I can do is help convict the guilty."

"Good attitude," Sara said. "You always did have the right outlook, Nick."

"I try."

Nick was driving, as he always tried to when he went out with Sara. He was the one who had rolled his car recently, but that was a fluke: run off the road by a drunk driver. Even with that, he was more comfortable with his own hands on the wheel rather than Sara's. For all her good traits, and there were many, driving wasn't high on her skill set. She navigated, with a map open on her lap, supplementing the vehicle's GPS unit's advice. "Turn up here," she said. "That right, up ahead."

A moment later, the GPS offered the same suggestion. "One of you is plenty," Nick said. "Someone's gotta go."

Sara turned off the GPS. "We're almost there. One more left."

Nick made the right, then the left. They were deep in it, now. Huge trees had been whittled down to little more than blackened toothpicks. The understory was gone, nothing but black scorch marks on bare earth remaining. The stink of char was everywhere, overwhelming all other aromas. Instead of the usual refreshing fragrance of mountain air, this place smelled like a barbecue gone bad.

He knew Catherine had given them this assignment as a kind of favor. He had been, as she put it, shot and blown up recently, and Sara had injured her hand punching a guy. The guy had undoubtedly deserved it, and Sara had been hoping for someone to punch, but still. Ray was the one who really needed to get away, to take time off, but there was no convincing him of that.

"There," Sara said. "That trailer. That's got to be the place."

Nick parked outside, next to a handful of other vehicles, all bearing government tags of various sorts. By the time they were out of the lab's Yukon, the trailer's door had opened and a man in a dark suit emerged. "You must be from the crime lab," he said.

"We are," Sara replied. "Mr. Castillo?"

"That's right."

"I'm Sara Sidle. This is Nick Stokes."

"Supervisor Willows said she was sending me her best. I trust you two are up to the challenge."

"We'll do what we can."

"And you," Castillo said, addressing Nick. "She said you have experience with wildland fires."

"A bit," Nick said. He and Catherine had once had to figure out how a scuba diver got into a tree-top, when he was found there after a forest fire.

"I've been studying the problem for months, now," Castillo said. "We were afraid something like this would happen, and we wanted to be ready when it did. I'm afraid that this case is the perfect one to apply our new policy to, tragic though it may be."

"You mean prosecuting for murder?" Sara said.

"Yes. You drove through the fire damage on your way here."

"We did, yes," Sara answered.

"We have the blaze mostly contained, but it's not out yet. So far, more than eleven thousand acres have burned. Twenty-one homes, and counting, are destroyed. Six people dead, that we know of. There might be more, but we won't know that until we sift through the ashes and the residents are allowed to return. The combined cost to the government, at a state and federal level, is already well in excess of three quarters of a million dollars. That number is going up every minute."

"It's an awful thing," Nick said.

"It's a tragic thing, but what it isn't is an accident. This fire was set with intent. Someone had to actively decide to burn a forest, and then follow through on that decision. Come, walk with me."

"Okay," Sara said.

Castillo led them away from the trailer and through burned trees. The smell here was even sharper. Ahead, Nick could see blue sky where the trees ended, presumably where the slope fell away. "For a hundred years, the Forest Service's official response to any fire, however small, was to put it out. A lightning-caused fire in the middle of five million acres of undeveloped forest? Put it out. Because of this policy, we have forests throughout the country, but especially here in the West, that have not burned in more than a century. Do you know the end result of that?"

"I would guess," Sara said, "a lot of area ready to burn."

"More than ready," Castillo corrected. "Anxious to burn. Fire is part of the natural life cycle of forests. It allows the germination of new seeds, clears away brush and dead trees. It's the way things are supposed to be. By preventing burns for so long, the unintended result was a huge increase in the available fuel. Then we have a year like this one, with a heavy monsoon season, lots of rain, followed by a hot, dry season—and yes, before you ask, experts believe that climate change is causing hotter, drier conditions that only exacerbate the situation."

"The rain grows more underbrush, grasses and shrubs," Nick suggested. "Which then dry out."

"And feed the fire. Forest fires tend to ladder. They start out burning low, but they'll climb, if there are rungs to climb on. Brush of varying heights, low branches—those are just what it needs."

They pushed past the final row of black trees and came to a drop-off. The ground sloped away at a nineteen- or twenty-degree angle, and below, for miles and miles, they looked down upon more blackened landscape. "This fire burned hot and fast. There are whole neighborhoods on this mountain that had to be evacuated with an hour to spare, sometimes less. Lives were saved, make no mistake about that. But homes were destroyed with everything in them. Irreplaceable things. Family photographs, videos. Things that had been in families for generations. Not to mention pets and livestock. There isn't always time, in a quick evacuation, to save them."

"That's hard," Sara said.

"It's terrible. Terrible. Let's go for a ride, I want to show you where those firefighters died."

"We do need to see that," Nick said. They'd been given a file to study, which included maps of the fire's progress, diagrams showing the positions of the different firefighting teams, and photographs—awful photos, hard to look at—of the dead firefighters.

"It's not far. Come on."

They walked back through the scorched forest, to the trailer, and got into the Yukon. This time, Castillo gave directions while Sara drove. They wound up the mountain for about ten minutes, then took a twisty side road into a neighborhood of buildings that were called cabins but were the size of small mansions. The fire seemed to have hopscotched around; some houses were intact while others had been reduced to nothing but ash and stone. Sara drove slowly down the road, weaving through mounds of debris.

Toward the end of a cul-de-sac, they stopped. A fire engine blocked the roadway. It was black, its tires gone, glass shattered, paint blistered and peeling.

"There it is," Castillo said. "Engine number forty-two. They were trying to get back in it, to escape, when the fire caught them. It came in a wall. They had no time for anything, not even time to pray. When the fire approached, the superheated air was probably fifteen hundred degrees or higher. Just fried them where they stood."

He waved toward the houses scattered around the cul-de-sac. "This is what they died for," he said. "Trying to protect these homes. Probably, these people shouldn't have built here. We call this the wildland-urban interface, and it's very dangerous. These homes are in the most fire-prone areas imaginable, in terrain where fighting fires is very difficult and sources of water can be hard to come by. We try to educate people, to get them to keep the brush trimmed back around their houses, to keep defensible space. But they like the trees up close to their homes, for shade and for the scenery. Fire rises, as I said, and it climbs hills as well as trees. When it does, houses burn. People need to understand that."

"I guess these people will, now," Nick said.

"Some of them. Some of the ones whose homes burned probably won't rebuild, not here. But the ones who were spared? They'll just think they're immune. That's how it usually goes."

"They're not immune, though," Sara said. "Safer

for a while, maybe, because this fire burned off the accumulated fuel."

"That's right," Castillo said. "But it'll grow back. The forest restores itself. And in the meantime, this is only one community, on one mountain. We're faced with this in every wildland-urban interface around the state. That's why we have to not only preach safety and prevention, but we have to prosecute the arsonists."

"I get it," Nick said. "We'll do whatever we can."

"Thank you," Castillo said. He looked like he meant it, like he took the loss of those firefighters very personally. He blinked back moisture, sniffled once, touched the end of his nose. "Your work here will save a lot of lives."

Later, after Castillo had told them how to find the area where Forest Service investigators believed the fire had begun, Nick and Sara stood outside the Yukon. "I didn't think we'd be back up here so soon, Nick."

A recent case had brought them to a different part of the mountain, closer to the city. "Let's just hope there aren't any werewolves around."

"Or any bloodsuckers bigger than a mosquito. But you know what's missing?"

"What?"

"Listen."

He did. "I don't hear anything."

"Exactly. When's the last time you heard a forest without birds?"

6

CATHERINE WAS WIDE awake, and getting back to sleep didn't seem like a winning proposition. She decided to shower and go in early. There was always plenty to do, and if she was busy in the lab, maybe she wouldn't be dwelling on the fact that her name was being blabbed all over the local news.

When she got there, the lab was still crawling with day shift people. She always felt a little like an intruder at such times, though her office was her own and her fellow criminalists never acted as if she were unwelcome. She returned the favor on those rare occasions that they showed up during night shift. Still, there was a definite sense of being a stranger in a foreign land.

She went into her office and dug into the paperwork that she typically ignored, in favor of fieldwork and lab work, until Ecklie started harassing her for it. Her overheard comment might have landed her in hot water with him and the department brass, so she would make sure they didn't have anything else to complain about.

She had been at it for most of an hour when a familiar, gruff voice roused her from her forms. "What the hell are you doing here, Cath?"

"I could ask you the same thing, Earl," Catherine said. She saved the document she was working on. "You did work the scene with us last night, right? Why aren't you home in bed?"

"Couldn't sleep."

"I know that feeling."

"I knew the pieces of this bomb were sitting here waiting for me and I had to get back to it."

"You really have a thing about bombs, don't you?"

"They're fascinating objects. The people who plant them tend to be interesting, too. Loners, often. Meticulous. Some of the finest craftsmanship I've ever seen has been put into devices intended to be used only once and destroyed by that single use. Takes a certain mindset to do that."

"I suppose it does."

"I'm not saying I admire the whole person, just the dedication to the craft."

"Well," Catherine said. "As long as you draw a line."

"Damn straight."

"Can you tell me anything about this one yet?"

"Come with me."

Catherine left her paperwork behind, delighted at the intrusion. Earl led her to a layout room where he had assembled bits and pieces taken from the scene into something roughly tubular, about eight or nine inches long. Beside it were shards of black plastic, melted and twisted into unrecognizable shapes. "That's our bomb?" Catherine asked.

"What's left of it," Earl replied. "It was originally a piece of aluminum pipe. Could have been used for all sorts of purposes, but our guy found his own use for it. He packed it full of ammonium nitrate—"

"Fertilizer."

"Not when it's used like this, but yes, that's its most common commercial use. He added diesel oil. Together, the two are a very unstable, explosive mixture."

"Similar to what that guy McCann planted at Officer Clark's funeral. The bomb that almost killed Nicky."

"And the same stuff Timothy McVeigh used in Oklahoma City, although he used a lot more of it."

"So it's the explosive substance of choice for domestic terrorists."

"Ammonium nitrate isn't just used in the States," Earl said. "It's common in terrorism cases around the world. It's not a controlled substance and it's not that hard to get. IED makers in the theaters of war in the Middle East swear by it."

"What can you tell me about the bomber?"

"Well, it's not McCann."

"I didn't think it would be."

"Or anyone who learned from him. His bombs were beautifully crafted. This one's pretty punk-ass by comparison. Amateur hour. Plans probably came from the Internet."

"You think so?"

"It's easily found out there. It's explosive, all right—we saw the results of that. But there's no style to it, no grace. It's just a big, destructive bang."

"What about the construction of the device itself?"

"Same thing. Effective but boring, and poorly made. If the bomber had been more skilled, no one in either vehicle would have survived. A bomb like that could have done damage to an up-armored Humvee, and neither of those vehicles had anywhere near that sort of protection. And the trigger was a garage door opener. The bomber's lucky— those don't have very unique frequencies. The wrong person pushing the wrong button at the right time could have blown him to bits before he even planted it."

"So we're looking for a bad bomber."

"We're looking for an inexperienced one," Earl corrected. "But they all have to start somewhere, don't they?"

"I suppose so."

"He—and I'm not being sexist; it's possible for women to become bombers, but it's so rare as to be virtually unheard of—he survived this one. Which means there's every likelihood that he'll do it again. And you know what they say."

"What's that?"

"Practice makes perfect."

Catherine drove downtown. Daniels and his administrative assistant, Maureen Cunningham—the woman driving the second car—remained in the hospital, but the other staffers had been released. She didn't know if they would be working, so soon after the attack, but Daniels Cable News was on the air twenty-four seven, so chances were good.

What Earl had told her about the bomb nagged at her. The trigger had been a low-powered device, the bomber inexperienced. Those two factors meant the bomber couldn't have had a lot of confidence in the attack—certainly not enough to be far from the scene at the moment of detonation. He would have needed to know exactly what route the Daniels party would take, and when they would be reaching his location.

She wanted to know how someone might have come by that information. And she figured his employees were the ones to ask.

As soon as she turned onto the road DCN headquarters was on, she realized her mistake. She had seen the protest on TV, but not in person. Up close, it was bigger and more chaotic than she had expected. There were hundreds of people thronging the street, many garbed in bright clothes or strange costumes, most carrying signs. They chanted and shouted and sang. Some were right up against the gates of the network's headquarters,. Their intent seemed to be intimidation, and Catherine would have been surprised if it wasn't working, at least to some extent. How could anyone get any work done in that kind of environment?

The idea of turning around and conducting these interviews over the phone flitted across her mind. She decided against it, though. She had come this far, and she had a job to do. She would make sure it got done, and an unruly crowd wouldn't stop her.

She eased toward the gates, and a couple of uniformed guards parted the sea of protesters for her.

She had hoped not to make eye contact with the protesters, but their garb—lots of Revolutionary War costumes, complete with knickers and tricorn hats, and an equal number of people decked out in red, white, and blue—grabbed her attention. As did the signs. "Hands Off Our $$$!" "Read Our Lips: No More Taxes!!!" "Re-elect Nobody!" "No Taxes For War!!" The people were mostly white, but not all of them, and they represented the whole span of ages, from toddlers through seniors—even senior-plus, if that was a category. Catherine drove slowly between them, wincing when hands slammed against her car. She thought she had a clear shot at the door when a stout man in his mid-forties blocked her way. He was staring at her through the windshield.

"Hey!" the man shouted. "Aren't you that cop?"

Catherine thumbed the window down a little. "I'm not a cop," Catherine corrected. "I'm a crime scene investigator. Can you move aside, please?"

"From TV. You were on TV."

"Occasionally."

"No, today. Hey, hey!" the guy called, raising his voice. "It's that lady cop, from TV!"

"Don't do that," Catherine said, the words coming out as soft as a breath. It was too late, and she knew it. The news spread through the crowd. Catherine steered around the man, but before she made it through the gates, people were blocking her way, their faces twisted in anger, some screeching at her and waving fists. The security guards were doing their best to control the protesters, but for a frightening moment she wasn't sure they would manage.

"Why do you think it was us?" one protester asked.

"Get the facts!" someone called out. "Don't make blind accusations."

Catherine took her badge off her belt and showed it out the window. "I haven't accused anyone," she said, keeping her voice level. There was an edge to it anyway, and she couldn't prevent it. "I *am* trying to get the facts, that's why I'm here. Now get out of my way." She was only seconds away from flipping on her lights and siren.

The shouting and stomping and banging on the car was frightening, and she thought again that it had to be intimidating to the staffers and volunteers who passed through every day to go to work. A couple of uniformed cops who had been standing off on the sidelines joined the security guards, and herded the protesters back. "Let her through, folks," one said. "She's here on police business. Back away." They opened a path for her, and Catherine gladly took advantage of it.

When she made it inside the building, the racket slacked off. The front lobby was expansive, marble-floored, with a reception counter constructed of some rich, dark wood and topped with a granite counter about halfway to the rear wall and an open-stepped staircase curving gracefully to the next level. Monitors suspended on poles, at different heights, all played DCN's programming. Catherine was astonished to see her own face flit across the screens. DCN's coverage seemed to be largely about the bombing. Given Dennis Daniels's notoriety, she wouldn't have been surprised if the same held true for the other cable news outlets.

Soft music played inside, and she suspected there were white noise machines at work, too—a gentle rushing sound blocked some of the hubbub from outside. She gave her name to the perfectly coiffed receptionist at the counter. A few minutes later, a man came down the stairs, his shirtsleeves rolled up over his wrists, collar open, no tie. He wore jeans and loafers and he had short, curly hair and an easy grin. His casual nature almost disguised the cuts and bruises on his face, neck, and hands. "Sorry about the trouble outside," he said. "I'm Eldon Wohl."

"Catherine Willows."

"Of course. From the Crime Lab."

"Is there anyone in Las Vegas who doesn't know me?"

"Probably not," he said. "You've been all over our air today. And the Internet. You're the topic *du jour* on the conspiracy websites."

"Another checkmark for my bucket list."

Wohl chuckled. "Also, Garrett Kovash told us about you. He said you might come around."

"Normally it would be a detective," Catherine said. "But they're busy, too. And I just had a few questions that tie in with my investigation."

"Sure, come with me." She followed him up the stairs and past glass-walled offices, in which people were either working or giving an effective imper-sonation of it. Down a short hallway was an inner conference room with its own glass walls facing in-side, but no windows looking out.

"Your job title is operations manager, right?" Catherine asked as he waved her toward a rolling chair. The conference table was sleek, also glass— someone in charge of interior spaces appeared to be a big fan of that. She supposed the business had a large budget for glass cleaner, and maybe a couple of full-time employees to use it.

"That's right. Operations manager, non-news division, if you want to get technical. I make sure salaries get paid and the lights stay on, that sort of thing. Dennis likes to keep the business side and the news side of the house strictly separated."

"So that commercial considerations won't affect the judgment of the news people?"

"Exactly."

"But the network has never pretended to objectivity," Catherine pointed out. "Daniels has always used it to advance his own point of view."

"There's a big difference," Wohl said, "between espousing one's own viewpoint because it's the right thing to do, and allowing an advertiser to dictate news coverage to its own financial ends. Dennis has always been clear that he sets the political tone at the network, and while the on-air personalities, on certain programs, are allowed to speak their minds, he is the one who hires and fires, which guarantees a certain consistency of outlook. He's opposed to extremism on either side. He supports commonsense, middle-of-the-road solutions. He advocates for social and economic progress and against backtracking or standing still."

Catherine had heard the network's slogan many times. "The world is changing. We either change with it, or it leaves us behind." She figured that progress was a safe enough thing to be in favor of—like motherhood and apple pie, it was hard to argue against. And the word was vague enough that everyone could define it in their own way.

"But you didn't come to talk politics," Wohl said. "Or the TV news business, I'm guessing. So how can we help you?"

"First, what's his condition?"

"Dennis is awake and alert. Probably driving the hospital staff nuts already. He's got some broken bones and some internal bleeding, so they want him to stay there for a couple of days. But he'll be fine. Maureen, too. Full recovery is expected in both cases."

"I'm glad to hear that."

"Yeah, you're only looking for an attempted murderer, not a murderer."

"I wish I could always be so fortunate."

"What can I do?"

He had not taken a seat, but paced around the conference table like a big cat in a zoo. She guessed TV news was not a profession for the lethargic.

"Who knew the route you would take last night?"

That brought his pacing to a sudden halt. He picked at his lip. "Let's see . . . Garrett Kovash chose the routes. He's been doing it for a couple of weeks, since the threats started coming in faster and meaner."

"Does he reveal the routes in advance?"

"Not much. We went in two vehicles, okay? Bryan driving one, Maureen the other. I guess before we headed out, he described the route to those of us who were going. While we were at the house in Lake Las Vegas, he told us all how we'd return."

"Why not just let the drivers pick their own routes?"

"People are creatures of habit. Especially when we're tired. Garrett's worried that we'll settle into our routines, drive our usual paths. So he stays on top of us, trying to keep us on our toes."

"And he told all of you? How many was that, six?"

"That's right. Two vehicles. We could have all squeezed into the Escalade, but I had a conference call here and I had to leave late. Maureen worked until I was ready, and we took off about forty minutes after the others."

"Is it typical for so many of you to attend a fundraising event?"

Wohl shook his head. He was pacing again, occasionally interweaving his fingers while he walked. "We haven't been involved in politics long enough to know what's typical. This wasn't strictly fundraising, it was more about taking the temperature. Dennis hasn't formed an actual campaign committee yet, so nobody's writing us checks. He just wanted to discuss his chances with some of the people who can write big checks when they want to."

"So this wasn't a dinner at which people hand you checks in envelopes."

"Not at all. It was a face-to-face with a potential ally and his very wealthy friends. I think it went well."

"Until you were on the way back."

"Yeah, that was a turn for the worse, definitely."

"And before you left Lake Las Vegas, Kovash told you the route he had picked out for the trip home."

"That's right."

"Did you tell anyone else?"

"I hardly listened. I was driving, but Maureen was navigating. I was involved in a discussion of economic stimulus, with an actress you've seen in a dozen movies."

"So you don't know if anyone else called home, called a friend, anything like that."

"No idea."

"Are the others who were with you that night here today?"

"Dennis and Maureen are still in the hospital. Garrett's there with them. Connie, Bryan, and I are here."

"Can I talk to them?"

"You might have a hard time getting Connie to put down her three phones. Apparently that's how she lives all the time. Bryan's a hard worker, too, but he'll talk to you."

"He's Dennis's driver?"

"Driver, man Friday, body man. He's there to know what Dennis is going to need before he needs it. If Dennis wants an umbrella or a breath mint or a pen or a flashlight or a pipe wrench, Bryan's supposed to fish it out of a pocket. And he does."

"I could use one of those."

"Who couldn't? Between Bryan Donavan and Maureen Cunningham, Dennis really doesn't have to do much of anything for himself. I'm afraid this one is taken, though. He's as loyal as an old hound dog. I think Dennis could quit paying him and he wouldn't care."

"Loyalty like that is a vanishing trait."

"Yeah, you're not kidding. Hang on, I'll get him for you."

7

CATHERINE COOLED HER heels for a couple of minutes in the conference room, before Wohl returned with a young, slender African-American man. He was dressed much like Wohl, in an open-collared shirt and dress pants, but unlike Wohl, he seemed absolutely calm, with a stillness at his center that Catherine supposed was an island of stability Daniels could cling to in the turbulent waters of the media business.

Wohl was introducing her to Bryan Donavan when someone started to scream.

Her first thought was that one of the protesters had come into the office, but then she recognized the shrill tone of utter terror. Wohl and Donavan both turned toward the conference room door. Then they all heard the word *Fire!* and Donavan ran from the room.

Wohl tossed her an uncertain look. "We'd better . . ."

"Right," Catherine said. Wohl hurried out the door, Catherine right behind. The smell of smoke already tickled her nostrils.

The screams had increased, and even before she emerged from the hallway, Catherine heard chairs falling over, drawers slamming, and people rushing from their glass-walled offices.

A muddy gray haze hung in the air of the reception area. Catherine hurried down the steps, appraising the situation. The smoke seemed thicker in the rear area, behind the reception desk. "Fire's in back," she said. "What's back there?"

"Then we'll go out the front," Wohl said. "There are storerooms back there, loading docks, that kind of thing." He raised his voice to be heard over the general din. "Has anyone called 911?"

"They're on the way," someone answered.

"This so sucks," Wohl said. "Everyone stay calm, stay orderly!"

"It looks like the fire's all outside," Catherine said.

"Let's hope it stays that way. Our whole operation is in this building. I'd hate to see it all go up in smoke."

They followed the others out the front doors. The mob was still right outside the gates, but their chanting and shouting had stopped when the exodus began. The mood had changed in what seemed like an instant, from one of ugly confrontation to one of human connection and cooperation.

Sirens wailed in the distance, growing nearer. Catherine scanned the crowd quickly, knowing that arsonists often liked to be at the scenes of their fires, to watch the damage and confusion they caused. But this scene was too chaotic; if one of the protesters had started the fire, there was no easy way to pick out which one.

She detached herself from the knot of campaign workers and went around to the rear of the building. First responders were arriving, squad cars and fire engines, and the gate guards were waving them through. Catherine held her badge up, directing them toward the back. When a uniformed cop approached her, she explained the situation and let him worry about controlling the crowd and securing the scene. She hurried toward smoke, billowing out from the loading docks, anxious for a look at the blaze before the firefighters trashed it.

The fire was small, but had the potential, as almost any fire did, to become much larger. It had been set right at the base of a steel loading door. She suspected that some sort of accelerant—kerosene, gasoline—had been splashed on a pile of rags and ignited. Scraps of scorched fabric were still in place. The door hadn't burned through, but there was wooden framing around it, and once that caught it could get into the walls and spread fast.

Firefighters brushed past her and attacked the fire with some sort of super fire extinguishers, tanks mounted on their backs. They blasted the flames, making an almost deafening racket and filling the air with cool, sharp vapors. They smothered the fire, preventing oxygen from reaching it, and it was out in no time.

And her crime scene was largely ruined.

Not entirely, though. Arsonists often believed

that their fires would cover any traces left behind, but they were usually wrong. Even DNA could survive a fire, as long as it wasn't soaked. She had a field kit in her vehicle, and she would go get it in a minute. But first she wanted a closer look. As the firefighters backed away, Catherine stepped up.

The loading area was pretty typical, if somewhat cleaner than those used for restaurants and supermarkets. Garbage dumpsters, pavement covered in oil and grease stains. A video surveillance camera was mounted above the dock, but its lens had been shattered. A rock on the ground beneath it might have been the culprit. Catherine crouched and found tiny glass shards on top of the rock, but when she fingered it aside, there were none beneath it, confirming her hunch. Other small stones were scattered here and there, so probably someone had stood back, out of the camera's range, and thrown them until one connected.

If that was the case, then the person who had thrown the stones knew where to stand. She would check the video, see if she could catch a glimpse of him, but if her guess was right, she wouldn't. She could also find out when the lens had been broken—if it was immediately before the fire started, or sometime earlier.

Initial indications pointed to someone on the inside, someone who had seen the video feed and knew the camera's range. On the other hand, wouldn't an insider have known that Daniels was still in the hospital, and not at work? She would know more after she did a more thorough investigation. After first making sure that the uniforms had secured the area, she hurried back to her car for her kit.

Whether the arsonist was a DCN insider or not, if it was the same person who had detonated the bomb, that person harbored a serious case of rage toward Dennis Daniels.

Rage like that wouldn't go away on its own. It would keep seeking an outlet until it was satisfied. She would need to find the person before that happened, or Daniels would pay the final price.

Ray Langston went into the lab early. Since he had been stabbed, he hadn't been sleeping well unless he was drugged. And he hated being drugged, because while the narcotics took the edge off the pain, they dulled his mind. When he did sleep, nightmares plagued him. So he avoided the painkillers and tried to work through the agony during his waking hours.

Catherine worried about him, which bothered him almost as much as the drugs did. Though he walked with a cane that Doc Robbins had given him, and he couldn't always conceal the pain, or the weariness that overtook him much earlier than it once had, he tried to hide the symptoms from his co-workers, and especially from her. They tried to baby him, and he didn't want any special treatment.

There were plenty of people working the bombing case, so he picked up where he had left off on the severed hand. He had left it in the morgue with Robbins. The medical examiner wasn't in yet, but he had left a file folder on Ray's desk.

Ray sat down—slowly and cautiously—and opened

the file. There was a sticky note affixed to the inside, saying simply, "Ray, I had some spare time on my *hands*. AR."

The file contained almost a dozen photographs. Robbins had made a cast of the bone at the end of the hand, the nubs of radius and ulna left behind when the hand was separated from the wrist. In the file, he had included photos of the actual hand, some made with a regular camera, and close-ups under a binocular microscope. With those, Ray could easily see what had attracted the medical examiner's interest.

Visible on both the actual bone photos and the cast were tool marks, tiny but distinct striations on the edges of the bones.

The hand had been cut off.

What the dog had found was definitely evidence of a crime.

He set Doc Robbins's file aside and found another one under it, this one from Carrie, a day shift DNA tech who had been helping with their caseload since Wendy's departure. She hadn't left a personal note, just a DNA report. Ray scrolled down the printout until he reached the most pertinent bit of data—a name and address.

He jotted those down on a separate piece of paper, then returned to the document for a more comprehensive study. Carrie had extracted DNA from bone marrow found in the hand, and used a short tandem repeat technique to analyze it. With short tandem repeats, one obtained fragments of DNA, which were then extended through polymerase chain reaction. Studying those with the single nucleotide polymorphism technique, she had isolated and printed out a graph, showing the STR peaks. Below that was another graph, this one depicting the STR peaks of a man named Carter Hawkins, who had submitted to a swabbing six years earlier, when a jewelry store he managed was robbed. The robbery was a smash-and-grab job, and the thief had cut himself on the glass, leaving behind traces of blood. Employees, Hawkins included, had volunteered their DNA to exclude them from suspicion. The thief had turned out to have nothing to do with the store. He'd been arrested while trying to sell the stolen jewelry to a pawnshop, and the DNA from the crime scene had helped convict him.

The Carter Hawkins DNA had remained in the system, though, and when Ray studied the peaks and valleys of the two graphs, they were identical. The chances that they didn't come from the same person were somewhere in the neighborhood of a billion to one.

Ray put the printouts back into the folder, and checked to make sure that his and Doc Robbins's were the only two that had been left on the desk during his attempt to get some sleep. They were.

Taking his cane in one hand and the sheet of paper with the name Carter Hawkins and an address in North Las Vegas in the other, Ray hobbled to his car.

The house was in a development that had been completed sometime in the last few years. The landscaping—what there was, mostly desertscapes, cacti and succulents in fields of tiny tan rocks—was not yet mature, and the houses had not been lived in long enough to develop individual personalities. There were four styles of house, all of them two-story, with a few additional options available, and they were painted in the same three approved shades of brown and tan.

He found the address Carrie had left for him and parked in the drive. The only distinctive thing about this house was that someone had run a bumper into the garage door, and the damage had not yet been repaired.

When he rang the doorbell, he had to wait only a few seconds for a response. The door swung open, and a silver-haired man stood inside. He was Caucasian, fit and tanned, and he wore a polo shirt stretched tight across his muscular chest and shoulders. Tufts of gray hair coiled out of the open collar, and sun-kissed curls on his arms nearly hid his gold watch. Chunky gold rings graced three of his fingers. His face was lined, his cheeks carved with deep dimples extending all the way to his firm jawline. He had two hands, and they were both real, Ray noted.

"I'm sorry to bother you, sir. I'm Ray Langston, with the Las Vegas Crime Lab, and I'm looking for Carter Hawkins."

"You found him."

"Is there someone else with that name? A junior? Your father or your son?"

"I'm the one and only, far as I know. My pappy was a pistol, and I'm a son of a gun. But his name wasn't Carter. If I have any sons, I don't know about 'em. And at this age, I don't want to find out."

"I'm sorry, I'm a little confused."

"You look downright lost, Mr. Langston."

"Honestly, I was expecting to discover that Carter Hawkins was deceased. Or at least missing a hand."

Hawkins clasped his together, flashing gold. "Got both of mine." He pantomimed a golf swing.

"I can see that."

"You mind telling me what this is about?"

"Before I do, can you prove that you're Carter Hawkins?"

"You want my DNA?"

Ray chuckled. "I already have that."

"Oh, from that heist at Gem Towne?"

"That's right."

The man reached into a back pocket and withdrew a fat leather wallet. He started pulling cards from it and handing them to Ray. "Driver's license, VA, gym membership, library card, Visa—"

Ray interrupted the man, handing back his cards. "That's fine, Mr. Hawkins. Apparently you are who you say you are."

"Damn straight. Now you going to answer my question? What's this about?"

"The thing is, Mr. Hawkins, we recovered a . . . a body part. Specifically, a human hand. We ran a test on the DNA from the hand's bone marrow, since the tissue was badly damaged and contaminated, and that DNA matched yours. I don't mean close, either, I mean identical. And yet, here you are, with both hands seemingly well attached."

Hawkins stared at Ray, as if he had just emerged

from an alien spacecraft and demanded to be taken to Earth's leader. "My DNA? In some chopped-off hand?"

"So it appears."

"Maybe you folks oughta wash out your test tubes more often."

"Lab contamination is always a possibility, but a very remote one. We do try to be very careful about such things."

Hawkins flapped his hands at Ray. "Well, obviously someone's made a mistake."

"I can see that. I'm just trying to figure out how."

"Yeah, well, you got me there, pal. I sell rings, watches, necklaces, earrings, jewelry of all kinds. I don't do the store thing anymore, just craft shows, gem shows, that sort of deal."

"Do you keep your inventory here?"

Hawkins appraised his own house. "Hell, no, it's in a vault."

"And you haven't been the victim of any crime?"

"Not since that one at Gem Towne. That's, what, five years ago."

"Six, but who's counting?"

Deep canyons appeared on Hawkins's brow. "So you say the DNA you took from the mystery hand was from the bone marrow?"

"That's right."

"Would it make a difference if I was a marrow donor?"

Ray had to consider the question for a few moments, to mentally review what he knew about blood marrow donation. "Did you donate to a family member?"

"No, it was one of those marrow drives. I donated, they matched me with someone."

"Did they collect with apheresis?"

"I . . . they might have told me at the time, but I don't remember all the mumbo jumbo."

"With apheresis, they'd give you an injection regimen for a few days ahead of time. The injections tease stem cells from the marrow into the bloodstream. Then you give blood more or less normally, through a needle. The blood is filtered to collect the stem cells, then returned through a needle in your arm."

"Yeah, that's what it was. Just like giving blood, almost."

"It's much easier than a straight harvest. That requires general anesthesia, and a big needle into your hip or breastbone. You'd feel that one for a few days, probably."

"No, it was the first, aph whatever."

"Apheresis."

"Right. Does it make a difference, which way I donated?"

Ray smiled. "Technically, no. Just professional curiosity. I'd have to do some checking," he continued, "but I believe that donated marrow can show up as the only marrow in the body. There are various possibilities—the DNA can be a combination of the two marrows, blended together. But if the patient underwent a procedure that killed his or her native marrow, then the donated cells would produce their own marrow, and the DNA would come back as the donor's, not the recipient's."

"That's strange."

"It's rare. But as precise as DNA matching is, that's one of the things that can interfere with it."

"So where does that leave us?" Hawkins showed a mischievous grin. "I don't have to cut off my hand or anything, do I?"

"Not on my account. But if you can tell me where you donated, that would be a big help."

"You wait a minute? I got it in here somewhere."

"Sure."

Hawkins disappeared from the doorway, shouting out reports of his progress every few seconds. Ray got the impression that he was a lonely man, holed up here in his house, maybe not getting out much except when he had a show. He was glad for Ray's visit, however brief it might be.

He returned shortly, carrying a brochure. Stapled to it were pages of medical records. "Place is called Indigo Valley Blood Center," Hawkins said. "They had a drive going, TV ads, that kind of thing. I figured, what the hell, if it'll help save someone's life, what do I have to lose? Nothing I can't replace, right?"

"That's true. And it truly is a lifesaver for some people."

"That's what they said."

"Can I see that for a second?" Ray held out his hand and Hawkins put the papers into it. Ray noted the date, a little more than four years earlier. "Thank you," he said.

"That's it?"

"That's it. I appreciate your cooperation."

"Hey, you find out who that hand belongs to, will you let me know?"

"I'll try to do that."

"If I helped someone, I mean, really helped? That'd be a good thing to carry with me. The knowledge, not the hand."

"I figured that's what you meant. I'll let you know, okay?"

"Okay, good."

"Thank you, Mr. Hawkins."

When he got back into his car, Hawkins was still standing in the doorway, watching him go. He raised one hand in a wave, then broke into a huge grin and raised the other—a double-handed farewell. Ray tossed him a salute—one hand, the other firmly gripping the wheel—and backed out of the driveway.

8

THE DAY GREW warmer as Sara and Nick trekked through the woods. Still, it wasn't nearly as hot as it no doubt was down in the city, where the sheer accumulation of concrete and pavement added to whatever heat the sun provided. Though the birds and mammals had fled the forest, the insects were already coming back, and as the CSIs worked, they found themselves slapping at flies and clouds of gnats.

They had decided not to start a close examination of the fire's origin point until they had scoured the area around it for signs of human activity. Sara was ducking under a charred live oak branch when she caught a glimpse of something through the burned trunks that looked wrong. She shoved the branch away, sending a cascade of crisp, brown leaves to the ground. They landed with a dry clicking sound.

"Nick," she said.

"Yeah?"

"Something . . ." She pointed. "Up there?"

Nick crouched, got at her eye level. "Yeah, I see."

"Let's check it out."

"Yeah, okay." They angled their course and headed up the slope, feet crunching in ash that was as thick on the ground as a fresh snowfall. Sara's shoulders were feeling the weight of her field kit, and her clothes were almost black.

"I don't think I'm ever going to get this stink out of my nose," Nick said. "I'll be dreaming about it."

"I know what you mean," Sara said. She had been thinking the same thing. "Where we're staying, there's a shower, right?"

Castillo had offered them a cabin, ordinarily used by rangers but temporarily vacant. They hadn't had a chance to get inside yet. "I hope so. If there isn't, I'm gonna be pissed."

"Worse comes to worst, we can always have a fire truck hose us off."

They passed through a thick stand of trees and found what had looked so strange from below. In a clearing was a campsite, and though the tent and some tarps had burned, other things were smoke blackened but otherwise intact—cooking pots, metal grommets, utensils. Detritus on the ground could have been the remains of clothing, boots, and cleaning equipment. A stone circle in the middle of the clearing was obviously a campfire ring.

"Someone's been camping here," Sara said.

"And not just for a little while," Nick added. He pointed out multiple rubbed marks on the trees. The campers had tied and re-tied ropes to them, possibly moving their tent or tarps, even hanging a hammock. "They've been adjusting to different weather conditions, maybe."

"Or different seasons."

"Could be."

"How many of them, do you think?"

"Hard to tell."

"It looks like there's just one tent," Sara observed. She indicated a smoothed area on the ground, covered with a fine layer of ash not as thick as in most spots. She'd had fairly recent experience with camping, in Costa Rica. Gil Grissom had found her there, before they had married and he'd gone to France. "It stood here. Not a big one, either. Two people, three at the most, and that would be crowded."

"Probably chased out by the fire," Nick said. "It's too pristine to have been empty for long. Not to mention it's unlikely people would have left so much stuff behind if they hadn't had to get out in a hurry."

Sara went down on one knee beside what seemed to be the remains of a crate. An assortment of knives, forks, and spoons had fallen from it, along with a couple of metal mugs. "It'll be hard to find useful prints on most of what's here," she said. "It's all so coated in ash." She picked up a mug by the rim, and blew ash from around the sides, where fingers would be likely to grip it. "Not going to find any by dusting, that's for sure."

"Doesn't look like it."

"Still, we could send some of it back to the lab, maybe get something through fuming or other techniques."

"ID whoever was camping here? You think they started the fire?"

"They might not have, but they might know who did."

"True."

"Let's bag the likeliest items, send them down the hill with a courier, see what we get. Can't hurt, right?"

Nick agreed. They selected items that would have been touched frequently, metal because those surfaces had survived the fire. In a couple of cases, Sara could make out friction ridge impressions on some things that had a surface in contact with the ground, protecting it from the ash fall. They bagged a handful of good possibilities, and Nick slung the bag over a shoulder. It clanked when he moved. "At least it'll scare away the bears," he said.

"Pretty sure the fire took care of that already, Nick." While Nick had been bagging the last of them, Sara had searched the surrounding area for signs of trail. "Hey, it looks like they went this way," she said. She twitched a branch that had snagged a bit of fabric on a broken end. "There's a sort of path here, maybe an old animal trail or something." She removed the scrap with tweezers, dropped it into a plastic bag, and labeled it.

"Makes sense, someone living in these woods for any length of time, it'd be easiest to get around on existing trails."

They followed the path. There were faint impressions of boots in the dirt, filmed with ash, as everything was. "A lot of tracks," Sara said. "Coming and going. They've used this for a while."

"But that fabric scrap you found, that was new."

"That hadn't even burned."

"So they were here after the fire started."

"It sounds crazy, but I think so. Probably getting out in a hurry, not watching where they were going."

"This trail keeps leading up, it's going to lead right to that neighborhood," Nick said. "Where the firefighters died."

Sara looked at the hillside, checked the position of the sun through the brittle trees. "Yeah, I guess so."

Although they thought they knew where the trail led, they followed it. Sara felt like a tracker of old, studying the landscape for faint signs, cracked twigs, and indentations in the earth. At one point she found a granola bar wrapper that the earlier inhabitants of this mountain region wouldn't have come across. They had been at it for almost forty minutes when they heard scrambling from up the slope.

"Hello!" Nick called. "LVPD Crime Lab! Who's up there?"

A muffled response drifted down to them. "Probably can't hear you over all the noise they're making," Sara suggested. "You think it's our campers?"

"Only one way to find out," Nick said. "Let's meet 'em halfway."

Sara groaned, but mostly in fun. She loved being outside, was glad Catherine had assigned her this duty. The only drawback was that the forest was so trashed from the fire, and she preferred them vibrant, greens so pure and rich they made your eyes ache, buzzing with the sounds and smells of fertile life. She and Nick kept climbing, the trail growing progressively steeper and rockier as it cut uphill.

A few minutes later, she got her first look at the man coming down. "Nick," she said in a loud whisper. "It's just one guy."

"I thought it was a platoon."

The man looked accustomed to forest hiking. He wore jeans with huge black streaks up the legs, from ash and char. His shirt was long sleeved, light cotton, and his boots were serious outdoor gear. A sheen of sweat coated his face, darkening his shirt at the sides. He cradled a shotgun in his arms.

"Sir?" Nick called. "We're with the Las Vegas Crime Lab. I'm going to ask you to put that shotgun down."

"Why?"

"Just put it down!" Sara said, her voice commanding.

Nick's hand drifted toward the service weapon at his belt.

"This is still America, isn't it?"

"We're only going to say it one more time," Nick said. "Put down that weapon."

"Fine," the man said. He bent over and gently rested his shotgun in a bed of ash. "It's going to be filthy."

"Yes, sir, I'm sorry about that," Nick said. "But we're more comfortable talking to people who aren't carrying firearms."

"Have you found them?" the man asked. He was on the burly side, but not fat.

"Found who?" Sara asked.

"Those hippies who were camping down here."

"Hippies?" Sara echoed.

"Whatever you call 'em these days. They had dirty long hair. Man and a woman, I think, but it was hard to tell."

"We haven't found the people who were camping below, if that's what you mean. Why do you ask?"

"Because they started this fire."

"They did?"

"I'm sure of it."

In Sara's experience, the more certain people were of things they could have no way of knowing, the less likely they usually were to be right. "We'd like to talk to them," she said. "Their trail seems to lead this way. You don't know where they might have gone?"

"I got no clue."

"We've just come from their camp," Nick said. "They're completely burned out."

"Serves 'em right."

"Can we get your name, sir?" Sara asked.

"Givens. Harley Givens."

"Do you live around here?"

He jerked his head back up the hill. "On the road up there."

"The evacuation order hasn't been lifted, as far as I know," Nick said.

"Well, nobody stopped me when I drove back in."

"That was probably an oversight. I believe the fire is contained, but it might not be safe yet to go home."

"What's left of my home, you mean?"

"Was there a lot of damage?" Sara asked.

"It's only about half gone."

"We're very sorry for your loss," she said, aware that she was using phraseology ordinarily reserved for survivors of the recently deceased. The grief had to be similar, though, if not exactly comparable. One of the stages of grief was anger, and that seemed to be where Harley Givens was stuck.

"I'll tell you what, sir," Nick said. "We're going to figure out who started this fire, and that person or persons will be punished. But having people tromping around the woods with guns is only going to make our job harder, and may obscure important evidence."

"Can you tell us what you know about these campers?" Sara asked.

"Not much," Givens said. "They have long hair, they're dirty, they're living in the woods like animals."

"How long have they been there?"

"It's been months. Five, six, maybe. I don't know what they live on. I guess they go to town for groceries once in a while. Mostly I think they hunt, or eat nuts and berries or whatever they can scrounge out here. Sometimes they steal, too. Most of us pay a pretty penny to live on this hill, and here they are, squatting in the woods for free, leaving their waste around, scaring off the animals."

"What makes you think they started the fire?" she asked.

"It just stands to reason. They had a campfire going every night."

"Mr. Givens, we were just at their camp. It looks like they had a pretty well constructed fire ring. They're in a wide clearing, no branches directly overhead."

"Doesn't take much of a breeze to pick up embers from a fire up here, carry 'em to the trees," Givens countered. "It's been so dry."

"I understand that, Mr. Givens. But the Forest Service investigators believe the fire was started intentionally, and they have a good idea of where. And it was not at that campsite."

"Yeah, they *believe*. But they don't *know*, right?"

"Not for an absolute certainty, yet," Nick admitted. "That's one of the things we'll be looking into."

"They gotta pay," Givens said. "You gotta find them and make them pay."

"We'll find the perpetrators, sir," Sara assured him. "Why don't you go back down the mountain until the evacuation order is lifted?"

"Guess I don't really have much choice, do I?"

"No, sir," Nick replied. "You really don't."

9

CATHERINE MET JIM Brass in a police department hallway. "Thanks for coming," he said. "You examined the first scene and you were a witness at the second, so I thought you might be able to help with an interrogation."

"Of who?"

"Guy's name is Alec Watson."

"I've heard of him."

"You're not alone. That's just the way he likes it."

"Is he involved in those protests at the DCN building?"

Brass stuffed his hands in his pockets and shrugged. "He's one of the movers and shakers behind them. If there's a right wing angle to be played, he plays it. I brought him in as a material witness, not as a suspect, so we'll have to keep this friendly."

"Understood," Catherine said.

"Come on, then." Brass opened the door to the

interview room, and Catherine followed him in. Alec Watson was already sitting at the wooden table. A paper cup of coffee stood on the table, steam slipping from the plastic lid's opening.

"How's the joe?" Brass asked.

"It's not home-brewed, but it'll do," Watson said. He was an athletic man, dressed in casual but expensive clothes. His long legs were stretched out under the table, and Catherine noticed that his shoes were barely scuffed on the bottoms. They probably hadn't cost much more than an average squad car. He had short red hair, combed back off his face, sparkling blue eyes, and a smile that seemed at the same time genuine and apologetic, as if he were somehow inconveniencing them. Catherine wondered why some political pundits who weren't nearly so attractive ended up on TV, while this one stayed behind the scenes, writing and publishing.

"Thanks for coming in, Mr. Watson," Brass said. He scooted back a chair opposite Watson, waited for Catherine to sit beside him, then took his own seat. "I'm Captain Jim Brass, and this is Supervisor Catherine Willows of the Crime Lab."

"Pleasure," Watson said. He didn't offer a hand, and neither did Catherine or Brass.

"I understood this would be a brief interview," Watson said. "So I didn't arrange for representation. If that was inaccurately described to me, I'd like to know now so I can call my lawyer. The hourly fees those sharks charge, you know."

"We'll try to keep it quick and informal," Brass promised. "But if at any time you don't want to go on without a lawyer, you certainly have the right to stop us until you can get one here. You're not under arrest or under oath—we're just looking for some information here."

"I'll do what I can."

"We appreciate that. Mr. Watson, you know there's been a bombing that seems to have been directed at Dennis Daniels. There's also been a fire at the DCN headquarters."

Watson studied Catherine through narrowed eyes, then pointed a long finger at her. "You're the one who thinks *we're* behind it."

"I was misquoted," Catherine said. "Taken out of context."

"Happens all the time. My side likes to complain about the liberal media, but that's really too facile a representation," Watson said. "The truth is more that we have an incompetent media, incapable of presenting either side accurately, or of understanding what they're getting wrong. They go to journalism school, when in fact the political reporters should be studying government, the science reporters science, and so on."

"We don't know who's behind these attempts, Mr. Watson," Brass said, pointedly ignoring the man's digression. "All we know is that somebody is. We know multiple groups are involved in the protests, some conservative and some liberal. We also believe that some of those groups are more mainstream, and some are more fringe. The concern is that someone, possibly someone associated with one of those fringe groups, has gone freelance. Maybe they felt that carrying signs and chanting slogans wasn't strong enough, and they wanted to put some real fear into Daniels. We can only guess at their motive—maybe trying to influence his channel's coverage, or trying to prevent him from entering the race for governor."

"That's always a possibility," Watson replied. "None of us can look into the heart of those around us, even those who agree with us on most of the fundamentals."

"And it didn't escape notice," Brass continued, "that the first attack was with a bomb, and the name of your organization is BOOM."

Watson shook his head. "Is this where I should demand a lawyer?"

"That's entirely up to you," Brass said.

"Seriously, BOOM stands for Because it's Our Own Money. We're opposed to excessive taxation, and in favor of revisiting the nation's tax laws in a major way. But we're not violent."

"I didn't say you were."

"The name is actually a reference to the anarchists of the late nineteenth and early twentieth centuries," Watson said. "The bomb throwers. Their methods and their ideologies were wrong, but they had one thing right. We could use a little more anarchy these days, a little less nanny government intruding upon the people's lives and business."

"I thought the anarchists were trying to disrupt the social system, but in favor of more regulation in certain areas," Catherine said. "The labor movement, for example."

"Worst thing that ever happened to the American worker," Watson declared.

"Didn't they bring us weekends, paid sick leave, the forty-hour week?"

Watson had clearly given plenty of thought to the topic, and he addressed it with a smooth, professorial air. "They came along just as the industrial revolution was making great strides. They made unreasonable demands of owners, who agreed to those demands because in the long run, it was to their benefit. Sure, they gave the workers weekends off. But the long-range impact of industrialization was to increase productivity, and therefore to increase profit. If those same workers had stayed loyal, they could have shared in the profits generated by streamlined manufacturing processes. They could have been owners, but instead they wanted to be removed from the whole process, to set strict limitations between a person's job and the rest of his life. If they hadn't done that, they could have been rich."

"Those who didn't lose their jobs to machines," Brass countered. "And if everybody was a millionaire, then the rich would have to be billionaires. I went to Italy for a law enforcement conference a few years ago, and I had a million *lira* in my pocket. But a decent dinner cost a hundred thousand *lira*."

"The point is," Watson went on, "the labor movement steered the workers wrong. The owners were trying to do the right thing, trying to keep people employed while the industrial revolution took hold. And those anarchists throwing bombs just got in the way. The people lost their chance, in those days, to be the ones who ran the world. I don't want them to miss out this time. So we could use some of that anarchic spirit, the idea that it's the people, not the powerful, who run things. That's the philosophy behind BOOM. It's not about literal bombs, it's about metaphorical ones—shaking things up, challenging the entrenched interests in Washington. The best way to do that is through tax policy. If we strangle the government economically, it'll have to listen to us."

"If we strangle the government economically, who pays for schools and roads? And police?" Catherine asked.

"There will always be money for the critical things," Watson assured her. "It's everything else that should be looked at carefully, with the understanding that every dollar spent came from the people. That's not so radical, is it?"

"Refresh my memory, Mr. Watson," Brass said. Catherine recognized his usual technique of changing the subject when an interviewee got carried away with his own words. "You run this activist group, but your main business is publishing, right?"

"I started out as a journalist," Watson said. "But I was never that good at it. Real journalism, in my mind, requires an objectivity that I couldn't bring. I was too damn opinionated for my own good. So I decided to become a pundit. After doing that for a while, I realized I was nothing but a hired gun, and I could make a lot more money working for myself. So I started my magazine, *Elementary*—as in 'Elementary, my dear Watson,' and things just took on a life of their own. Now there's the magazine, the book line, the online presence, dozens of bloggers, and so on."

"So you went from writer to mogul."

"That's as good a summary as any."

"And you basically precipitated these demonstrations against your fellow mogul, Dennis Daniels."

Watson chuckled. "I'd like to think there was some equivalency, but the truth is the TV business will always generate far more profit than publishing. My website does okay, but it's no internet behemoth. As for precipitating demonstrations, he did that himself, by consistently using his air to push for programs that will have the effect of raising taxes. In case anybody hasn't noticed, we're struggling with a weak economy and high unemployment, and these are likely to be with us for some time. The last thing anybody needs right now is an increased tax burden."

"Right," Brass said. "But he's not a politician, at least not yet. He's promoting an agenda, but he's not casting votes. And he didn't put out a message saying, 'come picket my office.' You did that, mostly through your online efforts."

Watson considered the comment before he nodded. Catherine guessed he was once again thinking about lawyering up. "That's accurate. And you're right that he isn't an elected official. But his actions can provide cover for elected officials who are directly casting votes for increased taxes."

"Did you think it would get as big as it has? Or last as long?"

"I really had no idea. I hoped we could turn out people for a weekend. The fact that they've been out there for three weeks is quite a surprise."

"Do you know most of the players?"

"Many of them, but certainly not all. There are groups represented there that I've never heard of, and others I know of but have never had any contact with. And of course some individuals who aren't connected to any group at all. There's even a liberal organization protesting the use of tax dollars for what they call the never-ending war."

"Speaking of war, you have war veterans in your group, don't you?" Brass asked.

"Of course. But I advise you to choose your next words carefully, Captain Brass. To accuse America's fighting men and women—"

"I'm not making any accusations. Given the nature of the bomb, though, it would be irresponsible to not ask the question."

"I understand that. I'm telling you, the people who represent BOOM in that demonstration are not violent people. I don't know every individual across the country who has joined online, but there's nothing in our policy positions, or in our collected writings, that would suggest to anyone that murder or violence are acceptable political acts."

"That's BOOM. What about the other organizations involved? And the people you mentioned who aren't affiliated? Has there been anyone all along who might have struck you as unbalanced in that way?"

"I couldn't say with any specificity. There are people who I'm glad aren't associated with BOOM. I'm not one for funny hats or Hitler comparisons, let's say."

"Is there any direction you'd point us?"

"Look, I don't know if anyone out there is

involved in these attacks. I hope not. But if you're asking if I think any of those groups might preach that sort of direct action, I would have to suggest that you take a close look at the Free Citizens of the Republic."

"They're pretty far out there?" Brass asked.

"It's my understanding—very thirdhand, not through any direct knowledge—that they've been stockpiling weapons. That's all I'm comfortable saying."

"Very well, Mr. Watson, thank you."

"Am I free to leave?"

Brass showed him a hungry shark smile. "One more thing. I'm sure you can tell us where you were this morning, between about midnight and one?"

"That's easy," Watson said. "The latest issue of *Elementary* had to go to the printer this morning. I was at my desk until after two, dotting *I*s and crossing *T*s."

"You're a very hands-on publisher."

"I'm a simple guy, Captain Brass. I preach personal responsibility, and that's how I conduct my life and my business. I have editors and proofreaders, but every page of the magazine crosses my desk before it goes to the printer."

"How about this afternoon?" Catherine asked. "Around two-thirty?"

"I was on a video conference call with associates around the country. I'd be glad to provide a contact list. And of course, I recorded the call for future reference."

"Of course."

"We were discussing how to save the country.

While, of course, selling copies of the magazine and books. The free market is a wonderful thing—"

He was about to go off on another tangent, Catherine realized, and she didn't think she could take it. "If you gentlemen will excuse me," she said, "I have a lab I should really get back to."

"Sure, Catherine," Brass said. "We're just about wrapped up here. I'll talk to you later."

"Okay. Nice to meet you, Mr. Watson."

"Likewise," he said. He flashed her a grin that seemed sincere at first glance. But it didn't touch his eyes. They glittered but looked as cold as the most distant stars.

She let herself out of the room and closed the door gently. She hoped Jim wouldn't be stuck for too much longer. It seemed that once Watson was wound up, he wouldn't stop talking until he had run out of juice. Unfortunately, he hadn't really said anything terribly pertinent to the investigation, with the possible exception of his comment about the Free Citizens of the Republic. Whatever, she didn't have time to be a captive audience to one of his political rants.

Outside the interview room, she checked her cell phone. She had received a message from Tasha Ames, an acquaintance who worked at the County Clerk's office. Tasha had asked for Catherine to call her back, and said it was urgent.

Catherine returned the call. "Thanks for getting back to me, Catherine," Tasha said. "I don't mean to pry, so if this is none of my business, just tell me."

That's never a good way to begin a conversation, Catherine thought. "What is it, Tasha?"

"Well, some paperwork just came across my desk, and I thought it was strange. Strange enough to check with you about, actually."

"What is it?"

"It's a lien. Against your house."

"A lien?" Catherine stopped in the hallway, moving over to lean against a wall. She tried to keep her voice low, but suddenly felt like everyone was watching her, listening to her every hushed word. "Tasha, what are you talking about? I don't owe anybody money."

"I'm still making my way through it, and some of it looks strange. Have you hired a contractor named—wait, this can't be right."

"What? I haven't used any contractors in ages."

"I don't know, this is weird. It says the contractor's name is John of Tipton, and then in parentheses, Bakersfield. Just like that. First name John of Tipton, last name Bakersfield, but in parens."

"I've heard some odd names before, but . . ."

"That's what I mean, Catherine, this whole thing just struck me as *off*, somehow."

"What's the worst that can happen?"

"The worst? He can force you into foreclosure, make you sell your house so he can collect his money."

"But I don't owe any money."

"It says here you owe fifty-eight thousand dollars."

"That's crazy."

"Cath, I can 'lose' this for a while if you want me to. A couple of days, anyway, if that'll help you find time to get over here and file a response. I know you're busy."

"I'm busy, but not too busy to fight some bogus sixty grand claim against my house. Anything you can do would be great, Tasha. It's too late today, but I'll be over tomorrow to see what steps I need to take."

"That's fine, Cath. It won't go anywhere, trust me."

"I appreciate the heads-up."

"If I were you, I'd check in with your bank. Just in case. If this is some sort of harassment technique—"

"I get you. I'll make a call. Thanks, Tasha."

When she ended the call, Catherine's hands were shaking. The idea that someone could file a claim against her, on completely nonsensical grounds, was infuriating. Part of living in a free country, she realized, was that people could bring all sorts of legal actions. Anyone could sue anybody else for anything, as long as they could get a lawyer to go along with it, or had the minimum legal knowledge to do it themselves. And although she worked with a number of attorneys and had a great deal of respect for the good ones, she also knew that slimy lawyers could be found under almost any good-sized rock.

When she had control of her own fingers again, she phoned her bank and asked for Carlton Weaver, the branch manager. He was on the phone in less than a minute. "Catherine, what a delightful surprise," he said. "What can I do for you?"

She explained her mission, told him about the fraudulent lien. "I wanted to make sure nobody's monkeying with my accounts," she said.

"Hang on, let me just have a look." She heard

him breathing on the other end of the line, heard the tapping of computer keys. In a moment, he made a huffing sound. "Oh. Oh, my."

"What is it, Carlton?"

"It appears that your accounts have been frozen, Catherine."

"What? Well . . . unfreeze them! Who the hell authorized that?"

"I'm afraid it will take me a bit longer to find that out. Don't worry, Catherine. I know you're financially stable. I'd advise against making any withdrawals or using a debit card for the next hour or so. But I'll be sure that you're liquid before I leave my office for the day."

"Thanks, Carlton," she said. "You're a lifesaver."

She didn't know how it had happened so fast, but she was convinced that these attacks on her had something to do with the offhand comment that had been reported in the news. Thanks to Benny the idiot, who would definitely have much to answer for.

And that name. *John of Tipton (Bakersfield)*. She thought she had read something in a law enforcement journal about people who used strange aliases like that. She couldn't recall the details—but she thought she knew who might.

She hurried back to the interview room. Only a few minutes had passed, and when she got there Brass was just seeing Alec Watson out. A uniformed officer waited to escort the publisher outside.

"Hold up a minute," Catherine said, rushing toward them. She had to bite back the anger or else risk exploding at him. "I have another couple of questions for Mr. Watson."

Brass couldn't contain his surprise. "Really?"

"Inside, please," she said. Watson obeyed, and Brass followed them back into the room. This time, Catherine didn't take a seat.

"Does the name John of Tipton Bakersfield mean anything to you?" she asked. "With parentheses. Bakersfield tacked on at the end in parentheses."

Watson tipped his head back, gazing toward the ceiling, and grinned. "Oh, dear. You've met the Free Citizens."

"What are you talking about?" Catherine demanded.

"I'd like to know what you're both talking about," Brass said.

"Some clown has taken a lien against my house. And someone's frozen my bank accounts. The same creep, I'm guessing."

"He's got to be a member of the Free Citizens of the Republic," Watson said. "They rename themselves that way. Their given name, then 'of' and their father's surname. Finally, for their last names, they use the parentheses and the place where they were born."

"Why the hell would they do that?" Brass asked.

"Because they're nuts," Watson said. "You think I'm joking. These people are so far out on the edge that they make me look like a bleeding heart liberal."

"Explain, please," Catherine said. "This is my *life* they're screwing with."

"Okay then, here goes. The Free Citizens of the Republic believe that there hasn't been a legitimate United States government since we went off the gold standard in 1933."

"I thought that was necessary to get past the Great Depression," Brass said.

"I'm not telling you what *I* believe—although that point is open to debate—I'm telling you what *they* believe. A government backed by a currency that isn't tied to something of real value—gold, in most cases—can't be legitimate, they claim. Without that legitimacy, they don't owe it any fealty. They refuse to pay into Social Security, or to carry Social Security cards. To use the names shown on their birth certificates would be an admission that the government is real, so they name themselves. They hate the idea of paying taxes, and most of them try to stay off the grid altogether. But they do surface from time to time, and they're happy to use the workings of the government they despise to net people in a web of bureaucratic red tape. Lawsuits, liens, and so on. They'll keep after people, sometimes for years, with little hope of ever winning any judgments, just for the sake of being a huge nuisance."

"That they definitely are."

"Every now and then, they do win a judgment," Watson continued. "That just makes them worse, because it puts money—money not seen as legitimate, in their eyes, although that doesn't keep them from spending it—in their pockets, and it encourages them to try it again."

"And they're after me because—"

"Because as of this morning's early news, you're the new poster girl for authoritarianism. You represent big, oppressive government, and you clearly have a grudge against freedom fighters."

"I didn't. But as of right now, if those people are freedom fighters then I could develop one in a hurry."

"If they've already initiated proceedings against you," Watson said, "your best bet is to challenge them. They probably won't hold up, and you'll be inconvenienced, but not destroyed."

"That's what I'm planning to do, Mr. Watson. Somehow, I had a feeling you'd be able to shed some light."

"Like I said, they're the fringiest of the fringe. I don't disagree with them on taxes and some other issues, but they take things way too far."

Brass stepped close to the taller man. "If you have any influence with them, Watson, make them back off Catherine."

"If I had any influence, I'd disband them. I'm sorry to say I don't. You're on your own, Supervisor Willows. Tread lightly."

"I'll do that," she said, her tone sharp. "Thanks for your concern."

She left the room again, this time joined by Brass. The uniformed officer was still there, and he escorted Watson out the front door. Catherine and Brass trailed behind. Outside, news crews had taken up residence, and they shot footage of Watson stepping out of headquarters. He waved to the cameras, but refused to engage in dialogue.

Catherine noticed someone else, almost as tall as Watson and much bigger around, watching him go. The man had his hands on his hips, flaring his suit jacket behind him. She nudged Brass. "Jim," she said. "One-fifteen. Isn't that Garrett Kovash?"

"I believe you're right," Brass said. "I thought he was at the hospital watching over Daniels."

"I thought so too. I guess we were both misinformed."

"Wouldn't be the first time," Brass said. "Not by a wide margin." He laughed. "In our business, it's pretty much a given."

10

THE INDIGO VALLEY Blood Center was located in an anonymously modern building, heaped with other, similarly nondescript structures into a medical office park. One-stop shopping for anything from a person's first days to last, and all points in between, as long as there was a physical, mental, or emotional problem which a trained professional could hope to repair or manage. Usually at a high price, of course—med school didn't come cheap, Ray knew from experience, and every doctor wanted to pay back student loans in a hurry, the sooner to reap the rewards of intensive study and hard work.

Ray didn't blame them for that mindset, but he was glad it was in his past. There was little in the way of material goods he longed for, these days. He owned books and music, good Scotch, and a home with plenty of space to move around in. His desires now were, he was happy to admit, more cerebral— even, if he could be so bold, spiritual. He wanted to help others; in particular, he wanted to help the victims of violent crimes, or their survivors, reach some kind of peace with what had happened to them. Their lives could never be put right, but they shouldn't have to carry difficult questions with them for all their days. Who did this? Why? To what end? With the exception of those who knowingly embraced a violent lifestyle, most crime victims were plagued by these concerns, as they sought to make sense of an inherently senseless act.

Ray's life—this stage of it, anyway—was dedicated to answering those questions, and to helping ensure that the people who had committed violence against others didn't get the chance to keep doing so.

He had been part of that medical establishment for years. More recently, he had seen it from the other side, as a victim and a patient. A psychopath named Nate Haskell had, in spite of Ray's experience and precautions, played him and attacked him, and Ray had not only lost a kidney but had, in a very real way, lost his innocence. He understood now, in a more immediate and visceral manner than ever before, the one-two body blow of powerlessness and violation that crime victims knew. He was gripped by grief and rage that finally gave way to a grudging acceptance of his new status in life: victim, temporarily disabled, weakened, and vulnerable.

Pulling into the medical park's lot, a momentary wave of nausea gripped him. He pushed it aside, knowing it was nothing more than a reaction to the environment, reminding him of his injuries, of seemingly endless physical therapy sessions, of the pitying looks people tossed him when they thought he couldn't see, as he hobbled with his cane from place to place.

When he passed through the glass front doors of the Indigo Valley Blood Center, a young woman eyed him from the far side of a window. She sat behind a counter, and as he neared, she slid the window aside. "Can I help you?" she asked. "Do you have an appointment?"

He let bemusement win out over the flash of misplaced anger that rose in him first. "I'm not a patient," he said, pulling back his blazer to reveal the badge holder hanging in his inside pocket. "I'm with the Crime Lab."

Her eyes saucered. They were a striking shade of blue, edging toward violet. "Has there been a crime?"

"Not here," he said. "But I am here on official business. I need to find out who the recipient of a marrow donation was."

"I'm sorry, but that's a privacy issue," she said. "We can't reveal that."

"I understand the privacy concerns, believe me. I'm a physician, and I volunteer at a clinic here in town. I'm completely sympathetic. But we have a situation here that trumps privacy. The recipient's life might be in danger . . . or it might be too late altogether."

"I . . . I'm afraid I can't help you."

"Who can? Please, I don't have time for a lot of bureaucratic runaround. Just send me straight to the top."

"Belinda Jones is our managing director," she said. "I'm not sure she's still on the premises, though."

"Please check for me."

She nodded and reached for her phone at the same moment. She touched a couple of keys, waited, caught Ray's gaze. "She's not answering," she whispered. Then, "Oh, hi Belinda. There's a police detective up here at the front. He'd like to speak with you. Okay, thanks." She hung up the phone and met Ray's eyes again. "She'll be right up."

He thanked her, without bothering to correct her misidentification of his job title. Most people, civilians, didn't understand the difference. Any police officer in a uniform was a cop, and any cop in street clothes was a detective, even if he wasn't a cop at all, but a scientist.

The receptionist pointed toward a bank of empty chairs. "You can have a seat there," she said.

"I'm fine," Ray said. Standing still for a long time was painful. But so was sitting and then standing again. Or lying down. Pain was a constant companion. At the moment, he thought standing was easiest, if it wouldn't be too long. And if it was, he would make the woman call Belinda Jones again.

In just a minute or so, he heard the clip-clop footsteps of a woman in heels hurrying down the tile-floored hallway. A trim woman in a conservative gray dress came around a corner. He watched her fix a smile on her face. Her hair was black with a few strands of silver showing, and her skin was smooth and pale.

"I'm Belinda Jones," she said as she neared him.

He let her see the badge, then allowed the jacket to close as he switched his cane to his left hand and offered his right. "Dr. Ray Langston," he said. "I'm with the Las Vegas Police Department Crime Lab."

"Would you like to come to my office?"

"That would be fine, thank you."

"Right this way." She led him back the way she had come, her pace slower, letting him keep up. People in the medical professions got used to being around the infirm. She didn't make small talk; not a word passed between them until they were inside her office with the door closed. Instead of sitting, she leaned against a corner of her desk, gestured toward a straight-backed leather chair. "Please."

"Thank you," Ray said. His gratitude was genuine; he was more than ready to avail himself of the opportunity.

"What is it I can do for you, Dr. Langston?"

"I need information. I'm a medical doctor, I understand all about patient privacy, but I also know the law. Someone's life is at risk, and if I have to get a court order, I will."

"Let's see if we can avoid that," she said. She still wore the same smile she had composed in the hallway, and it had all the authenticity of a horsehair wig.

"That would be my preference, as well. Here's the story. A severed hand was found here in the city, and when we tested the bone marrow for DNA— the tissue was too severely compromised—we came up with a match to a man named Carter Hawkins. Mr. Hawkins has both of the hands he was born with; however, Mr. Hawkins has also been a bone marrow donor, through your facility."

Belinda Jones blinked three times. "I'm not sure I'm following you."

"Under certain circumstances—to which, in this case, I think we have to stipulate, barring other information—donated bone marrow can completely replace native marrow. The DNA of the recipient matches that of the donor, as long as that DNA is derived from marrow. Which, in this case, it was. In order to discover who the hand belongs to, and to find out if its rightful owner is alive or dead or perhaps in serious need of medical attention, we need to know who received Mr. Hawkins's donated marrow."

She was, he noted, a very composed woman. Medical administrators tended not to be emotional types, he had found. They had to stay calm in times of crisis, had to keep cool heads. Ms. Jones's was positively arctic. "I understand."

"So, will you help me? Or do I have to come back with a court order, and sheriff's officers to help me enforce it? It would be unfortunate to have to disrupt your operations for even a day or two, much less weeks, but if we had to search through every file . . ." She came off as so unflappable that he was playing it tough, trying to flap her anyway.

"I'm sure that won't be necessary," she said. She didn't appear the least bit flapped, but she shifted off the corner of the desk and walked around it, sat in her chair, and opened a laptop computer. "The donor's name was Hawkins?"

Ray spelled it for her, and gave her the address and date of birth. Her fingers tap-danced on the keyboard. "The patient's name is Ruben Solis."

"Can you brief me on his circumstances? It might help to find him."

She wrote something down on a sheet of paper, tore it from her pad, and slid it across the desk toward Ray. "There's his address and phone number. He was diagnosed with aplastic anemia. His body stopped producing new red blood cells, because of some damage—"

"Damage to the bone marrow, I know. So his native marrow was depleted—"

Her turn to interrupt, and she seemed glad to do it. "With radiation, in his case."

"And then the donated marrow introduced. It set up housekeeping and generated new blood cells, new stem cells, reproducing itself."

"And so his marrow's DNA would match that of Mr. Hawkins. Very strange, but I guess it makes sense."

"It's an extremely rare occurrence, but not unheard of."

"Well, there's Mr. Solis's contact information. I hope you can find him, and give him back his hand."

"I'm afraid it's a bit worse for wear," Ray said. "But I would like to know how he lost it, and what his present condition is."

"I would appreciate it if you didn't tell him how you found him. We perform an essential function here, Dr. Langston. Getting people to donate blood is a walk in the park compared to marrow donations. People are terrified of the whole idea. They imagine that we're going to have to carve into their bones and scoop it out with spoons, or something. Patient privacy is something that I take very seriously, but I know you could prevail in court if you tried. I gave in, but not happily."

"Noted," Ray said. "Thank you for your cooperation."

"I've never met Mr. Solis, but I hope you find him well."

"As do I, believe me. As do I."

Ruben Solis's home was between Indigo Valley Blood and the crime lab, so Ray swung by on his way back. The neighborhood was the polar opposite of the medical park with its sleek, modern buildings and lots full of new, pricey cars. Approaching Solis's street, Ray covered block after block of run-down homes, neglected yards, corner liquor stores with barred windows and graffiti-stained walls. The few pedestrians eyed him as he passed, their skin mostly brown, hair mostly black, expressions ranging from curious to hostile. This was the Las Vegas the tourists never saw, the neighborhood where hotel maids and dishwashers and landscapers went when their shifts ended.

Ray parked in front of a small house covered in cracked brown stucco, falling somewhere in the architectural range between Santa Fe style and cardboard box. The front yard was poured concrete, painted green. It made a certain sense in a desert climate, but there were more elegant ways to go about it. He crossed the concrete, pulled open a flyspecked screen, and rapped on the door. He could see light through a peephole, and then it went dark.

"What do you want?" a female's voice asked from the other side.

"I'm with the police department's Crime Lab," Ray said. "I'm looking for Ruben Solis."

"I don't know no one like that."

Ray held his badge to the peephole. "Please, ma'am, this would be easier if you could open up. If you want, I can give you the lab's phone number so you can call and make sure I am who I say."

She was quiet for a moment, but then the door opened a few inches, to the length of the security chain. A pretty face appeared in the gap, a mane of thick black hair, brown eyes with laugh lines at the corners. "What?" she asked.

"Doesn't Ruben Solis live here?"

"I told you, no."

"What's your name?"

"Lucia."

"Lucia what?"

"Lucia Navarre."

"Ms. Navarre, I'm Dr. Langston. I'm not a cop, I'm a scientist." He held up the cane, as if to demonstrate his harmlessness. "It's very important that I find Mr. Solis. He's not in any trouble, but he might be in some kind of danger."

Lucia closed the door again. Ray heard her release the chain, and then she opened it. She was short, on the heavy side for a city that idealized tall, thin, and leggy, but with hints of a lush figure beneath a baggy Las Vegas Chiefs jersey and black jeans. She was probably in her twenties, but had the kind of skin that could stay youthful well into her forties. She kept her gaze aimed somewhere toward the ground behind Ray. "I told you already twice, I don't know him."

"Do you live here alone, ma'am?"

"Since my husband went away, yes."

CSIs were trained to notice things that others might miss. In this instance, Ray noticed that although she had willingly opened the door, she clutched it in a death grip so tight that her knuckles were blanched. Her weight was on her left leg, and the heel of her right foot was tapping fast enough to power the city, should Hoover Dam fail. She was nervous. There were plenty of reasons for a Latina to be anxious in the presence of law enforcement, but the most common involved immigration status, which was no concern of Ray's.

"I really need to find Mr. Solis," he said again. "I'm not here to make trouble for you or anyone else."

She met his gaze at last, giving him an exasperated look. He knew why—because he wasn't buying her story. Maybe it was the truth. But this address was the only thing Ray had to go on. And Lucia was so nervous he couldn't help thinking she was hiding something. Maybe Solis was the husband who had moved out.

The place was furnished inexpensively, with little in the way of decoration. But on shelves in the living room there were dozens of strange little constructions, wooden boxes with scenes inside them. There were street scenes and desert scenes, interiors and out, all the people fabricated with what looked like found objects—pieces of hardware, nails and bolts and bits of shredded screen, scraps of wood, melted plastic, chunks of tire. "Those are interesting," he said. "Did you make them?"

"My . . . my husband did."

"What was your husband's name?"

She didn't hesitate. "Enrique."

Ray decided to play a hunch. She wasn't being honest with him, he could tell that much. If he tried to push too hard, she would just clam up. She was certainly within her rights to do so. He didn't want that to happen, and if he had to employ a little subterfuge of his own to find Solis, he would do so. "I'm sorry to be a bother, Ms. Navarre. Since I was injured . . . I wonder if I could use your restroom." As if thinking better of it, he turned away. "No, I'm sorry, that's so rude—"

"It's fine," she interrupted. "Go ahead."

"If you're sure."

"Yes, of course." She stepped back from the door and indicated a dark doorway down the hall. "It's just there."

"Thank you," he said. "Thank you so much."

He moved past her, went into the bathroom and turned on the light. Inside, he ran water at a trickle for a few moments, while he scanned the medicine cabinet to see if Ruben's name appeared on any prescription drugs. It didn't, but his gaze landed on a hairbrush, thick with black hair. Some strands were long and lustrous, like Lucia's, but others were short and coarse. He took the piece of paper on which Ruben's name and address were written from his pocket, put the hairs in the middle, and folded up the lower one-third of the sheet. He folded the upper third over that, then repeated the process with the sides. When he was finished, he tucked one end into the other. The result was called a druggist fold, and it was accepted in the forensic science field as a good way to secure small evidence samples, without fear that adhesives from tape or glue might contaminate them.

He flushed the toilet, washed his hands, plucked a few more stray long hairs from the brush and emerged from the bathroom. "Ms. Navarre, I wonder if I might take a few hairs from your brush?" he asked, displaying the ones in his hand. "Just to run a DNA test, to make sure that I can exclude you."

"Exclude me from what?"

"Well, the truth is we're not positive that Ruben Solis is who we're looking for." Which was true, as far as it went—Ray had thought he was looking for Carter Hawkins at first. Until he found Solis, he wouldn't know for certain.

"So you might be looking for a woman?"

"It's hard to say. I don't think so. But if I can test these then I'll know for sure it's not you."

"Well . . ."

"I promise you, I'm not looking to create any problems for you. I don't know what your citizenship status is, and I'm not going to ask. I don't know if you are employed, or where. All I want is to answer some questions about the whereabouts and condition of Mr. Solis—or whoever—and leave you in peace."

"Okay, I guess," Lucia said.

"Thank you." He tucked the hairs into his shirt pocket, patted it. Entirely useless, for evidentiary purposes. But she had granted permission to remove hairs from the house, and he was doing so.

The long hairs, he was pretty sure, were hers. The

shorter ones, almost certainly not. If Ruben Solis's DNA—his *own* DNA, not the borrowed stuff—was in the system, then he could find out if they belonged to him. And if they did, Ray would be making a return visit to Lucia Navarre's house, sometime very soon.

11

DETECTIVE LOUIS VARTANN walked close to Catherine as she made the rounds of the lab, checking in on her people. Though they were dating, Catherine and Vartann were too professional to let the depth of their attraction show in public, especially at work. But Vartann spoke in quiet tones, most of the time, and she didn't mind keeping him near so they could speak freely. He seemed to like it as well.

Her immediate concern—besides looking in on the progress David Hodges was making with trace evidence recovered at the bombing site, and seeing Archie Johnson's progress enhancing security video from there and the alley where the fire was started—was trying to figure out who had targeted her for harassment, and why. She had described the broad strokes, and he had asked some pointed questions, many of which she couldn't answer.

"Here's what I'm thinking," she explained. "Maybe someone is just mad at me for whatever I said, or they think I said, or I was reported to have said—and believe me, by now I've heard so many different versions of it that even I'm not positive what I really said. If that's the case, fine. I said something I shouldn't have, and I'll take my lumps. But what if whoever has filed these actions against me is doing it to steer me away from the investigation, to distract me? Then it might be the bomber himself. If we can find out who this John of Tipton is, that might lead us directly to the bomber, or to someone who knows him."

"And in a case like this, whichever angle gets you there fastest is the one you want to use," Vartann added.

"That's right. So far he hasn't killed anyone. I'd love to keep it that way."

"Well, I haven't found John of Tipton yet. But I've been doing some digging into the Free Citizens of the Republic group, and I have to say, they've got some strange ideas."

"I gathered that." Catherine stopped behind Archie, who was intent on a video monitor. "How's that going?" she asked.

"I can run it back for you," Archie said. "This is the street scene, an hour before the bomb went off. I've got video from two different angles, but unfortunately neither of them shows the whole street. There are people moving in and out of frame, but I haven't been able to pin down anyone placing or detonating the explosives." He paused the video and tapped the screen. "This is the only guy who keeps appearing and reappearing."

Catherine angled for a better view. The man

Archie had indicated looked homeless, his clothing ragged, face unshaven. He pushed a baby buggy, but the buggy's occupant didn't look like any baby she had ever seen. "Is that a dog?"

"Sure is."

"Oh, that's Dogman," Vartann said. "He's harmless."

"He's hanging around the bombing scene."

"Dogman's mildly schizophrenic, but he's no trouble when he takes his meds. He definitely doesn't have the capacity to construct a bomb."

"He might have seen something," Catherine pointed out.

"Could be. Whether or not he'll remember it is another story. And you wouldn't want to have to rely on his testimony in court."

"What were you doing before we interrupted, Archie?" Catherine asked.

"Looking for reflections."

"Of what?"

"There are a lot of reflective surfaces on the block. Car windows, shop windows, polished chrome, that sort of thing. I'm trying to find and isolate those, then enhance as much as I can to see if maybe our guy appears somewhere."

"Good thinking," Catherine said.

"Oh, and I have this for you. Those ISPs you asked for." Joanna Daniels had turned over threatening e-mails that had been sent to her husband, and several letters of the same nature that had come by regular mail. Those were with a Questioned Documents tech, but Catherine had asked Archie to run down the ISP addresses from which the e-mails had originated.

"Thanks. That was quick."

Archie turned and gave her a smile. "I do what I can."

"Best we can hope for." With a subtle nod, she and Vartann kept walking. The lab was cool, and one of the city's most advanced air circulation systems kept it virtually odor free, scrubbing every liter of oxygen several times an hour. "What have you learned?" she asked Vartann when they had moved out of Archie's earshot.

"Watson told you about the Free Citizens' belief that the government turned traitor when they abandoned the gold standard," Vartann said. "But did he tell you about the North American merit?"

"What's that, some kind of bird?"

"It's the currency that they believe is scheduled to replace the American and Canadian dollars, and the Mexican peso."

"Merits? Where did that come from?"

"Who knows? Somebody with a high fever, I'm guessing."

"When is this supposed to happen?"

"Soon, apparently. The black helicopters will bring North American United Army troops to our neighborhoods, and the jackbooted thugs will go door to door collecting dollars and replacing them with merits, legal tender in Mexico, the U.S., and Canada."

"Wow," Catherine said. They passed by the ballistics lab, where Earl was running computer simulations to measure the explosive blast, in an attempt to figure out just what substances were involved, and in what precise quantities.

"They're getting ready for the changeover by buying precious gems, especially diamonds. Those, they say, will never go down in value, no matter what. There'll always be an international market for them."

"I don't understand how people come up with such bizarre ideas, Lou. Or why other people ever believe them."

"There's pretty much no limit to what people will believe."

"I guess that's always been true."

"Something else Watson said is true, too—they are hoarding weapons and ammunition. Most of it seems to be purchased legally, and there's a paper trail. They go to states where gun laws are the most lax and buy up whatever they can. Nothing illegal about it, but when you put a lot of weapons together with a paranoid, extremist mentality, then you have the building blocks of a scary situation."

They reached Catherine's office and went inside. She took her usual chair behind the desk. Vartann folded his arms over his chest, leaning against a filing cabinet. "A couple of their top dogs are in town tonight," he said. "Giving a seminar, of all things. They call it an informational session on the coming economic crash—"

"I thought we already had that."

"I guess they mean the one that'll happen when the merits come in. Anyway, the guys leading the seminar are Steven and Troy Kirkland. Father and son. Steven's the dad, and the grand old man of the Free Citizens movement. They travel around the country, seeking out recruits for the cause."

"And staying one step ahead of the IRS, I'm sure." Jim Brass slouched in the doorway, though Catherine hadn't heard him approach. For a big man, he could move as silently as a summer breeze.

"I should go," Catherine said. "See if they can call off this John of Tipton fellow."

"No way," Vartann said.

"He's right," Brass added. "You're already a target. The last thing you should be doing is stirring up that particular hornet's nest. I can go, poke around, see if I can find anything out."

"I'll go with you," Vartann said. "You need to stay away from those people, Cath. At least until the crosshairs are off you."

She understood their point. They were right. She had already become personally involved in this case in a way she shouldn't have. Going to that seminar, confronting the group's leaders, would just be digging herself in deeper.

At the same time, she had been a grown-up for a long time. She didn't like relying on anyone to look out for her interests, and the fact that those people had drawn her into their drama—and threatened the home she and her daughter lived in—infuriated her. Confrontation might be a bad idea, professionally. But it would feel so good.

"All right," she said with reluctance. "I'll stay away from them. For now. But if you get a line on this Tipton joker—"

"We'll let you know, Cath," Vartann promised.

"Good."

"I found out another interesting tidbit," Vartann said. "You should stick around for this, Jim."

"I got a few minutes."

"Apparently the Free Citizens and BOOM have a history. And not a happy one. They've been feuding for years. Both groups came up during the 1990s, originally. The Free Citizens have always been fringier, a little farther out of the mainstream. And although they share some common goals, their approaches have made them practically mortal enemies, with the Free Citizens accusing BOOM of selling out to big business and politics as usual, and BOOM calling the Free Citizens dangerous nutbags. The rivalry has been physical, at times, with group members assaulting each other, planting pipe bombs in mailboxes, that sort of thing. The Free Citizens are suspected in a couple of larger bombing plots, as well, though there's never been enough evidence to bring charges on those. There have been some arrests on both sides, but no one's been able to connect those incidents to the group leaders."

"That is interesting," Brass said. "So when Watson told us that the Free Citizens are stockpiling weapons . . ."

"That's definitely true. But it calls into question his motive for telling you. Was he just being an upright citizen—?

Catherine finished for him. "Or was he trying to sic us on his rivals?"

"Exactly," Vartann said. "Either way, I'm working on getting a warrant. Considering what's been going on, it would be good to know if the Free Citizens armory includes ammonium nitrate."

12

SEAN VOET LOOKED like an unlikely rebel.

When Brass rang the doorbell of his ground floor apartment in a brick apartment building, painted aqua and named Tradewinds Apts., the man who answered the door did so on one leg. He supported himself on wooden crutches festooned with colorful stickers and phrases written in marker. His left leg, Brass noted, was leaning against a threadbare couch in the living room behind him. The prosthetic went up to mid-thigh.

Voet's arms and shoulders looked to be in pretty good shape, though his left forearm was more scar tissue than skin. His desert camo fatigue shirt hung open, displaying a distinct paunch and a latticework of scars climbing his chest. His hair was straight, brushing his collar in the back, more gray than brown. He looked at Brass through thick-lensed, metal-framed glasses and wiped a lock of hair off his forehead. "Yeah?"

"Are you Sean Voet?"

"Yeah."

Brass showed badge and ID. "I'm Captain Brass, LVPD."

"You outrank me," Voet said. "I never made it past specialist." He tapped his left thigh. "The war ended for me before I had much of a chance to move up."

"Which one?" Brass asked. "Vietnam for me."

"Desert Storm." Voet replied. "Third Squadron, Second Armored Cav. At 74 Easting, our Bradley took fire from the Republican Guard—bastards were eager to surrender in some places, but not there. They crippled us, then opened up on us with the seventy-three millimeter gun of a Russian-made BMP-1. Scored a direct hit. Two guys were KIA, and I was—well, you can see. Guys were scraping me up to put me in a body bag when I surprised them by not being dead."

"Sorry," Brass said. He truly was. Soldiers who went to war knew the risks going in—it was what they had signed up for. But he always preferred them to come home in one piece, and upright. Too often, it didn't happen that way.

"Is what it is," Voet said. He made his way back over to the couch, sat down beside the leg. "Damn thing itches sometimes, especially if I've been on it all day."

"While demonstrating outside a cable news office, for example."

"That's right." Voet glared at him, chin angled up. Defiant. "Something on your mind, Cap?"

"I respect your service, Mr. Voet. And I would defend your right to protest until my dying day. But these e-mails you sent to Dennis Daniels . . ." He drew some printouts from an inner jacket pocket, scanned down the first page. "This is choice. 'Your head should be on a pole to warn the other lapdogs of industry not to screw with the American people.' Or how about this one? 'When we're done with you there won't be enough left to fill an airplane barf bag.' Come on, Sean, you really think that's an appropriate thing to say to anybody?"

"It is if that's the way I feel."

"You really want to kill Daniels?"

Voet shook his head, clearing that wayward lock from his eyes. "Okay, it's hyperbole, for the most part. I'm trying to make a point, all right? Guys like this, they pretend to be on the side of the people. But when push comes to shove, they're carrying water for Wall Street, for the coal companies and the oil companies and the big defense companies, just like the rest of them."

"It's a free country. Nobody's making you watch DCN or any other channel."

"No. But they can use their power to influence elections, and that does affect all of us."

"You got an answer for everything, don't you?"

"Dude, I gave my leg for this country. I spent nine months at Walter Reed after I was finally stateside. Long enough for a woman to have a baby, right? Only in my case, it was me who was being born. Reborn. I had been headed for a middle-American, middle-class life. I had a wife and a dog waiting for me in Columbus, Ohio. But while I was at Walter Reed, my wife sold the dog and divorced me and moved to Rhode Island with a truck driver."

"That stinks," Brass said.

"Tell me about it. Anyway, while I was there, I realized a few things. Walter Reed was a dump then. Nobody took care of you guys when you came back from Nam, and no one was looking out for us, either. This country had decided that wars shouldn't happen, so even when they do, most people try to pretend they're not real. If they accidentally see anything on the evening news, they imagine it's a movie, and Brad Pitt or Ben Affleck is the grunt on the screen taking fire. We don't ask the country to make any sacrifices, or even to acknowledge the effort. We run our wars off the books, passing on the cost to future generations instead of paying for them with new taxes or spending cuts."

"I'm with you so far," Brass said. He needn't have bothered; Voet was wound up and would have continued without the prompt.

"So I came to the conclusion that we just shouldn't have any more wars. I mean, if we're not going to take them seriously. Why not just disband the armed forces, pull everybody out of Iraq and Afghanistan? We can beef up the Coast Guard and the Border Patrol, in case anybody tries to attack us. But as for playing policeman to the world? There's no stomach for it anymore. We're better off not funding a military than sending people out to die for a country that won't even acknowledge the sacrifice."

"So that's your beef with Daniels?"

"I moved to Vegas after I got out of Walter Reed. Figured what better place to start life over? There was nothing left for me in Columbus. So here I am, and there's Daniels, just another cog in the machine, pushing for programs that dump more tax-payer money into the military-industrial system that chews up people like me and spits us out. As long as he backs bills that raise taxes instead of slashing the military budget, I will keep protesting him."

"And threatening his life," Brass reminded him. "Because he's in town, and it's convenient for you."

"Like I said, the threats are hyperbole. I'm trying to make a point, to get his attention."

"So when you said you'd bury him up to his eye-balls in the desert and let the rattlesnakes and scor-pions get him—"

"I mean, how can you take that seriously? Espe-cially now that you've met me? I don't know if you've ever tried to dig a hole with just one leg, but let me tell you, it ain't easy."

"I'm sure."

"What else did I say in those? Something about tying him to my rear axle by his ankles and driving to Guatemala, right?"

"I think that was in there."

"Come on, man."

"Some of your threats are pretty far out there, Sean, I'll give you that. But there are others. 'I'll kill you.' 'I'll rip your lungs out.' 'I'll cut you into pieces and drop them in a shark tank.' Those are more be-lievable, and more sinister. You sure had Mrs. Dan-iels concerned."

"I'm not a genuinely violent man, Cap. I used to be, but after Desert Storm I gave that shit up. Now I talk a good game, but that's it. I'm just trying to scare the dude."

Brass had not been invited to sit, but he parked

himself on the arm of a big, overstuffed chair. "Where were you last night? Midnight to one, say?"

Voet barked a short laugh. "Here. What, you think maybe I was out dancing?"

"Dancing would be better than here, unless you've got a witness."

"Just me and the tube. I don't sleep much these days, Cap. Lots of late movies. Last night I spent time with Ronald Colman and Marlene Dietrich."

"*Kismet*?" Brass asked.

"No, I looked in the program guide." Voet laughed again. He sounded like a strangled seal. "See, kismet means fate or destiny, and—"

"I know what it means."

"Yeah, I was watching *Kismet*. Fell asleep during it, in fact."

Brass nodded. "I've seen it, so I'm not surprised. It's better than the Howard Keel remake, though. Still, Sean, that's a pretty weak alibi."

"It's what I got."

Voet had not been the only person who had threatened Daniels, not by a long shot. He had been one of the most persistent, however, and he had been local. And he'd been photographed at the demonstrations on multiple occasions. Those factors were the ones that had set off Joanna Daniels's radar, and Brass's as well. The next most frequent threat-maker lived in Kentucky, and had been making similar threats toward people in industry and politics since 1979. Brass had a couple of other Las Vegas residents to check out—and of course, it was possible that the bomber had traveled to the city to pull off his attack, or was one of the quiet ones who didn't broadcast his intentions. Those sorts would have to be dealt with through a wider-ranging investigation, and increased security around Daniels.

Brass considered himself a pretty fair judge of people. The impression he got from Voet was that the man was telling the truth. He was opinionated, maybe obnoxiously so. He sent messages without thinking them through. But he was most likely harmless. At any rate, although his alibi was weak, failing the discovery of some evidence placing him at one or more of the crime scenes, it was good enough.

"Okay, Sean," Brass said. "Do me a favor, will you?"

"What's that, Cap?"

"Stop threatening people. If you have a cause, then work for it all you want, but don't threaten the lives of people you disagree with."

"I'll try, Cap. I honestly will."

"One more thing, Sean?"

"Yeah?"

"Stop calling me Cap."

13

NICK AND SARA followed Harley Givens back up the hill. As he climbed, Givens clutched his shotgun like it was a lifeline and he a drowning man. He threw glances their way from time to time, as if making sure they weren't gaining on him. Nick understood that Givens was within his rights to carry the weapon, but he was still a little sensitive about shotguns, having recently been leveled by one. Only his Kevlar vest had saved his life, that time. He was wearing it again, even though it was a bit bulky for backwoods hiking.

As they neared the top, they heard voices and vehicles—engines cutting out, doors slamming. Sara caught Nick's eyes. "Maybe the evacuation's over?"

"Could be."

Givens must have heard the exchange, because he shot them an angry look. His face was flushed, from the climb, his anger, or both. "I told you nobody stopped me!"

"We were supposed to be told, Mr. Givens," Nick said. "Apparently that didn't happen."

"I think we're the low heads on the communication totem pole out here," Sara said quietly. "The rangers and Forest Service firefighters are used to talking to each other. They *have* to talk to Castillo. But they haven't figured out how to bring us into the loop yet."

"I hope they figure it out soon. This wasn't a big deal, but if there's something serious—like they lose control of the fire again—I'd sure like to know about it."

"Best thing we can do is try to stay on their screens. Make sure we check in once in a while, make sure they see us around."

"Yeah, you're right." Nick smiled at her. "It's kind of like old times, isn't it? You and me out here."

"Kind of," Sara agreed.

Most of the men at the lab had had crushes on Sara at one time or another. Greg's had been a serious one. Nick had appreciated her smarts, her wry sense of humor—so subtle sometimes that hours could pass before anyone figured out she had told a joke—and her physical beauty, but he had never longed for her the way some others had. They had been friends, as close as siblings, and that was how they'd liked it.

Grissom, of course, was the one she fell for. She had left town, and then he had as well, chasing her into the jungles of Costa Rica before they finally reached the understanding that everyone else at the lab had already decided was the only sensible one.

There had been times Nick had missed having her

around, and the fact that she was back, working beside him, was a source of joy. He had resolved not to take her for granted, and the same went for the rest of the team. Coming close to death sharpened one's intellect in that way—made a person understand that time with anyone precious was always too short. Nick hadn't always been careful enough about that, but he was determined to try.

Givens reached the crest of the slope before them and disappeared. By the time Nick and Sara made it up, the sounds of conversation from the street were continuous. When they cleared the rise, they found out why.

There had been fourteen houses on this stretch of road leading up to it. With the evacuation order lifted, most of the families occupying them had returned. Every house had suffered at least some damage when the fire roared through. Seven were completely totaled, nothing left but charred timbers, stone chimneys, and ash. Most of the residents hadn't gone inside their homes yet, or if they had they'd come right back out again. They stood in the street, talking to neighbors and friends, as if to weigh the damage individually would be too hard to bear.

Close to the path they had taken up the hill, a young man—a boy, really, not out of his teens—stood at the cliff's edge, looking down into the burned forest. While Nick watched, he shook a cigarette out of a pack and shoved it between his lips, then drew a disposable lighter from his pocket and thumbed fire from it. The sudden lick of flame struck Nick with the force of a curse word shouted in church—to be lighting a fire, here and now, with those people who had lost everything so close by, seemed inappropriate at best.

"Let's have a talk with this kid," he said.

"Okay." Sara walked toward him. The kid saw her coming and turned away from her. "Hey," she said. Nick picked up his pace, in case the kid tried to run.

He didn't. He stayed where he was, eyeing the forest and ignoring the CSIs. "Excuse me," Sara said.

He finally deigned to acknowledge her, letting a billow of smoke issue from his nose and mouth. "'S'up?"

"I'm Sara Sidle from the Las Vegas Crime Lab," Sara said. "That's Nick Stokes."

"Long way from home."

"We're here on special assignment."

"Congratulations." The kid sucked in more smoke, leaked it out through his nose. He was heavyset and he stood with his feet well apart, as if bracing for a cannonball to be fired at him. Nick thought he just might be able to keep his balance. His hair was long and dark blond, and he had an unruly wisp of beard and whiskers that reminded Nick of photographs he had seen of Civil War officers. He seemed to be squinting against his own smoke, but Nick got the impression that it was his usual expression, a sort of bored superiority.

"What's your name?" Nick asked.

"Kevin."

"Kevin what?"

"Cox."

"You have any idea how the fire started, Kevin?"

Kevin wiggled his shoulders. "I don't know. Lightning?"

"There hasn't been a storm up here in more than a month," Nick said.

Kevin gave another shrug, sucked on his smoke. The end glowed bright orange.

"Do you know anything about those people who were camping down the hill there?" Sara asked. "The ones who've been there for a couple of months?"

"Seen 'em a few times."

"That's not really an answer."

Kevin took another king drag on the cigarette. "Best I can do. Seen 'em, don't know 'em."

"Do you know where they went, after the fire started?" Sara asked.

"Nope."

"Okay, Kevin," Nick said. "You think of anything that might help us, you let us know. Think you can do that?"

Kevin dropped the cigarette, half-smoked, to the ground. "Guess so." As if just realizing that the CSIs were paying attention, he pressed his hiking boot onto the cigarette, crushing it into the ground with an exaggerated motion. When he had thoroughly pulverized it, he moved his foot and examined his work. "It's out."

"That's good," Sara said. "Living up here, you should make sure they all are."

She and Nick left Kevin staring over the edge, and went toward the largest knot of local residents. Harley Givens was there with his shotgun resting against his shoulder. There were about twenty-five people in all, Nick judged. One woman sat on the ground near the group, her face buried in her hands, softly weeping. Others had marks on their faces where tears had tracked through dust or ash. All around were grim expressions and clenched fists. Even those who had fared the best had little reason to celebrate.

"You ask me," Givens was saying, "it's those damn hippies. Cops wouldn't let me hunt 'em down."

"We're not cops," Nick interrupted. "We're CSIs. Crime scene investigators."

"Whatever," Givens shot back. "You work for the cops. And you're way out of your jurisdiction."

"Gee, Nick," Sara said. "Do you suppose everyone we meet up here will remind us of that?"

"We're on special assignment for the state attorney general's office," Nick explained. "So there are no jurisdictional issues with us being here."

"Well, I hope they were burned to a crisp," Givens said. "There a law against that?"

"No, sir."

"Harley's right," another man said. He was thin and reedy as a sapling, tanned to a tree bark-brown, and he wore white tennis shorts, a T-shirt, and a gray cardigan. "Just about all of us have had some sort of run-in with that pair."

"What kind of run-ins?" Sara asked.

"I caught 'em using my hot tub one night," the thin man replied. "Janey over there had 'em picking from one of her fruit trees a couple months ago."

"And someone stole my bicycle," another resident added. "A ten-speed. Never saw it again."

"I didn't see a bike down at the campsite," Nick said. "Anybody else ever see them with it?"

"Maybe they sold it in the city."

"The thing is," the thin man went on, "they just plain don't belong here. I mean, how is it right? We pay hefty mortgages to live here, and they come along and mooch off the land, steal from us."

"I see your point, Mr.—" Sara said.

"Collin Gardner." He pointed to a house that was mostly intact, except for a black patch in the shake roof. Nick was pretty sure the roof was a goner, and it would have to be replaced before winter came along. "That's my place there."

"I think I understand how you feel, Mr. Gardner," Sara said. "But if you had complaints about them, I'm sure there are appropriate mechanisms for that around here. You could have called the sheriff if you suspected them of crimes."

"We're not all mountain folk," Givens said. "Some of us are, I am, others retired up here. We're from all over. But we all got something in common with mountain folk. We see a problem and we want to handle it ourselves."

"I did call the sheriff," the woman Gardner had called Janey said. "He said if I hadn't seen anyone at the fruit trees, how did I know it wasn't birds, or raccoons?"

That seemed like a legitimate question to Nick, but he decided to let it lie.

"I'd like to get my hands on those two," Gardner said. "Show them how we feel about them around here."

Some of the others shouted their support for his

attitude. The whole scene made Nick uncomfortable, as mobs promising frontier justice always did. He supposed that most of the neighbors genuinely believed the campers had started the fire, but he had serious doubts. For one thing, it appeared that they had still been at their campsite after the fire started, and had fled as it came toward them. If they had started it, they wouldn't have done so in a place where it was sure to burn directly toward their camp. And they wouldn't have sat there waiting for it.

Given the nature of the complaints, he thought it was much more likely that someone else had started it to burn them out. They seemed to have a good thing going, and little motivation to ruin it. If anything, the campers seemed more like targets to Nick than villains. He knew he had to keep an open mind, to let the evidence dictate the theories, but so far, the idea that the campers were at fault seemed a stretch.

They were still standing there, one person expressing an opinion, then another, sometimes talking over one another, when a forest-green Suburban pulled into a driveway. A woman got out from behind the wheel with a ferocious look on her face. "Mrs. Fontaine," someone said. "I'm so sorry about Ty."

Nick recognized the name—Marc Fontaine had been the fire captain who had died.

"Are you okay, Marla?" someone else asked. "Do you need anything?"

Marla Fontaine ignored the words of concern. She strode directly to where Givens stood, and tilted her face toward his. She was about eight inches shorter, but she didn't look like someone to take lightly. "This is your fault, Harley Givens," she said. "You and Marc, you were always at odds. He tried and he tried to get you to cut back the brush, the trees, to build in defensible space around your homes." She swept her arms in a circle, encompassing the whole gathering. "All of you. Some were worse than others." She poked a finger toward Givens. "But Harley was worst of all. Telling Ty that his advice was unwelcome and unneeded. Calling him a worrywart. A little girl, isn't that what you said last time? That he sounded just like a little girl worried about the boogeyman in the closet. You didn't like it because he reported you a time or two, and you had to pay some fines. If you had worried a little more and argued a little less, he might still be here."

"Now, look, Marla," Givens began. "I'm sorry as hell for your loss. We all are."

"That's right!" someone else added.

"But you got no call to be throwing blame around," Givens continued. "Hell, a lot of wildfires are started by contract firefighters, just to make sure they got work coming in. I'm not saying that's the case here, but for all I know . . . anyhow, I'm just saying that until you know all the facts you shouldn't be throwing around accusations."

Marla's face went a shade of crimson, and she slapped Givens across the face, her hand moving faster than he could react to. The slap was as loud as a rifle shot in the sudden silence. "You know full well Ty never did such a thing," she snapped.

"Everybody take a step back," Sara said. She waded into the crowd, shouldering her way between Marla Fontaine and Harley Givens. "Tensions are high right now, and there's a lot of work to be done rebuilding, so let's not make things any harder than they have to be. Mrs. Fontaine, I am so sorry for your loss, believe me. If I were you, I would go home and remember the good things about your husband, and not let anyone around here aggravate you for a while."

"That," Marla said, "sounds like excellent advice. Thank you."

"We're with the Las Vegas Crime Lab. Do you mind if we talk to you for a minute?"

"No, that would be fine."

She let Sara steer her away from the crowd. Nick held his ground a moment, letting his presence serve as a reminder that Marla Fontaine was not to be messed with, then stepped to the side to join the huddle.

"Some of those people are perfectly nice," Marla was saying. "But that Givens man just peeves me so. He's lived up here for a long time, decades, so the others look to him, as if he were the ultimate fount of knowledge. There's a way that mountain people are—I suppose country people, pioneers of any sort, really. They like to do things their own way, and they don't like anyone coming along and telling them differently."

"I'm familiar with the syndrome," Sara said.

"I'm sure. Anyway, that's Harley in a nutshell. When he moved up here, the concern about wild-land-urban interface fires didn't really exist. Hardly anybody lived in the danger area, and it was a different time, with different standards. In those days, if a forest fire burned your house, you were just out of luck. Now those transition zones are so crowded, developments pushing right up to the edge of the wilderness, and everybody expects that their homes will be just as safe as if they were in a suburban neighborhood somewhere near the city, with underground pipelines and functional hydrants. People like Harley encourage the others to ignore the warnings that Marc made, that *everyone* familiar with the danger makes. He tells them that there's never been a bad fire on this part of the mountain. Does that mean there never will be? Of course not. It just means when it does come, it's going to be a doozy. And as you've seen, when it does come, they aren't prepared for it." She waved a hand at the house she had parked in front of. It looked like a textbook example of the principles she had described, and the fire hadn't so much as skinned it. "We were, thank goodness, and that saved our home. But it didn't save my husband."

Her eyes were tearing up as she spoke. "We're very sorry," Nick said, although he knew Sara had just said it a few minutes ago. Sometimes it couldn't be repeated enough.

"Thank you. Anyway, I haven't any proof or anything like that, but that man has been such a thorn in our sides, I wouldn't be the least bit surprised if he started the fire to get back at Marc."

"Get back at him for what?"

"There are laws about maintaining one's property, so that it doesn't become a danger to others. Ty turned Harley in recently—again. Harley will be stuck with a hefty fine. His neighbors could sue him, if they can prove that his willful neglect harmed their homes. But he knew about the report and the fine, and I think he was so angry with Ty that he could have started the fire, just out of pure meanness. Or spite. Or maybe he thought he could frame Marc for it."

"That's a very serious accusation, ma'am," Nick said.

"I'm well aware. It's what I believe. It may or may not be true, but I feel in my heart that it is."

"We'll certainly take it into consideration," Sara promised.

"That's all I can ask for. Thank you for your time."

She turned on her heel and walked past her Suburban. At her front door, she fumbled momentarily with the keys, then managed to open it. Once inside, she tossed a final, bitter look at the gathering, then slammed the door. Nick hoped she didn't have a shotgun handy.

"That could have been quite a scene," Nick said later, as he and Sara were starting back down the hill. "You handled it well."

"I just didn't want to see it escalate," Sara said. "Sometimes a slap can turn into a brawl."

"I hear you. What do you think about her theory?"

"I think," Sara said, "that we'll have to check it out. It's just a gut suspicion—but so far, my gut thinks there might be something to it."

14

RAY FOUND HIMSELF back at Lucia Navarre's house sooner than he had expected.

The DNA lab had been able to get to the hairs he'd brought back almost immediately. They didn't have time to run enough tests to narrow down the identity of the donors—if they were even in the system—but they did manage to discover one significant fact.

Hair that had been yanked from a head was often missing the follicle, which was the best source of nuclear DNA. But the shaft itself contained mitochondrial DNA, passed down from the mother. And the mitochondrial DNA located in the two distinct hair samples Ray had found in Lucia's brush showed that the people to whom those hairs had been attached had the same mother.

She answered the door almost immediately. "You again?"

"Me again," Ray said. "Sorry to trouble you so

soon, Ms. Navarre, but I'm afraid that you weren't straight with me last time."

"What do you mean? I told you every—"

Ray cut her off. "You didn't tell me that your brother either lives here or stays here sometimes."

"What brother?"

"The one whose hairs were in the hairbrush in your bathroom."

"You said you were taking my hairs."

"I'm afraid I wasn't specific about which hairs I was taking. But I did ask your permission, and you granted it."

"Not for that."

"It's done," Ray said. "The point is, you weren't honest with me. If Ruben Solis is your brother, then you've got to trust me, because he could be in a great deal of danger."

She eyed him for several long moments. "How do I know? That I can trust you, like you say?"

"You don't have much choice," Ray said. "I could turn you over to the LVPD or Immigration."

She visibly flinched when he mentioned Immigration and Customs Enforcement. Her reaction did not come as a surprise. "I haven't . . . I'm not . . ."

But Lucia couldn't finish her sentence. She sucked in a couple of deep breaths and then backed away from the door a few steps, turned her back to Ray, and buried her face in her hands. Ray followed her inside and closed the door.

"I'm really not here to make your life difficult," he promised her. "I just want to find Ruben, before it's too late. If you come clean with me, I'll do everything I can to help you both. That's all I can offer you."

Without looking back, she led Ray into her tiny living room. She collapsed onto a plaid fabric-covered chair with arms so worn Ray could see the wood beneath the cover. Ray stepped behind a sofa mostly occupied by two big bags of clothing that had probably recently come in from a Laundromat, and studied the bookcase full of odd little art pieces. Up close, he could see that the figures had distinctive personalities: one redheaded woman was playing an accordion made of folded paper, with a painted smile on her face. In another, a heavyset man made from a crushed soda can drooped in a chair while wire children scampered around him.

There were grooves in the floor of each box, which he hadn't noticed before. "Do these figures move?" he asked.

"There's a key in the back," she said. "You wind it up."

"May I?"

"Sure."

He took the one with the big, sad man off the shelf. The key in the back looked like something from a music box. When he wound it, he felt tension build. He released the key, and the wire children circled around the aluminum can man in a stuttering dance.

"That's impressive," he said. He looked at the others, probably thirty in all, and they all had similar tracks for the figures to move on. "Did you make these?"

"Ruben did."

"He's very skilled." He almost added "with his hands," but he caught himself in time. He put the box back on the shelf. A stray thought flitted through his mind—that someone who could make these could also construct a bomb. But there was no earthly reason to link this case to the attack on Dennis Daniels.

Lucia breathed in and looked toward the ceiling. She was afraid of something, but was it him? Afraid for Ruben? Or just afraid in general, living with perpetual fear, like many undocumented people? "All right," she said. "It's true. I don't have any papers. Only the thing is, I've lived here all my life, almost. Ruben, too. Our mother brought us here when I was, like, four and Ruben was just a baby. Then she got busted and deported. She left us here so we'd have a chance for a better life. She was going to come back again, but before she could, she got sick. She died down there, and my aunt Esmerelda raised us here. She couldn't get us papers because she wasn't a parent or a legal guardian, but she took care of us like she was.

"I finished high school, and went to community college. I got an accounting degree, and I figured there would be a career for someone like me, who was smart and ambitious. A country as big and rich and wonderful as the U.S. should have room in it for me, shouldn't it?"

"It seems like it should," he said.

"Seems like. But I work as a maid for a few families that don't have much more money than me. Enough to hire someone to clean their houses, but not, like, rich people. I have more education than most of my clients. But I can't use my degree, because none of the big companies want to hire me."

"You are undocumented," Ray reminded her. "That's always going to be a problem for legitimate employers. I'd think there would always be a place for a skilled accountant, but that's a significant strike against you."

"Yeah, I guess so." She came across as angry but resigned. "Still, it's better living here, even this way, than going to Mexico. My mother was the only family I had down there, and Esmerelda was her only sister. I would be lost there."

"What about Ruben?" Ray asked.

"Same goes for him. He wasn't even two yet when we came here. He doesn't remember anything about Mexico. He just wanted to build his boxes, and now there's an art gallery at the Marrakech that wants to sell them. They sent Ruben a contract. But it came this week, and he hasn't been here to sign it."

"Where is he?"

Lucia looked at him for the first time since she had let him inside. Her eyes were deep-set and haunted. "I don't know."

"How long has he been missing?"

"A week, I guess. I was afraid maybe he was deported, but I don't have any way to check. Still, if he was, he would call me when he got to Mexico."

"Let me ask you this—was he very sick? About three years ago?"

"Yes!" Lucia said. "He was. He had to get a . . ."

"He got a blood marrow donation."

"That's right! How did you know?"

"It's my job to know. What was the matter with him?"

"It was . . . something plastic."

"Aplastic anemia?"

"That's right. He had to get these blood transplants all the time. He always looked so much better after one that I thought he was well."

"But it didn't last, did it?"

"No. He kept on getting sick again. Finally he needed a bone marrow transplant, or I was going to lose him."

That matched what Belinda Jones had told him. "How could he afford the treatment?"

"There's this community center in the neighborhood, the Friends of the East Side Community Center. Mickey Ritz, the guy who runs it, he tries to take care of people. He arranged some money, when Ruben got sick. That paid for his treatment, and the place that provided the marrow took care of that end."

"The Indigo Valley Blood Center, right?"

"I think."

"So he got his medical needs taken care of, even though he had no papers."

"That's right. That's part of why I love this country."

Ray's emotions were torn. The money that went into Ruben's care might have gone to a citizen. But he and Lucia had been raised here, educated here, and Lucia seemed as patriotic as anyone he'd met, maybe more so because she understood the flip side, what might be waiting for her if she were ever forced to leave her adopted nation. Was there a right side of this situation? Or just a question of degree, of one thing being slightly less wrong than another?

Ray's Hippocratic oath told him that making sure Ruben's aplastic anemia got treated was the less wrong option. He was a law enforcement official as well as a doctor, and he was a taxpayer. But he had grown up as a military brat, born in South Korea and raised on bases around the world. He had been a boy without a country, American in name only, his fellow citizens the people in uniforms and the families who stood behind them. He knew something of what she must have felt as a girl, coming to this strange land, and the outsider status she still lived. Besides, the clinic he volunteered at treated people without regard to citizenship.

"What about the husband you mentioned earlier?" he asked. "Was he even real?"

"He's real," she said. "Sometimes I wish he wasn't."

"You couldn't get citizenship through him?"

"He was illegal too. He took off. I don't know where he went and I don't care."

"Okay, let's get back to Ruben. You have no idea where he is?"

"Not where."

That was a dodge. "What do you know?"

Lucia chewed on her right index finger, looking away from Ray again. She wanted to tell him, but she was scared. Terrified, more accurately.

"Come on, Lucia. I'll find out one way or another. You know that, right?"

"I guess so."

"Tell me what you know."

"Okay, fine. Only you can't ever say it was me, all right?"

"I can't promise that. Depending on what you tell me, you might be asked to testify in court."

"Then I'll be deported for sure."

"Possibly. Or possibly the district attorney would be able to make some sort of arrangement. I don't know, that's not my field. All I do know is that Ruben's in trouble, and if keeping quiet would help him, he would be home already."

"Yeah, I guess that's true."

"So tell me."

"Okay, there's these smugglers, this gang. *Coyotes*. They brought one of our cousins over, a few years ago. We helped make the arrangements, helped pay them. I guess that's how they knew who we were, knew that we didn't have papers. Once they know, they don't forget. Some families I know, undocumented, like us—they approach the family, and tell them that if they don't pay them off they'll turn them in to Immigration. If the family resists, they'll abduct a family member and the price goes up. They already know we won't go to the police. They want the ransom money from family here or back in Mexico, they don't care."

"And that's what happened to Ruben? They took him?"

"I think so, because they came to us and said they wanted five thousand dollars to keep quiet about us. We don't have money like that."

"But some families meet their demands?"

"You have to understand. Ruben and me, we don't have anybody in Mexico, but a lot of people do. The families in Mexico, they depend on money from here that people send back home. To them, five thousand would be a fortune—but to pay it, any way they can, would be better than not paying and losing the money being sent back every month."

"Only you don't have people to send money to."

"That's right. And because we don't, we don't have people who can scrape the ransom together for us."

Ray was almost afraid to ask the next question. "This gang—what do they do with the people they abduct? If they don't get the money?"

Lucia's voice quavered as she answered him. "The first thing is, they'll cut off a hand, and send it to the family. That's the last warning. They leave one hand so the person can still work. When a family gets that in the mail, usually they can find the money."

"Have you received one of Ruben's hands?"

"No. But every day, when I get the mail, I worry that it will be in there."

"What next?"

"Sometimes the person dies, after their hand is cut off. Sometimes the money comes in and they let him loose. You see people, men mostly, around the neighborhood with one hand. But if the person dies, then they hide the body somewhere and dump the hand. When a hand is found, word spreads, so we are all worried all the time that we'll be next."

And they were, Ray knew. She hadn't heard about Ruben's hand yet. Which probably meant Ruben was dead, that his hand had been left out in the street somewhere as a warning to others, and the dog had found it before any people did.

The trouble was, he had to tell her. The time had come. If he kept it from her now, it would be dishonest, and any trust he had built up would be shattered.

"I'm afraid I have some bad news for you, Lucia."

Her hand went back to her mouth. When she bit down on the finger, it reminded Ray of the dog gnawing the hand, and he had to try to block that image from his mind. "What?"

"One of Ruben's hands has been found. His left one."

"Oh, God, no!" Tears ran from her eyes, soaking her cheeks. She let them flow, unhindered, and spoke through her sobs.

"I'm very sorry. That's how I found you in the first place."

"And you know it's his?"

"We haven't been able to match the DNA to him yet. But it's his, I'm quite sure."

"So . . . so he's dead?"

"I don't know. I hope not. It might be too late, but the more I can learn about this gang you mentioned, the better our chances are of finding him in time."

"I don't know anything about them."

"You said they approached you."

"That's right, but they come to you. They don't leave a business card or anything like that. You don't find them, they find you."

"I need more than that," Ray said. "I've got to have something to go on."

"Why? What's the point? If they left his hand someplace instead of sending it, then he's dead!"

"Maybe he's not dead yet. And if he is, then at least you'll know. If we can find them, we can arrest them, stop them from doing this to other families. Isn't that worth it?"

"It won't bring Ruben back."

"If he's already gone, then nothing will bring him back. All we can do is try."

"But I don't know who they are! Or how to find them."

"Where did they grab Ruben?"

"From here," she said. "I came home from cleaning a house and he was gone. He must have fought like a tiger. The place was a mess, furniture every which way, some things broken."

"And you didn't call the police?"

"Like I said, when you don't have papers, you don't call the police."

"I understand. Where did the struggle take place?"

"Here. Right here, in this room. He must have answered the door, and when they tried to grab him, he came back inside. They came in after him."

"But you cleaned up?"

"That's right."

"Do you mind if I look around?"

"I just said I cleaned up."

"And I recognize that you're a professional housecleaner. Still, you'd be surprised at what people can miss."

"Be my guest. If it'll help find Ruben, you do whatever you want."

"I can't guarantee anything," Ray said. "But it can't hurt, and it might help."

"Go for it."

"I'll have to go outside, get my field kit. Then I'll try to make it fast."

"Faster the better."

"I know. Ruben might not have much time left, if he's still out there."

The whole thing was a long shot. If they only dumped the hands of those who died from the process, then it was long since too late for Ruben. But if something else had happened—say they had removed the hand, then decided there was no point in mailing it because they had already ascertained that Ruben had no family to raise the ransom—there might still be a chance.

It was a chance Ray had to take.

He returned from the vehicle with his field kit. Getting down on hands and knees was painful. But if she had missed anything in her clean-up job, it would likely be small, and close to the floor. Nothing he found could be used as evidence in court, because the scene hadn't been secured in the interim. That didn't mean that there weren't clues that might point to Ruben's abductors, though. Crime scene investigation served multiple purposes, and this could be one of the most crucial.

The floors in here were hardwood, with carpeting that didn't quite reach all the way across. Ray started at the edge of the carpeting, then moved to the baseboard along the bottom of the wall. He moved slowly, tweezers and a magnifying glass in his hands.

As he had told Lucia, he found things she had

missed. The first was blood that had leaked between floorboards and turned blue-green when he swabbed with tetramethylbenzidine. TMB was only a presumptive test, and the presence of blood would have to be confirmed, but it was a good start. Once it was confirmed, the identity of the person who had shed it would have to be determined.

"Did someone bleed over here?" Ray asked. "That you know of?"

"I found blood on the floor when I came in that night. I cleaned it with floor cleaner and bleach. You found some?"

"Yes."

"I scrubbed and scrubbed."

"People often do," Ray said. "Especially when they're trying to hide it from us. They're rarely successful."

He went back to combing the floor. He turned up some tiny fibers that looked, at first glance, to be a polyester-cotton blend. Tangled with those, which he had to draw from beneath the baseboard, were two tiny, sparkly metallic disks. He bagged them and kept looking. The next thing he found were minute bits of what looked like skin, little flakes of tissue that might have been scraped off in the fight. He put these in a paper envelope. They'd be tested back at the lab, along with everything else. If they had come from one of Ruben's attackers and not from the victim, they might help locate him.

Ray searched for another twenty minutes, but found nothing else that appeared pertinent. "Thanks for your cooperation, Ms. Navarre," he said.

"Did you find anything that might help?"

"I'm not sure yet, but maybe."

"I hope so. I'm worried."

"I hope so, too." He didn't mean to be short with her, but he wanted to rush back and get the trace and DNA techs going on what he had found.

He didn't want to have found Ruben Solis, only to have lost him. Somewhere out there, a man needed to be reunited with his left hand, even if it was too late for him to use it again.

15

Louis Vartann called some people he knew at the Las Vegas ATF office, and arranged to pay a casual visit to the local headquarters of the Free Citizens of the Republic. Of course, most casual visits didn't involve four vehicles screaming into the front parking area and a dozen flak-jacketed men and women leaping out with warrants and weapons. But Vartann wanted to get the Free Citizens' attention, and he figured a big show would do that more efficiently than a quiet conversation.

Headquarters was a freestanding, one-story, stucco-sided building on the west side of Interstate 15. At night, a person would be able to see the lights of the Strip from there, but not much else. The neighborhood was largely blighted: an abandoned used car dealership sat next door, and on the other side was an empty building that had once been a chain restaurant. The liquor store beyond that remained in business, its windows barred, its walls painted a garish yellow that almost glowed in the afternoon sun. Vartann had been inside it once, investigating a hold-up. A third of the store was walled off by bulletproof glass—the owners held court on that side, pulling booze from the shelves for customers who shouted their orders through metal slots and paid through cutaways in the window.

The Free Citizens had a small wooden sign with their insignia—an eagle, though not a bald one, wings spread, rifles clutched in one talon and a scroll in the other—mounted beside the door. Except for that, the place could have been any small business that didn't rely on customers seeking it out in person. With LVPD SWAT cops and ATF agents fanning out around the building, Vartann tried the door. It was unlocked, so he announced himself and went in.

Inside was chaos.

There was a reception area in front, with thick carpeting and comfortable chairs and a chest-high counter behind which, presumably, a receptionist usually sat. No one sat there at the moment; instead, Vartann heard running footsteps and shouts from down the hallway beyond. He started down the hall, only to be met by a man in a brown suit, white shirt, and red-and-black striped tie, striding briskly toward him with a fierce scowl on a round, pudgy face. Behind that man were some others, less respectable in appearance. They were bull-necked guys with shaved heads, built like linebackers, wearing dark suits and glaring at Vartann through small eyes. One had a thin, dark mustache riding his upper lip, the other tattoos climbing up from under his dress shirt. The muscle, Vartann figured, to back up the boss.

"What's the meaning of this?" the man demanded.

Vartann held out the warrant. "This is a warrant to search the premises," he said. "If you'd like to call an attorney, feel free, but we're going to be looking around in the meantime."

"Search for what?" the man asked. "We've nothing to hide here."

"Then it'll be easy."

"This is an egregious violation of our rights," the man said. Vartann liked how he did that—went from nothing to hide to being violated in an instant.

"We've been informed that you might be in possession of some illegal firearms, sir. If you can show us proof of legal purchase for any weapons on the premises, we'll be out of your hair in no time." He chose, for the moment, not to mention that they were also looking for ammonium nitrate or other bomb-making materials. If the man read the warrant carefully enough, he could reach that conclusion on his own.

"Let me see that!" the man said, grasping for the warrant. He scanned the pages for a minute, then threw it back at Vartann. "We don't even recognize your authority! Leave these grounds immediately."

"You don't recognize the Clark County courts?"

"Their authority is not grounded in anything. It's vapor, nothing more."

"Sir, I have a dozen armed men and women here with the full force of the law behind us. If you don't recognize that authority, I recommend taking another look."

"It's people like you who are the problem," the man said. His thugs hadn't said a word, just stood behind him glowering like extras in a music video.

"Sir, you're going to have to ask these men to step aside and let us in, or I'll have to put all of you under arrest."

"Try it."

The more the man pulled the defiant act, the more tempted Vartann was. But he hadn't come looking to make any arrests—he just hoped to ask some questions about the attack on Dennis Daniels, and to warn the group against harassing Catherine. "What's your name, sir?"

"My name is Caleb of Leland, Tulsa."

"Oh, right, that whole parentheses bit. Clever."

"Once again, I'm going to have to insist that you leave these grounds."

"Does that mean you don't intend to comply with the warrant?"

"I've seen nothing that makes me believe you have the authority to enforce it."

"Okay, Mr. Parenthesis, on the floor, hands over your head."

"Excuse me?"

"It'll be easier on you if you do it yourself."

The man's face was turning so red he was starting to look like a kickball. "Now see here . . ."

"All right," Vartann said. He was out of patience. He reached for the man's wrist, caught it and gave a yank. Leland, if that was really his name, spun around and Vartann slapped a cuff over the wrist.

Leland began to struggle then, so Vartann twisted the arm a little harder and snapped the man toward him, then reached for his other hand. He caught it and brought it behind the man, cuffed that hand, and pushed him against a wall—not hard enough to hurt, just enough to immobilize him. The muscle men stood and watched. "You guys supposed to do something, or are you just decor?" Vartann asked.

"Okay, okay," Leland said. "You can look around, just take those things off me."

"Not yet, Mr. P.," Vartann said. "You and I will have a little chat while my friends search the premises. Is there someplace private we can go?"

"My office," Leland said.

"Where?"

"It's back here," one of the muscle guys said. "I'll show you."

Vartann broke into a smile. "Cooperation. That's what I like to see."

The men broke their blockade, and ATF agents filed past them into a warren of offices and warehouse facilities at the rear of the building. Enough time had been wasted to allow the Free Citizens to have hidden a truckload of elephants, but with agents surrounding the building, at least none were leaving the premises.

The muscle man, dark-haired and fair-skinned, with a neck as big around as a telephone pole, led the way to Caleb of Leland (Tulsa)'s office. It had a window with a view of the empty car lot, a big steel desk, a filing cabinet, and a pair of mismatched visitor chairs. The walls were graced with anti-government posters, some of which appeared to be patriotic and

pro-government unless the coded message was understood. Others were less subtle, like the one depicting the president of the United States with a tall black
hat and a villainous mustache, tying a bound woman
labeled "Freedom" to a railroad track. A train labeled
"Socialism" bore down on them. Even a quotation
from Thomas Jefferson printed on a poster took on a
chilling tone, in this context. On top of the desk were
an open laptop computer and a legal pad with some
scrawls on it.

"Thanks," Vartann said. "We'll just have a little
chat in here."

"Should I leave?" the muscle asked.

"Doesn't matter to me."

"Go," Leland told him. "Get the lawyers."

"Okay." The man left the office, shutting the
door.

"That's better," Vartann said. He unlocked the
cuffs. Leland sat behind his desk, rubbing his wrists.

"You storm troopers are all the same."

"Storm troopers?"

"You know what I mean."

"I think you could use a history lesson, sir. To
compare us to storm troopers is—"

"You barge in here with no legal authority,
and—"

"I don't know what you consider legal authority,
but Clark County, the state of Nevada, and the
United States of America have signed off on what
we're doing here. You don't accept any of those?"

"An occupation government? Hardly."

"Are we going to find any illegal weapons here?"

"I can't imagine that you would."

"Then there's no problem."

"The problem is you storm troopers think you can stomp all over our rights!"

"So we're back to that?"

"I call it like I see it."

Vartann moved toward the desk. Leland tried to wheel his chair away but he got snagged on the edge of the knee well. "We're not the bad guys here," Vartann said. "I don't know if you are, either. But whatever you think we're up to, we're not. We're trying to keep the peace. We want to make sure you didn't have anything to do with an attack on Dennis Daniels, or the harassment of a law enforcement officer. Did you?"

"Of course not."

"Is there any ammonium nitrate on the property?"

"I don't even know what that is."

Leland was spreading the fertilizer on pretty thick, Vartann thought, but he moved straight to the next question. "Do you know someone who calls himself John of Tipton, Bakersfield?"

"Should I?"

"Think about it. How many other groups do you know with that kind of naming system?"

"Well, I'm sorry. That name doesn't sound familiar."

"Right. Tell you what, if you happen to run across him, tell him that I strongly suggest he rethink what he's doing."

"Sure, if I happen to run across him."

"I'm not convinced you're taking this whole thing seriously," Vartann said. The man was infuriating. "I could still arrest you."

"I'd like to see you make it stick."

"Trust me, twenty-four hours in captivity is no picnic, even if we end up not filing charges. Like I said, that's really not why we're here. I'm trying to make this easy on you, and you seem intent on making it difficult."

"Because I'm not letting you and your fascist thugs bully me into admitting anything?"

"Just pass on the message," Vartann said. He had to get away from the man before he lost his temper. "We'll be out of your way as soon as we finish our search. For your sake, you'd better hope we don't find anything."

Although the swing shift had just started, everyone on Catherine's team had been on the job for at least an hour. She appreciated their dedication, but some part of her would have preferred that they were either resting up for the night, or out enjoying themselves, having lives away from work. She wanted her people well rounded, not obsessed with the job.

But she couldn't call them on it, having been at work since mid-morning herself. She knew she'd regret it later, when three or four o'clock rolled around and her body's natural cycle wanted her to be asleep. Working night shift, she had retrained herself to an extent, but ultimately, humans were made to function best in daylight, and the hours got to everybody once in a while.

On the other hand, it wasn't every day they had to deal with what might have been an attempted assassination.

She was at her desk reading over the various

reports that the case had already generated when her phone rang. She raised it to her ear. "Willows."

"Catherine," Jim Brass's gravely voice said. "Remember Alec Watson?"

"From earlier today? Sure. Why?"

"Because that's all that's left of him," Brass said. "Memories."

"Jim . . . ?"

"He's been murdered," Brass clarified.

"Where?"

"His office." Brass read off an address, which Catherine jotted down.

"I'm on my way," she said.

"I'll be here."

16

RAY LANGSTON SWUNG by the Friends of the East Side Community Center before heading back to the lab. He was intrigued now—this whole Ruben Solis thing had taken on twists he hadn't expected, and he wanted to see what he could find out about the missing man. If Mickey Ritz at the community center had arranged his marrow transfusion, maybe he could provide some answers.

The building was an inviting shade of rose, with tan trim. A tall fence shielded a well-kept playground, and the grounds were refreshingly clean. Had he been young and poor, he'd have felt comfortable coming here.

Through a large wooden door was a big, open room. People played cards at a table, a board game at another, and a couple of others were watching sports on TV. At a different table, a young Hispanic woman was helping some children with a craft project involving construction paper, beads, and copious amounts of white glue.

Something smelled marvelous, and Ray followed his nose to a busy kitchen. Six people, most of them young, were involved in the preparation of what looked like a Mexican feast—beans and rice, tacos, burritos, carne asada, and more. "Hi," a woman said. She was probably in her late teens or early twenties, a light-skinned African American with a fetching smile. "Can I help you?"

"I'm looking for Mickey Ritz," Ray said.

The oldest person in the kitchen, a Caucasian woman in her fifties, hair going gray and hanging in her face, waved a wooden spoon down the hall. "Back that way, last door on the left before you find yourself outside again."

"Thanks."

Ray reluctantly tore himself away from the tantalizing aromas and continued down the hall. He passed a couple of older folks, grizzled white men who appeared to be homeless. They gave him a wide berth, but greeted him when he spoke to them. Then he stopped in front of the last door on the left, and knocked.

"It's open!" a voice called.

Ray pushed the door wide. "Mickey Ritz?"

A sturdy bald guy stood there. He had been sweating profusely; his sleeveless sweatshirt was dark with moisture, and beads of it ran down hairy, tanned legs. He held a damp towel in his hands. "That's me."

"I'm Ray Langston, with the Las Vegas Crime Lab."

"Forgive me if I don't shake," Ritz said. "Just played some one-on-one with one of our better hoopsters. Damn near wore me out."

"It's a demanding sport," Ray said.

"You don't look like our usual clientele."

"I'm afraid I'm here on official business."

"Cop business?"

"Something like that."

Ritz toweled off his face, which was still bright red from exertion. "I'm pretty protective of the privacy of my people."

"Believe me, I appreciate that," Ray said. "I wouldn't be here if it weren't literally a matter of life and death."

Ritz lowered the towel, more interested now. "Whose life?"

"You know Ruben Solis?"

"Yeah," Ritz said. His voice took on a guarded tone. "What about him?"

"You arranged a marrow transfusion for him." Ritz didn't respond. "Lucia told me."

"Okay, yeah, I did. What about it?"

"He's in danger. Someone's abducted him, cut off his hand."

"Oh, no." Ritz's legs turned to rubber. He sank back against an overflowing bookcase. The office was cluttered with papers, sports equipment, games, and more. One of Ruben's constructions sat on a shelf—a basketball court, with a figure who looked quite a bit like Ritz at its center. Another door was open on the far side of Ritz's desk, light streaming through, but Ray couldn't see what was beyond it. "God, no."

"You know what that means? About the hand?"

"I hear a lot of things here. I don't believe them all."

"But you know Ruben is undocumented."

"Sure."

"And therefore easy prey for the kind of people who Lucia says are responsible."

"If the whole thing is real, yeah. I suppose."

"His hand is real. We took it away from a dog."

Ritz ran the towel over his head again. "God, no, this can't be happening."

"If you can tell me anything, Mr. Ritz, about Ruben or whatever you know about these people, it'll help."

"You don't know where he is?"

"We have no idea. We don't know how far the dog carried the hand, and we don't know how far it was dumped from Ruben's location."

"He's a good kid."

"I'm sure he is."

"No, I mean, really. Sure, he's here illegally. But he's smart, he's ambitious, and he's damn talented. He cares about others. He used to come here just to take advantage of our facilities, to have a safe place to go after school, someplace that wasn't the streets. We try to steer kids away from gangs here, Mr. Langston. He was an easy sell. Then, these past couple of years, he's been volunteering here, helping make the same pitch to the generation coming up behind his."

"Do you know anything about where the gang might be located? The one running this blackmail scheme Lucia told me about?"

"Can you close the door, Mr. Langston?"

"Sure." Ray did as the man asked.

"I trust our clients and staff with my life. This place *is* my life. I live here." He flipped the towel toward the open door behind him. "I work here. Sometimes it seems like I never get away. But I love it. Still . . . there are people out in the world who I don't trust, for a second. And some of them have hooks into some of my people, despite my best efforts."

"So you don't want our conversation overheard."

"It's probably not a problem at all. Still, some chances I'd rather not take."

"What do you know?"

"I've heard the guy who runs it is called Oz, or Ozzie. Something like that. And of course, I've heard what they do, how they blackmail undocumented aliens. And how they'll cut off hands to prove they've got them."

"And if the hands aren't mailed to the family—"

"That usually means they're dead. Then it's a warning to the rest of the community. Keep quiet, don't make waves, this could happen to you."

"Anything else?"

"Just this. If you find Ruben and he's been killed—then I hope to God you kill whoever did it. I'm not a violent man, Mr. Langston. I've had my troubles in life, like everybody does. There was a stretch for over ten years that I'm really not proud of. If you knew me in my twenties, you'd be astonished that I'm alive today. But I came through it, and I've turned things around. That's how I know that anybody can do it, because I did, and I'm noth-

ing special. And I've never laid a hand on anyone in
anger since then. If I had this Ozzie here now,
though . . ."

"When we find him, Mr. Ritz, we'll arrest him
and let justice take its course."

"Sometimes that's not good enough."

"It'll have to be. And let me assure you, Mr. Ritz,
we're good at what we do. When we make a case
against this Ozzie, we'll make sure we have the evidence in hand to nail him to the wall."

"Supervisor Willows," Jim Brass said. "This is Justine
Marie Taylor."

"It's good to meet you, Ms. Taylor," Catherine
said. "I'm so sorry for your loss."

"He was a great man, Ms. Willows. Not just a
great American, but a great man."

"I'm sure." She didn't yet know the woman's
connection to Alec Watson, but she looked like she
had been crying for hours. She was stout, solid, the
kind of woman who looked like she couldn't be
knocked over by anything short of a major hurri-
cane. Her hair was short and blond, her fingers
thick.

"Ms. Taylor was Mr. Watson's office manager,"
Brass explained.

"Our relationship was purely professional," Justine
said, answering a question that hadn't been asked.
"But I had the deepest respect for him. And something like love, I suppose. Not physical love, but spiritual. He was just . . . such a dear, devoted man."

Catherine had a hundred questions, but Brass
had probably asked them already, so she let them

slide for now. She had brought Greg along, and he was already photographing the office in which Watson had been shot.

Watson's office was an upscale affair in a private building. The plaque outside that announced *Elementary Magazine* and BOOM looked like solid gold. Inside, the floors were marble, the furnishings top of the line. Early American art graced the walls—originals, and most of it stuff Catherine would have expected to see in museums. She was sure she had walked past a Grandma Moses in the corridor, and something that looked like a Currier and Ives.

"I'm going to see what I can learn in the office," Catherine said. "I'll be there if you need me."

"Okay," Brass said. He took Justine's arm and steered her away. "They're the best in the business," he was saying. "If there's anything to be found in there, they'll find it."

She appreciated the vote of confidence. Brass had shown her where Watson's private office was, and she went in. Greg's electronic flash was going off as she entered. "Are you about done with that?" she asked.

"I am," Greg replied. He put the lens cap on the camera and tucked it into a bag. "Glad I put on two pairs of booties, too."

"It's definitely a mess." Catherine had double-bootied, too. These days, any scene at which bodily fluids had been spilled had to be considered a potentially toxic zone. There were bodily fluids in copious amounts in Watson's office, and protecting their own health was just as critical a decision as any other when it came to working the scene.

Watson had been sitting behind a massive wooden desk, one that looked like something the signers of the Declaration of Independence might have gathered around to put their signatures on that document. His body was on the floor behind the desk, now, where it would stay until Catherine released it into the care of the medical examiner's office. When she went around the desk, she could see at least a dozen bullet holes in him. There were more in the wall behind the desk, some glazed with blood spatter and brain matter. Somebody had opened up with an automatic weapon at close range, and the result was a body that was barely recognizable as human.

Blood had pooled around the body. Plasma and platelets beginning to separate, and the process would continue until it was cleaned up. The center of the pool was so dark it was almost black; toward the edge, where it was mostly plasma, it verged toward pink. The dual death smells of copper and sugars—common in plasma, along with every protein found in the body—hung heavy in the air.

Slugs had chewed up the desk's surface and struck the desktop computer that sat on it. Papers were strewn all over the place, knocked about by the bullets or by Watson's death throes.

Catherine set her field kit down on a clean wooden cabinet across the room from the carnage. The office was vast and decorated in a style that might have been called early American Patriot, if it had a name at all. Behind and to the left of the ornate wooden desk were crossed flags of the United States and Nevada, causing Catherine to wonder if

Watson had suffered Oval Office envy. She took latex gloves from the kit, pulled a pair on over her hands, and then a second pair over those. There was no such thing as too much protection, and if the outer pair were contaminated she could remove them and replace them with a second outer pair.

She scanned the whole room once again, looking for her starting point. With two of them, one could work on recovering trace while the other focused on the body, the bullets, and the spatter. It seemed, at first glance, fairly obvious what had happened to Watson, but that was just the kind of assumption a criminalist had to guard against. That first glance could prove to be wrong. They had to let the evidence dictate what had taken place, not let their initial biases dictate what evidence would be found.

As she let her gaze travel the room, mentally dividing it into sections so she would look at everything in detail, and not allow her attention to be focused on any one area to the detriment of another, it landed on what first appeared to be a scrap of paper, well away from the desk and the various bits of paperwork that had fallen from there. She moved closer to it and squatted down. "Did you see this, Greg?"

"I got a shot of it," he said. "Looks like there's some blood on it."

She took forceps and lifted the small white shape. It was no more than a half-inch square, with ragged edges. Greg was right, a couple of brownish spots at the center of it could have been blood. "It's gauze," she said. "I thought it was paper at first."

"Like a bandage?"

"That's what it looks like."

"Well, Alec Watson could have used some bandages, but I'm not sure that one would have helped. I'm pretty sure no one tried any first aid on him, though."

"So it came from someone else, maybe the shooter. I'll have one of the unis outside get it back to the lab, see if we can get a quick ID on that blood." She dropped it into a paper envelope from her kit and opened the office door to summon Brass. He was standing within earshot, and after the uniformed officer had been dispatched to the lab, Brass stayed in Watson's office.

"Ms. Taylor says that Watson had been in here for a little more than an hour," Brass said. "He was working on a speech. There were a couple of other staffers in another part of the building, but there was a lot of machinery going, computers and printers and scanners, and they wouldn't have heard people coming and going over here."

"Security looks pretty lax for a relatively high-profile guy," Catherine observed.

"That's just how he rolled, according to Ms. Taylor. A man of the people. Anyone who wanted his ear could come in and usually find him in his office."

"An admirable policy," Catherine said. "But it obviously turned out to be a dangerous one."

"She's been after him for years to put in security cameras. He finally agreed, but the installation appointment is scheduled for next week."

"Too little, and way too late."

"Somebody heard the gunfire, but by the time

they got over here, the shooter was gone," Brass continued. "Taylor says he didn't have any appointments this afternoon or this evening. He wanted to be left alone to work on the speech, so she stayed out of his hair."

"Maybe she should have stayed closer," Greg suggested.

"But if she had, maybe they'd both be dead," Catherine said.

"True." Greg stepped gingerly around the desk, touched a key and peered at Watson's monitor. "Looks like a round penetrated the casing but didn't hurt the guts. His speech is still up on the screen." Greg read for a moment, then reported, "It's a response to the bombing. He's asking for an end to the culture of violence and personal attacks, asking for a reconsideration of the rhetorical heat going on these days. He's afraid that extremist language might lead to a situation in which violence is not only tolerated, but inevitable."

"He was right about that," Brass said.

"Too bad he had to prove it the hard way," Catherine added.

Brass opened the door. "Well, I'll leave you to it. I still have to interview a couple of the staff members who were here. Doesn't sound like anybody saw any visitors, so I hope you two can find something."

"We usually do," Catherine said.

"That's what I'm counting on."

When Brass was gone, Catherine returned her attention to the task at hand. With no security camera, an open-door policy, and the discretion of a staff that left him alone to write, Alec Watson hadn't made things easy on her. But it wasn't the responsibility of the dead to tell their own stories. The burden of doing that was on the CSIs, who had to take the blood and bullets and brains, the faintest tracks and traces, and compile them into a narrative that would make sense to anyone who saw it.

"Let's get to work, Greg," she said. "Somewhere in this room, there's got to be a clue."

"You'd think so, wouldn't you?"

"I know so. All we have to do is find it."

"That's all," Greg said. "Nothing to it."

"It won't go any faster if you wait to get started."

"I know," Greg said. "I'll take the body."

"Be my guest." She would have done it, but was just as glad to hand it off. It was going to be an unpleasant job. Not that the rest of the office would be a walk in the park.

The job was the job, though. She knew it going in, and still she went back every night. Sometimes people asked her how she could stand it. She never had a good answer to that question.

The truth was, though, she could no longer quite imagine life without it.

17

NICK AND SARA went back down the hill, to where the Forest Service investigators believed the fire had been started. The CSIs had requested that the Forest Service hold off on their investigation so they could study the scene before it was compromised.

The fire had begun in a hollow, a small depression in the earth. The area below it was full of dry oak leaves and downed branches. If the same was true above, it wouldn't have taken much to get a good blaze going. Sarah pointed this out to Nick.

"You're right," he said. "And check the trees right around here."

Sara did. "They're hardly burned at all."

"So it began as a surface fire," Nick said. "Burning loose debris as it gathered strength. The burn moved uphill—"

"As fire tends to do."

"That's right. And as it did, it found ladder fuels, shrubs and low branches, that helped it climb into the crown. Some crown fires burn almost independently of surface fires, but this one seems like it covered every elevation once it got going good."

"And it gained strength as it went uphill," Sara added. "Creating its own air flow. The heat must have been intense, up above."

"Hot enough that those firefighters never had a chance."

"Are we convinced that it was human-caused?"

"The Forest Service people were. No reported lightning strikes in the area. No other reason for a fire to start on its own. Either it was accident or arson."

"Let's find out which," she said. "Because if it's arson, then someone's got a lot to answer for."

They gloved up and went to hands and knees, inspecting the transition area between burned and not-burned. After about thirty minutes, during which Nick began to suspect he would never breathe freely again, so caked with soot were his nasal passages, he heard Sara's voice.

"Nick?"

"Yeah?"

"Take a look at this."

He rose, a little creaky from having been down for so long, and walked over to her. She had brushed a circle in the ash about fifteen feet in from the edge of the burned area, revealing a bundle of tiny, pale sticks in the center of the circle. "Matches?"

"Matches," she said. "But they're stuck together, and they didn't burn all the way."

"I guess that's our good luck and the firebug's bad luck. I wonder why, though."

"From the size of these matchsticks," Sara said, "I'm guessing they're the strike-anywhere type. These days most matches have to be struck on a special surface."

"That strip on the matchbook," Nick said.

"Because the strip contains red phosphorous. The friction converts it to white phosphorous, for a fraction of a second."

"White phosphorus, that's bad stuff." Because it generated a lot of smoke, it was commonly used in battle to make smokescreens. But it was also highly incendiary, and it had a tendency to cling to surfaces, resulting in a lasting, extremely destructive burn. Most civilized nations didn't use it in that way anymore—at least, not officially. That didn't stop others from claiming that they did. What the truth was, Nick couldn't know.

"You're not kidding. Early matchboxes were made of metal, because matches had a habit of igniting themselves whenever they wanted. Now they're more stable, but the strike-anywhere kind, like these, have the red phosphorus added to the match head instead of on the striking surface. They're still not stable enough to be allowed on airplanes." She picked one of them up with a gloved hand. "There's something on them." She rubbed the wooden matchstick. "Feels like wax."

Nick tried to envision what had happened. "Someone bunched them together and dipped them in melted wax? Then after it cooled, brought them here and lit the fire. The wax melted again, smothering the wooden matchsticks, so they didn't burn all the way. And the fire was racing up, away from the matches, so even if the wax had completely run off them, the matches still might not have burned."

"The firestarter thought the evidence would go up in smoke, but it didn't." Sara put her head close to the ground and felt around in the soft earth. "Match heads often survive fire as well," she said. "If we can find some of those . . ."

"Then we'll be able to narrow the suspect pool to anyone who has ever bought a box of kitchen matches," Nick said. "Don't get me wrong, if you can find any, do it. We can use everything we get. But it won't exclude many people."

Sara held something up, her expression triumphant. Nick couldn't even see the tiny object between her fingers. "Got one! Now we just have to check every convenience store, supermarket, drugstore and camping supply place in a three-hundred mile radius, and we've got him."

"You know," Nick said. "I remember reading about an old-fashioned fire-starting device. You'd take a few matches, tie them together with string, and dip them in paraffin wax. Everything but the heads. That way, they were waterproof. You'd strike one of them and they'd all burn, including the paraffin wax, which is very flammable. These days there are plenty of better ways to light a fire, but the wax on these—"

Sara held the matches close to her nose. "Smells like candle wax to me. It's been melted more than once, but there's still a little bit of a floral scent. Berries, maybe."

"And candle wax is more likely to melt than to

burn. Maybe the person didn't have access to paraffin wax. It's not exactly commonplace these days."

"Or maybe it was someone who didn't know the difference."

"Nobody ever said your average criminal was any kind of genius."

"Let's get these couriered down to the lab," Sara suggested. "Maybe identifying the wax will pay more dividends than identifying the matches."

"We should send both," Nick said.

"Right." Sara started packing the matchsticks and a couple of match heads for transport. "Might as well keep them busy—they're probably in for a boring night without us around."

While she did that, Nick cut a wide circle around the spot where she had found the matches. The forest floor was different than paved surfaces or hard floors. Although people could leave tracks in those places, too, it was far harder to walk on dirt without leaving a sign.

Someone, however, had done a good job of it. Possibly the wind created by the fire had blown dirt and leaves and ash around, obscuring the trail. Nick managed to find one toe-print, very close to where Sara had been kneeling when she found the matches. His guess was that the arsonist had gone down on one knee, and by putting most of his weight on the other toe, had embedded that track more deeply into the ground. But there wasn't much to it—not enough tread to identify a shoe or boot brand, or tell the size for sure. What it did have were distinctive wear patterns and cuts on the tread, making it as distinctive as a fingerprint.

"It's better than nothing," Sara said. "When we have a suspect it'll help confirm, and it might exclude some others."

"Yeah," Nick agreed. "I was just hoping for more. Whoever this is, he's pretty light on his feet."

"The ground's been dry for a long time," Sara pointed out. "It's packed almost as hard as cement."

Nick was about to answer when he heard something crashing through the burned forest. Bear, he thought, or maybe deer. He drew a weapon, in case of the former—not that he wanted to shoot a bear, but if he had to warn it off, a gunshot might be more effective than shouting and waving his arms.

It was not a bear, however, but Harley Givens.

"Mr. Givens," Sara said, "didn't we ask you to stay out of the woods?"

"I believe what you said was that I should go back down the mountain until the evacuation order was lifted. Well, it's lifted."

"I think maybe you got the letter of that without the spirit," Nick pointed out. "We're trying to investigate a crime, and having you barging around could make that more difficult." He holstered his sidearm. At least Givens hadn't brought the shotgun this time. "Not to mention dangerous."

"I just wanted to see if you'd found any sign of them yet."

"Who, the campers?" Sara asked.

"Of course!"

"No sign of them."

"And we still don't know that they started the fire," Nick reminded him.

Givens stood with his hands on his hips, frowning. "I guess if you two were smarter, you'd be real cops instead of whatever it is you are. Some sort of errand runners, it looks like."

"Yeah," Nick said, holding in a laugh. "That's right. We have this job because we're the stupid ones. Show me your boots, Mr. Givens. The bottoms of them, please."

Givens raised one, then the other. Nick got a quick glance, enough to see that the tread on them didn't match what he had found.

"Mr. Givens, I'll ask you nicely one more time," Sara said. Count on her to try to defuse the tension. "Go home. Deal with your house as best you can, and let us do our jobs."

"Is there an 'or else' there, missy?"

"Or else, we'll put you under arrest for obstructing our investigation. By the time you get back home, there's no telling what'll be left of your house—or what woodland creatures will have decided to move in."

Givens caught Nick's gaze. "You might just be dumb, mister," he said, tilting his head toward Sara. "But that one? She's downright mean!"

18

THE RAID ON the Free Citizens netted a handful of automatic weapons of uncertain provenance, and the arrests of a couple of people who objected overly strenuously to the search. While Vartann was there, Catherine called and told him that Alec Watson had taken about a dozen 7.62x39-mm rounds. The ATF agents had found a stash of AK-47 knock-offs, which fired that ammunition, so those were confiscated as well. They would be returned to their rightful owners after ballistics testing. No traces of ammonium nitrate had turned up, and neither had any of the other items that had gone into the construction of the bomb used against Dennis Daniels.

For as much flak as Vartann took from the Free Citizens, the ATF people had it far worse. They kept telling the Citizens that they weren't there to abridge their Second Amendment rights—they weren't looking for legal guns, just ones that hadn't been rightfully purchased or, after Catherine's phone call, ones that might be a murder weapon. They said it in a monotone, by rote, and Vartann had the feeling that they probably repeated those words as often as he did the Miranda warning.

He was on his way out when he got another phone call, also from Catherine. "Twice in one evening," he said. "I must have done something right."

"You always do," she said. "But did you ever stop to think that maybe I'm just calling because I wanted to hear your voice? Maybe it's got nothing to do with what you do."

"That's okay, too."

"Then again," she said, all flirtation gone from her voice in a split second. She sounded tired, now. "Maybe I'm calling on business."

"That would be a shame."

"I know. We'll just have to make it up to each other later."

"That works for me. What's up?"

"We found a fragment of bloody bandage at the Watson scene," she said. "I had a quick test run. You'll never guess whose blood it is."

"I'm sure you're right."

"It belongs to Dennis Daniels."

Vartann was quiet for a moment, taking that in. "Isn't he still in the hospital?"

"As far as I know," Catherine said. "I'm still here at Watson's office. I was hoping maybe you could swing by the hospital and make sure Daniels is there."

"I can make a phone call . . ."

"Louis . . ."

"I know. In person is better. I'm on my way, Cath. I'll let you know what I find out."

"Good. Whoever shot Alec Watson is bad news. Guy's got more holes in him than a whole room full of bowling balls."

"I'll check it out," Vartann promised. "You finish up there. Maybe you can get some rest tonight."

"Somehow," Catherine said, "that doesn't seem very likely."

Dennis Daniels was indeed still in the hospital, and according to the nursing staff, he was a gigantic pain about it.

"He won't stay in bed for ten minutes," one of the nurses told Vartann, practically as soon as he flashed his badge. "I must have told him fifty times, he'll pop his stitches, he keeps roaming around like he does. Thinks he can run his whole business from here."

"Has he left the building at any point?"

The nurse shook her head vigorously. "Hells, no. He's stupid, not crazy. No, I take that back, he's a smart guy, he's just got too much energy for his own good."

"Probably why he's so successful."

"You could be right."

"I'll see if I can get him to calm down a little," Vartann promised.

"That'd be good. If not, you got handcuffs, right?"

Vartann shot her a knowing grin. Cops and nurses tended to get along, because both professions dealt with people at their worst. People in those jobs had to develop thick skins, good senses of humor, or both, just to get by. "I got 'em."

She directed him to Daniels's open door. Vartann

greeted the uniformed officer sitting beside it, tapped twice and walked in. Daniels was sitting up in bed, cross-legged, with papers scattered around him. Vartann recognized him from all the media coverage. He also recognized Joanna Daniels, a pretty blonde whose picture was in the paper almost as often as her husband's. She was involved in a number of charities around town, and seemed to be a social butterfly. A woman clad in a hospital gown sat in a wheelchair beside the bed with a stack of files on her lap, and another man slumped in a visitor's chair in a corner, holding a paperback book.

They were all looking his way. "Mr. Daniels, I'm Lou Vartann. LVPD."

"It's always a pleasure to meet a dedicated law officer," Daniels said. He was as slick as a politician, tossing off a slick smile even though his face looked like he had been using it to hammer nails. "Something I can do for you?"

Vartann glanced at the other people in the room. Daniels got the hint. "Sorry, where are my manners? This is my wife, Joanna, Maureen Cunningham, my administrative assistant—really, my professional lifeline, and Maureen's husband, Brett."

That explained why the other man wasn't injured or part of the work party. "Pleased to meet you," Louis said, shaking their hands. "I'm sorry about your injuries. Believe me, we'll find the perpetrator."

"Thank you," Maureen said. Vartann took a closer look at her. She had been banged up in the accident; a bandage clung at a diagonal over her left eyebrow, and that side of her face was discolored, bruising turning it shades of black and purple. But beneath the bruising and swelling, and despite blond hair cut in a conservative style, between chin and shoulder-length and seemingly designed not to call attention to her, she was, Vartann suspected, an attractive woman, with even features and clear, brown eyes. Her husband looked like he might have been a college athlete, broad-shouldered, narrow at the hips and waist. He had sandy blond hair, small eyes, and a neat brush of a mustache.

"Thanks," Brett Cunningham said. "You can't imagine how terrifying this all is."

"We'll be on it night and day," Vartann assured him. "We've got an amazing criminal investigation team, and honestly, what usually undoes people who do things like this is that they can't keep their mouths shut about it. The whole point is that they're after attention for some cause or other. Once they start bragging or making demands, it's only a matter of time."

"I hope you're right," Daniels said. "What brings you here?"

"Just checking in, really," Vartann said. "I see there's an officer outside."

"That's right. There's been someone there non-stop."

Vartann scanned the floor. There were bits of white gauze strewn here and there, like the remnants of a gentle snowfall. "And you've been up and around quite a bit, I've heard."

"Sitting still is hard for me," Daniels admitted. "Always has been. I think most business executives suffer from ADD, if you want to know the truth. In the media game if you can't multitask, jump from one thing to another with no downtime in between, you simply aren't doing your job."

"Must be hard for your employees to keep up with you."

"We don't even try," Maureen Cunningham said. "We all become specialists in one area, or a few of them, so we can offer advice where we're strongest and then back away."

"But isn't an administrative assistant a generalist almost by definition?" Vartann asked.

"I suppose so," Maureen said. "I don't get too deep into the weeds, though. I couldn't run a camera or an editing board if my life depended on it. But I can make hotel reservations like nobody's business."

"Travels too much, that's for sure," Brett said. "She's never at home."

Maureen chuckled. "He's right, I'm sorry to say. Most of my time is spent here, but there are always regulatory issues in DC or industry conferences in New York or somewhere else. Anyplace Dennis goes, either I have to go, or Bryan does. Sometimes both of us."

"We all do at least two jobs," Daniels explained. "We have to keep the programming on the air, which means gathering news and sometimes massaging the egos of our on-air talent. And we have to do the other things, the behind-the-scenes business that keeps the cameras rolling. The routine business elements, the advertising sales, and so on."

"This week, you're getting the kind of publicity money can't buy," Vartann pointed out. "Maybe it'll boost your ratings, make those ad sales a little easier."

"We all like ratings," Daniels said. "But I'd rather it was for what we do, not for having a car fall on top of me."

"Understandable," Vartann said. "While you've been not sitting still, you haven't left the hospital, have you?"

"I'm headstrong, not stupid," Daniels said. "One of those nurses would tackle me if I headed for the door. The instant I'm cleared to leave, I will, but until then I follow doctor's orders."

"Sounds like a wise policy. Thanks for your time, Mr. Daniels. Mr. and Mrs. Cunningham." Vartann offered a smile and left the room.

He stopped at the nurse's station on his way out, to warn the nurse that Daniels would continue pushing his boundaries. As he was finishing up, the elevator opened and Garrett Kovash emerged.

Most cops recognized Kovash. He had been on the force for several years, a star of his Academy class, rising quickly to detective. But he had always been a little too ambitious for his own good, and that ambition had led to corner-cutting and allegations—never proven—of greater improprieties. Eventually he and the LVPD had decided that it was best to sever connections all the way around.

"Lou," Kovash said. He wore a broad grin and stuck a hand out. "How's it hangin'?"

That was a question to which there had never been any good answers, and Vartann didn't try. "Garrett," he said. Noncommittal and safe. "I thought you were on bodyguard duty."

"My services extend to a wide range of activities,"

Kovash said. Equally noncommittal, Vartann noted, if not more so. "Did I miss anything?"

"Your client's driving the nurses crazy."

"How do you think I feel? If I could keep him in a bunker, it'd be a hell of a lot easier to do my job."

"It'll just get worse if he runs for office, won't it?"

"I'd love to talk him out of that. He's stubborn enough to make mules look like pushovers."

"How long were you gone just now?" Vartann asked.

"Why?"

"Just curious."

Kovash shrugged. "Couple hours, I guess. You folks have a uni parked outside the door."

"Right." Vartann was intrigued by the timing of Kovash's absence. "You mind showing me your shoes?"

"Always happy to do my part for law enforcement," Kovash said. He held one of his leather shoes out for Vartann. It was black, buffed to a high gloss. "They're Prada. Like 'em? I can get you a sweet price."

"I meant the soles," Vartann said. "But thanks anyway."

"Your loss." Kovash turned and showed Vartann the sole of his right shoe, then shifted and raised his left.

There was a tiny shred of white cotton stuck to that shoe. "Hold that pose a second," Vartann said. He addressed the nurse at the counter. "Do you have a clean envelope?"

"Sure," the nurse said. She rummaged around, came up with a business-sized paper envelope, and handed it to Vartann.

"Just another second," Vartann said.

"Good. I feel like I'm frozen in a game of hop-scotch. Or what's that one where you have to stop when the kid in front turns around? Simple Simon."

Vartann plucked the cotton from Kovash's shoe and dropped it into the envelope. "You're good," he said. "Simple Simon says thanks."

Kovash put his foot down. "What was all that about?"

"Let's just say I'm a Prada fan," Vartann said. He tucked the envelope into the inside pocket of his jacket. He was no CSI, but he knew the lab could compare the sample to the one found at Alec Watson's office. If they were a match, that would suggest taking a considerably closer look at Kovash's recent whereabouts.

Joanna Daniels emerged from her husband's room with a smile on her face. She looked tired, but otherwise resembled the photos Vartann had seen on the society page. "I thought I heard you," she said.

"I was on my way in," Kovash said. "But Lou waylaid me."

She reached Kovash and put a hand on his arm. "I worry when you're not around, Garrett," she said.

Kovash nodded toward Vartann. "The PD has a handle on things. Nobody's touching Dennis while they have someone outside his door."

"It's not the same. Besides, what if the officer has to go to the bathroom or something?"

"I'm here now," Kovash said.

Vartann broke in. "Well, you will be in a minute." He turned back to the nurse. "Is there a private place where we could talk briefly?"

The nurse contemplated for just a moment. "There's a private room down the hall. Four-seventeen. It was vacated this morning and there's no one in it yet."

"That'll work."

Kovash was staring at Vartann with concern. "What's this about?"

Vartann hadn't planned to say anything to Kovash. Not yet. But when he saw the way Daniels's wife reacted to Kovash's arrival, he decided to change his play. A friendly greeting didn't necessarily add up to an affair—but if the two of them were involved, that could amount to a motive. The mogul's wife and his bodyguard would have plenty of opportunity to take him out. And it had already been established that Kovash determined the route Daniels and his people would take back to the office after the fundraiser. "He'll be there in a couple of minutes, Mrs. Daniels," he said. "Come on, Garrett."

Joanna Daniels sighed but returned to her husband's room. Kovash followed Vartann to room 417. When they were inside, Vartann closed the door. Kovash's expression had changed from one of acceptance to an angry scowl. "What the hell is this, Lou?"

"I took a bit of gauze off your shoe."

"Thanks, I guess. It's all over the place around here."

"It's all over Daniels's room, anyway."

"That's where I've been spending most of my time."

"It's the time away from there I want to talk about. Where were you, for, say, the last three hours or so?"

"I've been doing a little digging on my own, trying to identify and mitigate threats to my client."

"Threats like Alec Watson?"

"I don't know that Watson's a threat, necessarily."

"But you paid him a visit?"

"I did. He's got a high profile and a large following. Of all the people who've been attacking Dennis—verbally, I mean—he's the most visible. I wanted to see if he knew anything about the bombing. How did you know?"

"The gauze on your shoe. We found some in Watson's office."

"Why were you looking at Watson's office?"

"I guess it hasn't made the air yet. Watson's dead, Garrett. Murdered."

Kovash blanched. "What, today?"

"Couple hours ago. We've been keeping a lid on it, but it'll be on the evening news, I'm sure."

"How?"

"Automatic weapon. He was hit something like a dozen times."

Kovash shook his head sadly. "He seemed like a pretty nice guy. I mean . . ."

"Right."

"You do know automatic weapons aren't my style, right?"

"I was hoping murder wasn't your style."

"I didn't think I had to say that. You know my record."

Vartann nodded. "I do. But you know I can't let the past determine my actions now. There's a first kill for every killer."

"I'm no killer, Lou."

"I believe you, Garrett. I just have to look at everything. Okay?"

"Sure, I understand."

"So Watson was alive when you left him?"

"Alive and complaining. He thinks—thought—Dennis was pushing more of a far-left ideology. I tried to set him straight. I'm a Reagan man myself, a law and order conservative. If I thought Dennis was some kind of commie, I might have turned down the job."

"Speaking of which, your job is to protect Daniels. Ours is to find the bomber. You do yours and we'll do ours, okay?"

"I can't promise I won't look into it," Kovash said. "That's part of protecting him, as far as I'm concerned."

"Well, keep it to a minimum, then. And stay out of our way."

"I'll make every effort," Kovash said.

"You do that."

Vartann offered his hand, and Kovash shook it. "I mean it, Garrett. You're not a cop anymore. We're on this, but if you run around leaving your footprints all over the investigation—almost literally, in this case—it could turn into a problem."

"I didn't kill Watson, Lou. You believe that, right?"

"I'm withholding judgment for now. I'll keep you posted if that changes. In the meantime, stick close to your client so I know where to find you." Vartann opened the door, walked out, and closed it behind him.

By the time he got on the elevator and the doors slid closed, Garrett Kovash had still not left room 417.

19

Ray had turned the trace he'd collected at Lucia's house over to Hodges for analysis. The organic, potentially DNA-bearing evidence went to Carrie, the day shift DNA tech, along with a plea for immediate analysis. "As close to immediate as you can manage," he'd added.

The tech was looking a little overwhelmed, and she nodded gratefully. "I'll let you know the minute I've got something," she promised.

"Thanks." Ray left her to her work and went to find Detective Sam Vega, who had agreed to meet him at the lab. Vega was in the hallway, chatting with Mandy Webster. "Sam," Ray said, "I appreciate you coming over."

Vega made eye contact with Mandy and shrugged. "Duty calls."

"It always does," Mandy said. "Usually at inopportune moments."

Vega chuckled, but joined step with Ray. "You healing okay?"

"I'm on my feet," Ray said. "Now it only hurts

when I laugh. Or breathe. Who needs two kidneys, anyway?"

Vega laughed. "What'd you want to see me about?"

"I was hoping to pick your brain a little—"

"Never something you want to say in the Crime Lab," Vega interrupted. "Or around Doc Robbins."

Ray let the jokes slide by. "I know you used to be with the gang unit, Sam. I wanted to see if you'd ever encountered a situation like one I'm facing."

"What is it?"

"A Latino criminal enterprise, or mostly Latino, anyway. They were involved in human smuggling."

"Bringing in undocumenteds?"

"Right."

"You used the past tense."

"Business has slowed there, so they've shifted their priorities. Now they're going after former clients, ones who have become established enough here to have something to lose, and blackmailing or abducting them, threatening to turn them into ICE if they're not paid off."

"That's downright sinister," Vega said. "Clever, but cruel."

"That's not the worst of it. When their victims, or their families, aren't immediately forthcoming, they have a nasty habit of severing hands. Apparently getting a loved one's hand in the mail can be quite the incentive."

"I can imagine." Vega's forehead furrowed. "I don't remember ever running into that sort of operation," he said. "It's been a while since I've been on the gangs detail, though. And this sounds more like an organized crime situation than a street gang."

"I understand that. I just thought it was worth a shot."

"Sure," Vega said. "I'll ask around. If I find out anything, I'll let you know."

"I appreciate it," Ray said. "I've got a brand new hand, and I'd like to find its owner while there's still something I can do for him."

"You think this is related to those other hands that've turned up?"

"I think so, yes. They spread them around as sort of an early warning system. People in the victimized community know what it means, and it encourages them to keep quiet and pay up."

"Nasty," Vega said. "I'll tap some of my CIs, and get back to you."

"Thanks, Sam. Anything you can find out will be a big help."

When Vega had left, Ray headed for the morgue. He hadn't forgotten about the series of unclaimed hands that had been collected recently, but he hadn't been focused on them, either. It was time to take another look.

"I need a hand, Albert," he said when he arrived.

Dr. Robbins looked up from the corpse he was studying, raised his hands, and clapped them together three times. "Good enough?"

"I mean a specific hand. Or a set of them, really."

"Which hands would those be, Ray?"

"Do you have many different sets? I'm looking for the ones that have come along lately without their arms attached. Or anything else."

"Oh, *those* hands." Robbins pointed a scalpel toward a bank of freezers. "They're in cold storage."

"Of course they are." Ray used the morgue sink to scrub up, then donned a pair of poly gloves. "You mind if I take a look?"

"Be my guest," Robbins said, bearing down on the corpse with the scalpel. "I'd give you a hand, but I'm up to my neck at the moment. Or this gentleman's neck, at any rate."

"Not a problem," Ray said. He shivered a little at the sight.

"Sorry," Robbins said. "Does that bother you?"

"It wouldn't have, a few weeks ago," Ray replied. "I guess it's just a little close to home at the moment." He started toward the freezer unit Robbins had indicated. "Actually, have the hands been thoroughly examined?"

"Examined for what?"

"Tool marks, I was thinking."

"Yes," Robbins confirmed. "Either I checked them, or David Phillips did."

"No need for me to duplicate the effort, then. I'll just review your reports."

"If you'd rather thumb through those than man-handle the real things, suit yourself."

"I will," Ray said. The medical examiner's sense of humor almost never failed him, even when it came mostly in the form of puns that would make a sane person groan. Ray always appreciated it—but there were times he didn't want Robbins to know that, because it would only encourage him. "Thanks for your help."

"If you need me, give me a call," Robbins said. "I believe you've got my digits."

* * *

Back at his desk, Ray read through the reports on the severed hands, closely examining the photos of tool marks on the bones. Four hands had bcen discovered, over the past six months. Three were male, one female. They were all left hands. All had been DNA-tested, but no identifications had been made. No one had come forward to claim the hands. In three cases, there had been enough skin remaining on the hands to determine that they had an olive complexion.

Tool marks on two of the hands, the second and third ones found, matched. They didn't match any of the others, though, and none matched the newest hand.

In the case of the third hand, epithelial cells had been found under two fingernails. DNA from those skin fragments had also been analyzed—another dead end. Ray had the reports spread out on his desk, trying to look at them through someone else's eyes, in case there was something that he just wasn't seeing, when Carrie walked in with a printout. "Here's what we've got on your samples so far," she said, handing the sheets to Ray. "Whoever they came from, he's not in the system."

"He?"

"I was able to determine that much. Male, probably Hispanic. But no ID beyond that. I can dig a little deeper into it, see if I can come up with anything else."

"Dig as deep as you can, but thanks for this," Ray said.

"Sure, glad to help."

She disappeared, and Ray studied the report

she'd handed him. The stats on the page looked familiar—lines of letters, others with numbers and letters, all of it meaningless to the average civilian and the average juror. Even now, so many years after the O.J. Simpson case, DNA technicians and CSIs still had a hard time explaining DNA sequencing to juries in a way they could understand. They wanted the process to be as simple as one of those pregnancy tests that showed a plus sign for positive. This result means the accused did it, that one means he didn't. Unfortunately, it didn't work that way. The best that could be claimed was that DNA offered a billion-to-one chance that the suspect was not the one who had left evidence at the scene. To which some defense attorney always asked, "You mean, there's a chance that it wasn't him?"

"A billion-to-one is hardly a chance," the beleaguered expert would contend.

"But it's not one hundred percent, absolutely positive."

"It never is."

"Thank you," the defense attorney would usually say at that point. "No further questions."

Ray pored over the report, wondering why the data on it rang a bell. Then, as if waking up from a nap, he shook his head and almost kicked himself. He turned back to the DNA profile of the person whose epithelial tissue had been found under hand number three's fingernails.

"It's the same person," Ray said softly. "I'll be damned, it's the same guy."

He studied both again, matching up the letter strings, the graphs. Identical. A billion-to-one chance that it wasn't the same man, maybe. Which was the same as saying no chance at all.

He still didn't know to whom the skin cells belonged. But it was a start.

It was better than he'd had five minutes ago.

Sara shielded her eyes against the sinking sun—another thirty minutes, forty at the outside, and it would be gone—and scanned the upper reaches of the mountainside.

"You lose a contact lens?" Nick asked.

She ignored the feeble gag. "Arsonists like to watch their fires," she said. "In urban areas, you always try to videotape the crowd outside a fire scene, right? Because chances are, he's there."

"True."

"Here, there was no crowd standing around watching."

"Too dangerous," Nick said. "A forest fire isn't easily contained to a single structure."

"Right. And it can be seen from a long ways off. So I thought, if I were the arsonist and I wanted to watch the fire, where would I stand?"

"Up there somewhere. Makes sense."

"Yeah, only most of the good vantage points have houses on them." She pointed out the most prominent ridges overlooking the origin point. "See? There, there, and there. I think that one, too, but if there was a house there, the fire burned it to the ground. I can't tell if those are burned trees or timbers."

"Kinda looks like a stone chimney," Nick said. "But it's hard to make it out, everything's covered in black."

"Point is, the houses were all evacuated. So even if the firestarter set it where he could see it burn, he didn't get to watch for long. As soon as it started up these slopes toward the houses, the Forest Service issued the evacuation order."

"And then they came in with air support, dumping fire retardant chemicals. Hoses around the houses. Firefighters everywhere, turning earth with shovels, lighting backfires."

"That's a hell of a job, but I'm glad they're out there," Sara said. "For us, though . . ."

"It means there's almost no such thing as an uncontaminated crime scene. Not outdoors, anyway."

"Indoors, you think?"

"I think the arsonist had to pour wax on the candles somewhere. Makes more sense to do that inside than out."

"True."

She eyed the houses more closely. They were large, luxurious. The cheaper homes, up here, were the ones without the primo views. "I think we can rule out insurance, as a motive," she said. "I wouldn't be surprised if some of these homeowners were underwater on their mortgages. Especially considering that some of these are probably vacation homes, second homes. But for insurance purposes you would start the fire closer to your house, you wouldn't count on it burning in exactly the path you wanted. And this is a pretty remote spot."

"Another common motive for arson is to cover up a prior crime," Nick said. "But the same reasoning applies. If you were trying to burn a house to hide a victim's body, you'd torch the house, not the woods three miles away."

"So what's that leave us?"

"A firebug. Someone who just gets off on seeing things burn. Or someone trying to smoke out those campers. Maybe someone with a grudge against the Forest Service, or against his neighbors. Though that'd be pretty risky, knowing your own place could go up just as easily as theirs."

It was all speculation at this point. They didn't have much to go on—some matches, some candle wax, and a lot of hunches.

Still, it was informed speculation. The physical evidence, combined with their years of experience at the interpretation of such evidence, steered them in a certain direction.

"I guess we're going up again," Sara said.

"You think it's time to knock on some doors?"

"I think you're probably right about the candle wax. If we can find spilled wax that corresponds with what we've got from down here, we'll be making real progress."

"If we're gonna knock on doors," Nick said, "I say we start with Harley Givens. I don't trust that joker for a minute."

"Works for me," Sara agreed. "Let's pay him a visit."

20

STEVEN KIRKLAND—OR STEVEN of Kirkland (Way-cross), as he billed himself at the seminar—was one of those men who had probably looked middle-aged by his late twenties, Brass thought. Now that he was in his sixties, he looked positively ancient. Deep canyons carved his face. His thin white hair showed patches of pale pink scalp. Brown spots mottled his lean, wrinkled hands, arms, and neck. He wore a baggy, short-sleeved white shirt that fit as if he had lost a lot of weight recently, but hadn't had a chance to go shopping. His brown pants were cinched up by his belt, and his brown loafers were scuffed and worn. For a guy who made plenty of money—and Brass couldn't help suspecting that was the underlying reason for starting and running the Free Citizens of the Republic, despite the group's protestations to the contrary—he didn't dress like it.

His son, on the other hand, displayed his wealth. Troy of Kirkland (Waycross) wore a cream-colored silk suit, a violet shirt, a striped tie, and shoes that matched the suit and had probably set him back five bills, minimum. He was sturdier than his father, though similarities were apparent in the closeness of his eyes, the thrust of his nose, and the almost absolute lack of discernible lips. When the Kirklands closed their mouths, they effectively disappeared, giving the impression that their faces were featureless in the shadows of their substantial beaks. When they spoke, they looked like Muppets.

The younger Kirkland's brown hair was thick and swept back off his face, and though his father rarely left his stool during the seminar, Troy paced the stage, strutting and squatting and waving his hands to make his points. He reminded Brass of an evangelist at a tent revival. That was not, as far as Brass was concerned, a favorable comparison.

If there were any Mrs. Kirklands, they were not in evidence. The audience crowding the Orpheus Hotel ballroom was a varied cross-section of Las Vegas residents, if by varied one could mean almost exclusively white males. They were of different ages, from a few kids of seven or eight, up to men in their seventies or eighties. A handful of women were scattered throughout the hotel ballroom, but none seemed to be there alone—they accompanied men, and a few of them had apparently been brought along just to keep an eye on the kids. The Free Citizens were not, Brass decided, the most socially progressive group of people he had ever seen.

Financially, more of them appeared to be of the class that the elder Kirkland seemingly represented more than the younger one. Brass saw a lot of blue collars and plenty of plaid, but not many suits and ties. The event was free, though Brass was certain a hat would be passed at some point, literally or metaphorically. Still, in Vegas not much came for free, and this seminar included bad coffee and dry cookies, to boot.

He and Lou Vartann had entered with the other attendees, most of them arriving in groups of two or three. They had mingled for a few minutes, helped themselves to the complimentary snacks, then secured chairs near the back of the room, where they could watch the audience, the dais, and the door. Two bodyguards flanked the stage, walls of muscle with short-cropped hair and dark suits.

"The day is coming," Troy Kirkland said. His tone was ominous, despite a shrill reediness in his voice. "And it's coming soon. On that day, long-established plans by the federal government in Washington will be revealed. But by the time they're made explicit, it will be too late to complain, too late to protest, too late to write your senators and congressmen. The White House switchboard will not, my friends, be taking calls on that day."

Troy paused, looked at his father, then turned dramatically to the audience. "The only response available on that day will be the same one that created this country, where there once was none." Another pause, for effect. "Revolution."

The father took over the spiel at that point, his voice ragged and phlegmy. "You might think we're exaggeratin' things," he said. "But we're not. If anythin', we're downplayin' 'em so we don't alarm folks too much. Make no mistake, though—if you're not alarmed right now, you're not payin' attention."

Steven took a sip from a plastic water bottle. Troy watched, his hands clasped behind his back, his posture one of respectful attention. When he was finished, Steven wiped his mouth with the back of his left hand.

"Here's the thing," he said. "When that day comes, it'll mean soldiers in the streets. Not American soldiers, either, but North American soldiers, and there's a big difference. It'll mean wholesale confiscation of our guns, and wholesale abridgement of our rights. That'll be the day that the Mexico/U.S./Canada superhighway opens up, connecting all three formerly sovereign nations with no border checkpoints. It'll be the day the new currency, the North American merit, comes into use and our dollars become worthless.

"On that day you'll either be prepared or you won't. You'll be ready to fight, or ready to surrender, to roll over like some damned rabbit, showin' the wolf your belly and tellin' it to go ahead and rip you open, eat out your heart."

"But they can be ready, can't they, Dad?" Troy Kirkland said, taking up the narrative once again. Brass was impressed with how well they had choreographed the give-and-take, probably over hundreds of similar presentations. "The good folks in this room *can* be prepared for that day. That's what the Free Citizens of the Republic is all about, isn't it? Fighting back, making sure that day never comes— or if it does, if all our efforts are for naught, that we're not taken by surprise."

"That's right," Steven said. Instead of addressing his son, he gazed out toward the audience. "You can be ready. You *must* be ready. And here's how. You need to get you some guns. Stockpile what you can, and ammo, and learn to shoot. Learn to hit your damn targets. Stock up on food, too, canned goods, stuff that won't spoil. It'll be some time before grocery stores reopen, those that survive the change, and when they do they'll only accept merits."

"Merits and diamonds, Dad."

"That's right," Steven said again. "Even under the new North American order, diamonds and precious stones will be accepted for goods and services. See, the United States never should have abandoned the gold standard. When we did, that was the beginning of the end right there, and that's the reason I don't recommend gold. The federal government is sitting on huge stockpiles of it—if they decided to release it all at once, they'd depress the value for years to come. But diamonds will serve you well. And maybe I shouldn't say this, since our stock is gettin' lower than I like to see, but—"

Troy whirled toward his father with the easy grace of someone who had done it a hundred times. "Dad, no!"

"I'm sorry, son, but these are good folks here. They've come of their own free will because they care about America, and we got to help 'em if we can. Thing is, we got some gem-quality diamonds, out in the truck. Around the time we're wrappin' up here, some of our security folks will bring 'em in. If you all would like to convert some of your dollars to diamonds, right here, tonight, why, we'd give you a favorable exchange rate on 'em."

At that announcement, the crowd broke into

hushed conversations, creating an overall buzz. "There it is," Brass whispered. "I'd like to test some of those diamonds, see if they're glass. Or plastic."

"How many laws do you figure they've broken so far?" Vartann asked. "Inciting armed rebellion against the government . . ."

"It'd go down as free speech," Brass replied. "They didn't call for an immediate taking up of arms, but for a theoretical one at some point in the future. Can't bust them on that one."

"They've got some pretty wild ideas."

"I wouldn't have them over for a barbecue," Brass said. "But so far I don't think they've crossed the line."

"All right, Dad," Troy Kirkland said, throwing his hands up with an exaggerated flair. "They're your diamonds. If you want to let them go for less than the going rate, that's up to you." He returned his attention to the audience. "But not quite yet. We'll do that when we've finished telling you what our research has taught us, these last few years.

"Republicans, Democrats, they're all the same. They've been bought and sold by those who are selling our country out from underneath us. They're powerful business interests, most of them based in New York, although they have their hands in Washington and Hollywood and everyplace else you see ugly high-rise office buildings full of drones. When they look upon this great land, all they see is a captive population of consumers for whatever made-in-China crap they want to sell us. They see Canada and Mexico the same way, and they see that it would be easier to sell more of it, if we were all one big country with a single currency.

"Now, I have nothing against the free market. Capitalism made this country great. But it was our country, and if they get their way, it won't be anymore. It'll be the country of North America, owned lock, stock, and barrel by those bankers and billionaires I'm talking about. We the people, we won't count anymore. If it's easier to steamroller us, that's what they'll do. If it's easier to take away our guns and move us into camps, that's what they'll do. As long as they can keep a population of sheep ready to shell out dollars—excuse me, merits—for their crap, they'll be glad to do it."

"They keep taxing us to death," Steven said. "But do you see where that tax money's goin'? There are potholes in every road, bridges fallin' down. We aren't winnin' wars, our schools are failin', and our borders are wide open. So where's the money goin'? It's goin' to outfit a secret army made up of American, Canadian, and Mexican troops, and it's goin' to build that secret highway and infrastructure, that's where."

Steven Kirkland came off his stool, for the first time since climbing onto the dais. "But we're not going to let them get away with that, are we?"

A couple of audience members shouted out their opposition, but it wasn't good enough for Steven. "Are we?" he shouted.

"No!" the audience responded.

"We're going to call them out, aren't we?"

"Yes!"

"We're going to protest the selling of our country, aren't we?"

"Yes!" the crowd thundered.

"And if we have to, we'll get our guns and go hunting for those who would do us harm, won't we?"

"Yes!" The crowd was into it now, stomping and clapping, whistling and shrieking.

Troy started making downward motions with his hands. When the audience finally quieted, he said, "That's what we like to hear. The Free Citizens of the Republic was formed, and exists today, to save our country from those people. We want America back—the United States of America that was founded in 1776, that adhered to a Constitution, and that promises all people life, liberty and the pursuit of happiness. That America. We thank you for your enthusiastic support. In the lobby when you go out, there'll be tables at which you can sign up for membership. For the low, low price of fifty dollars—that's nothing, pocket change for a couple of weeks—for only fifty American dollars you'll get an embossed membership card and a subscription to all of our publications, so you can stay up to date on the threats facing America and how we can combat them. There'll also be a table set up where you can exchange some of those dollars—while they're still worth something—for diamonds, which will never lose their value no matter what. Our supplies are limited, so act today. Thank you all for coming, and God bless the USA!"

Once more, the room erupted. The Kirklands exited through a door behind the dais, and the audience started filing out into the lobby area.

"Sounds like a pretty good racket," Brass said.

"For the Kirklands," Vartann agreed. "What do you want to bet those Free Citizens publications are just full of ads for more things to spend your money on? Things benefiting old Steven and Troy, of course."

"I wouldn't take that bet, Lou. I've got nothing against con men fleecing suckers as long as it's legal, and in this case it looks like the suckers are lining up to be fleeced. What bothers me is the rhetoric. They're stirring these folks up. When you've got a lot of loaded guns around and a lot of fearful people, sooner or later there's going to be trouble."

"I hear you," Vartann said.

"You want to try to catch the Kirklands, put some pressure on them to call their dogs off Catherine?" Everybody knew Lou and Catherine were dating, and he didn't blame the detective for wanting to look after her. Brass did, too—he and the CSI team had had each other's backs for years.

"I think I sent that message pretty clearly this afternoon," Vartann said. "And that's a local deal, anyway—the Kirklands just got into town, from what I hear."

"Okay," Brass said. "I still think we'd better keep an eye on them while they're here, and stay on top of the situation with Catherine. Last thing I want is for law enforcement to be afraid that doing our jobs will make us into targets for harassment. But if you want to get out of here, I'm okay with that. I don't think we're exactly popular in this crowd."

"Definitely not," Vartann said with a grin. "Let's go pull our shift on that superhighway and earn some North American merits for our retirement. . . ."

21

"I THINK I'VE got something here," Greg said.

He was leaning over Alec Watson's desk, bent almost double, aiming an alternate light source at the shiny wooden surface. "What is it?" Catherine asked.

"I'm not sure yet. Maybe he just spilled coffee or something, but it's pretty far back for that." He indicated an area about sixteen inches from the back of the desk, nearly two feet from where Watson would have sat. "He'd have to have had pretty long arms to put a cup down back here. I don't think he was part gorilla. But there are a couple of drops of some dried liquid over here."

"More blood?" She was almost used to the smell of it pervading the room. Every now and then she had to step outside to breathe in some fresh air.

"Doesn't look like it. It looks clear. And from the looks of this desk, it gets dusted and maybe polished every day, so they must be pretty recent."

"What do you think it is, then?" Catherine was on her knees, dusting the armrests of the two visitor chairs facing the desk, looking for friction ridge impressions. She had already dusted the edge of the desk nearest the chairs, and come up empty. The chairs were made of wood, with padded leather arms, back, and cushion. It was almost impossible to sit in a chair and not leave impressions somewhere, unless a person took great pains to sit with hands folded, or wore gloves. The difficulty was in the fact that the sealed, polished wood was a nonporous substance, and therefore easily powdered for latent prints, but since leather was porous, powders and chemical agents could backfire, hiding or erasing whatever impressions might have been left.

Greg disappeared behind the desk for a moment. She heard him rummaging around in his field kit. "My guess is saliva. Maybe whoever shot him was spitting mad. I'll test for it, see what happens."

"Good call," Catherine said. "It'd be nice to get some DNA from this room that doesn't belong to Watson. Or Dennis Daniels, who we know wasn't here."

Greg brought a wet swab to the desk's shiny surface and wiped an edge of one of the spots he had found, leaving plenty of the material behind in case other tests were needed. Then he touched the swab to an immunographic test strip he had prepared. Catherine recognized the technique, which was new but had tested well. Almost every organic compound found in plasma was also found, in trace amounts, in human saliva. The test Greg employed looked for the enzyme called human salivary alpha amylase, or hAMYI A. He had already put a drop of a detection antibody on the strip. The captured antibody, from the desktop, merged with the detection antibody, and if hAMYI A was present, the sample would move by capillary action to a test line.

"I get a gold star," Greg said after a couple of minutes. Catherine had stopped watching him and returned to her own work, trying to dust upside-down on the undersides of the chair arms. It was tricky work, because when she swirled the brush to lightly deposit dust without actually touching the surface, gravity interceded, and more dust fell back onto her gloved hand than stuck to the chair arm.

"It's positive?" she asked.

"It's human saliva. Don't know whose yet, the lab will have to tell us that. But maybe it's the killer's."

"We can hope." Catherine was glad he had persevered and identified the saliva. He was right; if it had come from the killer, then it could be analyzed for DNA and a possible identification could be made. She might still be able to make an ID, and quicker, with fingerprints.

She poured a little more of the light gray powder she was using onto a clean sheet of paper she had spread on the floor. The gray contrasted nicely with the dark wood of the chair. She touched the very tip of her brush to the powder, picking some up, then shook the brush to release any excess. Once again, she tried to twirl it onto the underside of the chair arm, and this time, some stuck. Thinking she had turned something up, she twirled one more time, moving the brush just a little to her right.

"I've got an impression here," she said.

"A good one?"

She withheld judgment on that until she had finished powdering it. "Looks like." The latent print showed up on the chair, where oils from the person's skin had left it. It wasn't magic, though it looked like it—she had made the invisible turn visible. She studied the whorls and arches. One loop slanting to the left was cut by scar tissue. "One full print and part of the next."

Her next step was to photograph the print, making sure she got good close-ups. Then she took lifting tape from her kit, placed one end beside the whole print, and smoothed it over that and the partial. She forced out a couple of tiny air bubbles, then lifted the print with one smooth, practiced motion. Because the powder was light gray, she chose a black mounting card to adhere the tape to. When she was finished, the print was preserved.

She would run it through IAFIS, the Integrated Automated Fingerprint Identification System, to see if the person who had left it was known to law enforcement. First, she had to document it—the least glamorous part of the job, but every piece of evidence had to be photographed and fully documented. On the lift card she wrote the case number, where she had taken the print, the address, the date, and her signature. She put the same information on a separate sheet of her notebook. One more step—now that she had found a latent print, she would have to take exclusionary ten-cards from everyone in the office, including the deceased, who might have sat in that chair.

And this was only the first print she had found. She was in for a long night.

Then again, in her business, they were all long nights.

Her documentation done, she shot one more digital picture of the lift card, then connected the camera to a laptop and transmitted the image directly to IAFIS. While the system searched for the print, she kept working on the chairs, looking for more latents. The search was fruitless; whoever had sat there had done a good job of keeping his hands to himself, or had wiped the chair down. The latter explanation made the most sense, because on most such chairs, her problem would have been one of eliminating dozens of prints left by innocents.

By the time she finished with the chairs, IAFIS had a hit.

"Interesting," she said.

Greg had moved on to examining the floor on her side of the desk—the side that wasn't covered in blood. "What is?"

She had pulled up the criminal record of the person who had left the print, and was scrolling down the page as she spoke. "My print belongs to Troy Kirkland. The son of Steven Kirkland, the founder of the Free Citizens of the Republic."

"That's the group that's been giving you a hard time, right?"

"Yes." She tapped a few more keys. "Looks like father and son both have pretty long sheets. Fraud convictions, assaults, stalking, various cons and scams."

"Are they allied with Watson's group?"

"Not the way Watson described it. Rivals is more like it, and not friendly ones." Catherine stood, reached for the ceiling, stretching her arms and legs to unkink the muscles. "I'll be right back."

She found Justine Marie Taylor in her office down the hall, flipping through file folders with one hand, while holding a handkerchief to her nose with the other. Her mascara was blurred around her eyes and streaked all the way down her cheeks.

"I'm sorry to disturb you," Catherine said. "But do you know if Mr. Watson had an appointment with Steven and/or Troy Kirkland this afternoon?"

"No, I don't think . . ." She let the sentence trail off. Setting the file folders aside, she checked the calendar grid on her desk blotter. "No, no appointments at all this afternoon. He doesn't like to have visitors when we're on deadline."

"Did you know Kirkland was here?"

"I had no idea."

"Have you ever met him? Did Alec ever meet with him?"

"I'm sure I've never heard the name," Taylor said. "And I make a point of remembering people Alec does business with."

"All right, thank you. I'm hoping we'll be out of your hair soon. Sorry to be a bother."

"It's no . . . no bother," Taylor said. "If you can find who did it, that's all I care about."

"That's the idea," Catherine said. "And you just helped a great deal."

She returned to Watson's office to find Greg dusting the individual shell casings left on the floor. "I think we got lucky," she said.

"Lucky enough that I don't have to do this?"

"Keep it up. If we get a print on one of those, it'll help seal the deal. But Troy Kirkland was definitely not an expected visitor. His aide says Watson didn't like setting meetings on deadline days, so Kirkland came by without an appointment."

"Sounds like we need to talk to this Kirkland guy," Greg said.

"And I think I know right where to find him." She fished her phone out of a pocket and punched up the number for Jim Brass. He answered on the second ring. Catherine could hear the steady rush of a car engine underlying his voice. "Are you driving?"

"Lou's chauffeuring," he said. "I'm enjoying being a passenger for a change."

"Does that mean you're not at the seminar anymore?"

"Seminar's over. I guess old Steven Kirkland is an early-to-bed kind of guy."

"Maybe you should go back and wake him," Catherine said. "At least wake Troy Kirkland. He was in Alec Watson's office today, in an unscheduled, secret meeting that even Watson's office manager didn't know about. It looks like he did a quick wipe job, but he left a latent on the bottom of the chair arm. Some cartridges were left at the scene as well; Greg's checking those now."

"I'll wake them both," Brass said. "They just got into town today, and I doubt they've been apart for more than ten minutes since they got here. From the looks of things, father and son are damn near inseparable."

"Both chairs have been wiped," Catherine reported. "So it's possible they were here together."

"We're on it, Cath. Thanks."

"What I don't get," Greg said after her call, "is even if the two groups are rivals, why go after Watson? They're both involved in that protest effort, right?"

Catherine had a suspicion of her own on that topic. She didn't want to think about it, because it implicated her, however indirectly, in a man's death. "Plenty of people saw Watson leaving headquarters today, and it was all over the news," she said. "After that, our people and ATF raided the local Free Citizens' headquarters. If they put two and two together, they might have suspected Watson tipped us off about their weapons cache."

"Which he did, right?"

"He did, yes. And one purpose of the raid was to persuade the Free Citizens to leave me alone."

Greg looked stricken. In other words, exactly how she felt. "Catherine, no. You can't . . . don't think that. Any credible tip that they were stockpiling illegal weapons had to be checked out. Whether or not you were in the picture."

"I get that, Greg. I do. But I also can't deny that Lou Vartann was the one who went to ATF with the tip, and the one who led the raid. And Lou and I are . . ." She left the rest unsaid, not certain who knew and who didn't.

"Just don't blame yourself, Catherine. Watson didn't have to come in. He could have lawyered up. He could have kept quiet. But he said his piece—intentionally steering us toward the Free Citizens.

Maybe he was trying to settle an old grudge his way, and they responded their way. The issues between them have nothing to do with you, though. And from the job they did on him, if they couldn't use this excuse, they'd have found another."

"I hope you're right, Greg." Even as she said it, Catherine knew that he probably was, that it was an act of egotism to assume that any part of their long-standing feud, or the violent climax it reached, had anything to do with her. She had a healthy opinion of herself—she was smart, capable, and tougher than she had ever dreamed she would be, in younger days. But she didn't believe the sun rose and set for her, and she didn't believe, in the long run, that the actions of the morally deranged needed her to set them off. At worst, she was an excuse for Watson's murder, but not a reason.

The best contribution she could make, at this point, would be to make sure she amassed the evidence necessary to convict his killer. She returned to the task at hand, determined to do just that.

22

HARLEY GIVENS OBJECTED to having his home searched without a warrant, but when Nick announced that he'd be glad to stand by the front door while Sara drove down the mountain, found a judge, got a warrant issued and signed, then drove back up, Givens relented.

"We just want to see your boots," Sara explained. "And your candles. Kitchen matches, too, if you have any."

"What about my collection of fishing lures?" Givens asked. "Science fiction novels? Chainsaw?"

"If you think those are germane to the case."

"You can't possibly still be working on the fire," Givens said. "Because if you were, you wouldn't be wasting your time with me."

"I think we'll decide what's a waste of our time," Nick said. He was fed up with Givens's obstruction and his general attitude, and he wouldn't mind finding evidence in his house if only so he could slap handcuffs on those pudgy wrists. "If that's okay with you."

Givens simply shrugged and admitted them into the house. "I got nothing to hide," he said. "If you find anything juicy, I'd love to see it."

The invitation was all-encompassing enough to allow Nick and Sara to search every inch of his house. But that really would be a waste of time. So far, the clues they had found were few—some matches, wax, and a boot print. They shouldn't have to spend more than a few minutes in Givens's house, and that was more than enough time for Nick.

Givens wasn't quite a hoarder, but he apparently had a hard time throwing anything away. His two-story house was overloaded with junk: things he might have found on the mountain, like old, rusted pieces of mining equipment, books that had been read and reread so many times their covers were frayed and falling apart, and tourist pamphlets from places as far afield as Disney World, a Louisiana alligator farm, a rodeo museum in Canada, and other unlikely spots. He probably really did have a collection of fishing lures, but Nick couldn't see it amid the clutter. The predominant smell was left over from the fire, but it had a different tone than the charred odor of the forest. Oilier. There had probably been plastic burning in the house, in addition to wood. Those fumes could be one of a fire's deadliest weapons.

In his bedroom closet, Givens had at least a dozen pairs of shoes and boots. Nick turned each one over and compared the toe to the photo he had taken of the print found near the fire's point of origin. None matched it. He checked every other room, looking for stray boots or signs of melted wax, without success. In a walk-in pantry off the kitchen, he found Sara. An overflowing, open wastebasket gave the pantry a sour, spoiled stink that overpowered even the burned smell. "Well, he's got safety matches," she said, showing him a box. "I've bagged some for comparison. But they're a common brand, so that doesn't get us far."

"Couldn't find any matching boot soles," Nick told her. "Or signs that he's been melting wax anywhere. Of course, he might have done that in the part of the house that burned."

"I don't see anything that merits a more extensive search," Sara said. "Which is fine with me . . . I don't think I can stand it in here much longer. The guy's got cans of beans that look like they go back to the sixties."

Nick was about to respond when he heard anxious, angry shouts from outside the house. "Sounds like trouble," he said.

"Just what we need." She put the box of matches back where she had found it. "Let's have a look."

Nick led the way outside, Sara following, Givens close behind her, carrying his shotgun. The sun's last rays sparkled in the charred tangle of branches beyond the road, like fireflies caught in a net. On the street, some of the same people they had encountered earlier were on the dirt shoulder of the road, surrounding a pair of young people Nick didn't remember having seen before. A man and a woman, both lean and blond, wearing dirty clothes that didn't quite fit. Nick knew at once who they must be.

"That's those campers," he said. "The 'dirty hippies,' right?"

"That's them," Givens replied. "They always return to the scene of the crime, don't they?"

"That's actually a myth," Sara said. "Some do, others don't."

"Here you go, officers," Collin Gardner called when he saw them coming. He was aiming a revolver at the pair. "We found 'em for you!"

"Put the weapon down, sir," Nick said. His hand snaked out, drew his own firearm from his belt holster. "Now. Anyone else carrying, please put your weapon on the ground right now."

"We have a right to carry arms," Givens complained.

"Haven't we been over that?" Sara asked. "You have a right. But we have a right to secure the situation, and that includes asking you to put your guns away for the moment."

Givens sighed and set his shotgun on the ground. "If this thing doesn't survive having you two around, I'm suing the department."

Collin Gardner was less cooperative. His arm trembled, but he kept the revolver leveled at the pair of campers. They stood with their hands raised, sharing anxious glances.

"Mr. Gardner," Nick said. "Lower that weapon. I won't ask you again."

"This pair here started that fire," Gardner said. "I want to make a citizen's arrest."

"We're standing right here," Sara pointed out. "If

there's any arresting to be done, we'll do it. So far, there's not a shred of evidence implicating these two."

"We did nothing," the young man said. He had a soft voice, with a German accent. "We started no fire."

Nick and Sara moved closer to them. Gardner finally lowered his weapon, but kept it in his hand. Nick decided to let that slide. "Let's break this up," he said. "All of you, go home. We'll talk to these folks and if there's action needed, we'll take it."

"Wish we could count on that," Givens said. "So far all you've done is hassle innocent locals, and make excuses for this pair."

"Mr. Givens, we know what we're doing. You've got to have a little faith in our judgment."

"You don't have much in mine."

Nick couldn't argue with that. "Just go home. This is under control."

The crowd began to disperse. At the edge of the group, Nick saw Kevin Cox. As before, he was by himself, watching but not participating. Gardner and Givens huddled together for a minute while Givens picked up his shotgun, speaking in low tones and casting angry glances toward the CSIs. When Sara took a step in their direction, they parted and each man went to his own home.

"Where have you two been?" Nick asked. "Since the fire began?"

"It came quickly toward us," the woman said. She spoke English with a more natural flair than her friend, her accent pronounced but less impenetrable. "We ran, up the hill to the house of a friend.

He said that we were to evacuate. So we rode with him, down into Las Vegas, and stayed in a motel. Today he said we could return, and he drove us back."

"You have anything to back that up?" Nick asked. "Motel receipts? Where's your friend?"

The man pointed to a house that had avoided any significant fire damage. "There," he said. "He lost his cat."

"I'm sorry," Sara said.

The woman fished a folded piece of paper from her back pocket. "This is from the motel," she said. She handed it to Sara, who opened it and read it.

"It's a receipt," she said. "They were at a motel for two nights."

"Doesn't mean they were there the whole time," Nick pointed out. "Although without their own wheels, it'd be a stretch. You two have a vehicle?"

"We have been hitchhiking, mostly," the woman said. "From New York. And using the train, sometimes."

"How long are you in the country for?" Sara asked.

"Six months. We will get to California, to the Pacific Ocean. From Los Angeles, we fly home. In three more weeks."

"What do you know about how the fire started?"

"Nothing," the woman said. "We were in our tent . . . reading. We smelled smoke, and when we came out, the flames were coming toward us."

The young man chuckled. "Something funny about that?" Nick asked him.

"Tell them the truth," the man said.

The woman turned a bright shade of crimson, and she turned her gaze toward the pebbled, ash-flecked ground. "We were making love," she said.

"That's cool," Nick said. "I'm all in favor of it."

"But the rest happened as I said. We smelled the smoke. When we saw the flames, we ran."

"All right. Are you going back to your camp?"

"If it's safe. What we left behind there is all we have." She shrugged under the straps of her back-pack. "Except what we could carry when we ran away."

"Don't leave the area without telling us," Nick said. He handed the woman a card. "My number's on there. We really want to get to the bottom of this."

"If we can help you, we will."

"Thanks. Be careful out there."

The two started toward the path down to their camp. Nick watched them go, and when he glanced toward Sara again, she was studying the ground as intently as the young German woman had just moments earlier. "What's up?" he asked.

"This isn't one of their footprints, I checked," Sara said, pointing to a spot near her feet. "And most of it's obscured by other prints, walking over it. But isn't this the same boot toe that you found down the hill?"

Nick looked closely, then pulled out the digital camera and checked his photograph. The print on the road shoulder did indeed match—same partial tread, same cuts. "Our arsonist was here," he said. "Part of that group."

"But they were all milling around and when we

sent them away, they were all walking on one another's tracks. We can't say which one it was."

"Maybe we can find that track again, after they went their separate ways."

"If we hurry," Sara said, looking toward the sky. The sun was almost gone; the half-light of twilight would be on them soon, then the dark of night.

They split up and tried to follow footprints, but most of the people had left the shoulder and headed toward their homes on the paved road. The boot print didn't reappear.

"Let's try that guy Collin Gardner," Nick suggested. "He's just as obnoxious as Givens, and he's awfully anxious to pin the fire on those campers."

"I take it you don't consider them viable suspects?" Sara asked.

"I haven't seen any reason to. None of the evidence points toward them."

"I agree. Just checking, since you let them go without even asking their names."

"If they're still here tomorrow, they're innocent," Nick said. "I think they are, and that they'll be down in that camp, trying to set it up again and to salvage what they can. You want to find out their names then, feel free. Seemed like a distraction to me."

"Okay," Sara said. "Let's pay a visit to Collin, then."

He lived three houses down from Givens, in one of the few places they'd seen on this road that actually looked like a cabin. It was good-sized, but constructed entirely of what appeared to be local wood and stone. The fire hadn't touched it.

There was no doorbell, so Nick pounded on the front door. Gardner opened it almost immediately, as if he'd been waiting. "Yeah?"

"We were wondering if we could take a look at your boots, Mr. Gardner," Sara said.

Gardner didn't budge. He was wearing black work boots, blue jeans, and a gray T-shirt under an open plaid flannel shirt. "I'm wearing them, see?"

"We'd like to see the soles, if you don't mind."

"I don't think so."

"Excuse me?" Nick asked.

"You have a warrant?"

"No, sir. We're just asking to see the bottoms of your boots."

"Come back with a warrant. You can park outside here day and night, if you want to. When you have a warrant, then you can come in and look at my boots."

"If that's how you want it, then—"

"That's how I want it." Gardner stared them down for another few seconds, then closed the door.

"Man, he's a peach, isn't he?"

"One of a kind," Sara agreed. "Or at least, we can hope so."

23

BRASS AND VARTANN hurried back to the Orpheus Hotel. Vartann parked at the valet stand, flashed his badge, and told the valets to leave the unmarked where it was. Inside, they rushed through the crowded lobby, diverting around the casino entrance, and took the stairs to the mezzanine floor, on which the Free Citizens seminar had been held.

There were still people milling about, talking over what they'd heard from the Kirklands. But the diamond-selling table was empty, and Brass didn't see any of the people he had identified earlier as members of the Kirklands' posse.

"Front desk," he said.

Vartann nodded, and the two men made their way back down and through the throngs in the lobby. At the desk, Brass shouldered aside a young couple checking in with six suitcases between them. "Sorry," he said. He showed his badge to the desk clerk, a woman in her mid-twenties, with dark skin and black hair. Her name tag identified her as Naveen, from Karachi.

"Naveen," Brass said, "I need to know, right now, what room Troy Kirkland and Steven Kirkland are in. Or rooms, if they're in separate ones. It's important police business."

"Certainly," she said. Her eyes widened a bit at the badge, but otherwise she gave no indication that this was anything other than her usual routine. Practiced fingers tap-danced across the keyboard. Finally, the eyes once again flared slightly, and she bit her plump lower lip. "I'm afraid they checked out. Twenty minutes ago."

"We need to see your head of security, then," Vartann said. "Quickly, please."

"Just one moment." She lifted a handset and spoke into it in hushed tones.

"You know, we were here first," the male half of the young couple said. "We're just trying to get our room key."

Brass gave the young man a scowl, and grunted a noncommittal "Huh."

"We'll wait," the woman said.

"Good idea," Vartann said.

Naveen hung up her phone. "Mr. Reese will be right here."

Vartann thanked her. He and Brass moved aside so the young couple could continue their check-in process. In less than a minute, a man approached wearing a dark blue suit and white shirt that would both have to have been custom-tailored to fit across a yardstick's worth of shoulders and around a neck the approximate diameter of a redwood's trunk. His copper hair was short, his face rosy and blotched. "You're Reese?" Brass asked.

"That's right. Chief of Security. What can I do for you?"

"Jim Brass, that's Lou Vartann. We came to arrest a couple of your guests for murder, but it turns out they left twenty minutes ago."

"Then they're not guests, are they?"

"Don't get cute, Mr. Reese. I want to see every second of video you've got from the time they checked out until they were off the premises."

"Okay, that's no problem. Come with me."

He led them through the lobby and out a door marked AUTHORIZED PERSONNEL ONLY. On the other side was a long utility corridor, concrete floored, with walls of concrete block painted a pale green. Their footsteps echoed in the empty hall. Reese stopped at an elevator and pushed the UP button. The door slid open immediately. He ushered the detectives inside. There were no floor selection buttons on the inside, but the doors closed and the elevator gave a little lurch. Moments later, it opened on another floor, and the three men stepped out into a room only slightly more technologically sophisticated than NASA Mission Control. Men and women sat in front of dozens of big video screens, with keyboards before them.

"This is security central," Reese explained. "The nerve center of the whole operation."

Brass regarded the screens all around them. Some showed static images, mostly shots of the casino and lobby. Others switched every few seconds between different scenes. There were cameras on every elevator, in service corridors, everywhere in the casino, in every cashier's cage, in the cash vault, and throughout the grounds and parking structures.

Reese stopped behind a handsome young man with neatly trimmed dark hair. "Josh," he said. "A couple of guests checked out recently. What were the names?"

"Steven and Troy Kirkland," Brass said, spelling the last name.

"Find exactly when they checked out, then bring up the footage from the front desk."

"Yes, sir," Josh said. He turned to his keyboard, and in less than a minute, the Kirklands appeared on his monitor. They were standing at the desk, clearly checking out. A clerk—not Naveen—handed Steven a receipt, which he folded and tucked into a pocket. Behind them, barely in the shot, stood a burly man holding a strongbox.

"That's got to be the diamonds. And the proceeds," Vartann said.

"Can we see where they go after this?" Brass asked.

"Stay on them, Josh," Reese instructed.

Josh fiddled with a joystick. Green lines appeared on the Kirkland's faces for a few seconds. "Got 'em," Josh said.

The on-screen image changed as the two men left the counter, the guy with the strongbox a short distance behind. As they walked through the lobby and then the casino, the image kept shifting, hopping from one camera to another but keeping up with their progress. Brass was getting dizzy watching, but he was impressed by the technology just the same. "Facial recognition?" he asked.

"That's right, sir," Josh said. "I told it to locate those faces wherever they appear. Now I'm just along for the ride."

It took the Kirklands several minutes to get out of the building. They crossed an elevated ramp into a parking structure, took an elevator, and then got into a brand new, gleaming Mercedes G55 AMG. The man with the strongbox put it into the cargo area and got into the backseat. Troy took the wheel and pulled the luxury SUV from its parking spot. As it drew away, the license plate was briefly visible.

"Nice wheels," Brass said. "South Carolina tags. Get that number."

Vartann jotted it down on a notebook he kept in his pocket. "Let's get out a BOLO," Brass said.

Vartann drew his mobile phone from another pocket, but its screen was blank. Reese chuckled. "That'll work again when you get out of this room," he said. "But in here it's completely jammed. They all are."

"Really," Vartann said.

"We don't take anything for granted when it comes to the security of our operation and the safety of our guests."

"Apparently not," Brass said. "We need to get the word out about that car, so if we could leave your dead zone . . ."

"Sure." Reese punched the elevator button. Once again, the doors opened right away, and the three got in. "Thanks, Josh," Reese said as the doors came together.

"No problem, sir!" Josh called back.

"Polite kid," Brass said.

"If they aren't, they don't last in my outfit," Reese said. The elevator glided to a smooth stop and the doors opened. "You should be able to use your phones now."

Vartann tried again. This time, his worked, and he called in a Be On the Lookout for the Mercedes. When he finished, Brass said, "One more thing. I want police protection on the head people in all the major groups involved in that protest. BOOM especially, but also the American Anti-Tax Party, the Patriots for Responsible Spending, and whoever else is there. I don't know if the attack on Watson was an isolated event or the first stage in a power struggle, but I don't want to find out by having more corpses turn up."

"I'm on it," Vartann said.

Brass shook Reese's hand. "Thanks for your help," he said. "If you could burn that footage to a DVD for me, I'll have an officer pick it up later."

"You got it. Anything else I can do?"

"Yeah. If you see the Kirklands again, detain them and call me. And if you take your time about calling me and they have to cool their heels in whatever passes for a jail around here, that's okay, too."

24

GREG DIDN'T LIKE hospitals. He didn't know any-body who did, except possibly for those whose lives or loved ones had been saved there. Even they, he suspected, would have more of a love/hate relation-ship with hospitals, glad that one had been available at the crucial time, but sorry that it had been needed in the first place.

Hospitals smelled, first of all. They tried their best to disguise the odor of disinfectant, but he always knew what it was anyway. There were always strange sounds, beeps and clicks and hums and whirs, emanating from devices that poked, prodded, and probed people in particularly private places. At any moment, there might be someone around a corner weeping or praying or arguing or screaming, or so lost in absolute grief that sound had become impossible.

So, hospitals? Necessary, but not places he would visit if he had any say in it.

In this instance, he did not.

Catherine had sent him to take a buccal swab from Garrett Kovash, bodyguard to the stars. And anyone else who might have been at Alec Watson's office. A quick comparison had showed that the DNA from the saliva found on Watson's desk didn't match the blood—which did indeed come from Dennis Daniels—on the bit of gauze from Watson's floor. Kovash had admitted being at the office, so if the saliva came from him, that was one mystery solved.

Greg's guess was that the saliva had come from one of the Kirklands. None of their previous court cases had involved DNA evidence, though, so it wasn't on file anywhere, and they had not yet been located. While he was at the hospital, he would swab any other members of Daniels's retinue who agreed to it, in order to eliminate them as suspects. But his money—figurative money, since he wasn't about to risk the real kind on a criminal investigation—was on the Kirklands.

Building a case like this, when there were no solid suspects and no witnesses, was always a matter of the accumulation of tiny pieces of evidence. Eventually, they could be put together in a way that painted a picture of the perpetrator. But the process could be painstaking and slow. And involve things like trips to hospitals, which Greg would rather not have to make.

He got off the elevator—even the elevator made strange noises and carried unpleasant odors—on Daniels's floor. A nurse pointed him toward the room, and when he started toward it, he saw Kovash standing outside, talking to a uniformed cop. Greg had met the cop before, at some crime scene or other, but couldn't remember his name.

"Mr. Kovash," he said as he neared. He showed his badge. "I'm Greg Sanders, with the Crime Lab."

"Oh, sure, how you doing, Greg?"

"Fine, thanks. I was just wondering, I know you were in Alec Watson's office today—"

"That's right."

"—so I was hoping I could get a buccal swab from you. We've got some unidentified saliva on Watson's desk. If it's yours, then it doesn't help us, but if it's not—"

Kovash interrupted again. "Understood. No problem. Just say when."

Greg had half a dozen capped swab sticks in his pocket. He was reaching for one when the elevator door opened again. Greg half-turned and saw a scruffy guy coming toward them, his wooden crutches plastered with stickers. His shorts displayed a smooth prosthetic left leg and a hairy, pale right.

"Voet!" Kovash said. His hand darted beneath his jacket and came out with a gun.

Greg didn't think, just moved a step forward, planting himself between Kovash and the newcomer. Brass had said something about paying a visit to a one-legged veteran who had sent Daniels threatening messages. He guessed this was the guy. But Brass had been convinced he was innocent of the attacks, all bark but genuinely a pussycat, not a dog at all.

"Hold on, Mr. Kovash," Greg said. The uniformed cop was on his feet, too, his weapon drawn. He didn't seem to know who to point it at. "Let's all just calm down."

"This guy threatened Dennis Daniels," Kovash said. "I've had my eye on him."

"Mr. Voet," Greg said. "You had a talk with Captain Brass earlier, didn't you?"

"I sure did. After he left, I thought about what I'd done. How shitty it was to write to Mr. Daniels like that, say those things. I never meant to do anything to him, but you shouldn't try to make someone else live in fear, either, and that's what I was doing."

"Are you armed?"

Voet laughed, then his laughter devolved into a raspy cough. "Hell, I ain't even properly legged," he said when he was able.

"What are you doing here?" Kovash asked.

"I just wanted to see him for a minute, apologize for my actions. It's important to me to take responsibility for the pain that I've caused others. If his wife is here, I'd like a word with her, too."

"You'll have to come back during visiting hours," the nurse said.

Greg was torn in different directions, but part of him wanted to shout at the nurse. There were people standing around with guns in their hands, and she wanted to talk about visiting hours? "That's not exactly helpful right now," he said. "Mr. Kovash, you want to put that weapon away."

Kovash glared at Voet, then at Greg. The rage behind his eyes was identical in both cases. "Officer," Greg said, "could you make sure that Mr. Voet isn't armed?"

"Sure," the cop said, seeming relieved to be told

what to do. He holstered his gun and patted Voet down. "He's clean."

"Mr. Kovash?" Greg said.

"Fine." Kovash made his weapon disappear under his jacket.

"What do you say we give Mr. Voet a couple of minutes with Mr. Daniels?"

"Okay, but I don't leave his side," Kovash said.

"Of course. I'm sure that would be okay with Mr. Voet."

"Long as nobody's pointing a piece at me, I'm cool."

"You keep your distance from Mr. and Mrs. Daniels," Kovash said. "And your hands where I can see them, and everything will be okay."

"Got it." Voet clomped across the floor, crutches and prosthesis, then good foot, then the same again. Kovash and the uni parted and made room for him to pass into Daniels's room, then followed him in.

Greg went as far as the doorway and watched from there.

Voet stopped several feet from the hospital bed. Mrs. Daniels was in the room, too, dressed in jeans and a loose sweater. Greg had seen her picture many times, usually taken at social events; without makeup, her hair down, suffering from lack of sleep, she looked like an entirely different person. More attractive, somehow, as if she had shed a veneer of plastic.

"Mr. Daniels, sir," Voet said. "Mrs. Daniels. My name is Sean Voet."

"What are *you* doing here?" Joanna Daniels demanded.

"I guess you remember my name. I shouldn't be surprised. I came to apologize, to both of you. You've got no reason to hear me out, and every reason to have your guys here throw me out on my ass, but if I could have just a minute of your time . . ."

"Take it," Daniels said. His wife started to protest, but he silenced her with a glance.

"Thank you, sir," Voet said. "I know the things I wrote to you were rude and offensive. That was nothing but bad manners on my part, and my momma brought me up better than that. I never meant to carry out any of the threats I made, but shouldn't have made them just the same. For any minute you lived in fear, any sleep you lost, any worrying you did on my account, I am deeply, deeply sorry."

"Apology accepted," Daniels said.

"I'm not saying I agree with all your viewpoints," Voet said. "Far from it. But I recognize now—brought on, I'm ashamed to say, at least in part by the terrible thing that's been done to you—that I was voicing my opposition in the wrong way."

"We all make mistakes," Daniels said. "It takes a brave person to admit them, sometimes."

"I might have been brave once, but I think I left that behind a long time ago," Voet said. "What I mostly am now is stubborn. When I had my mind set on you being wrong, I figured I could do or say anything to make you change what your announcers said on the tube. Now that I've realized what a mistake that was, I'm too damn stubborn to not say my piece. So I'm sorry, and I won't do it again. You'll hear from me—you can be sure of that—but my tone will be civil, not threatening. I promise that, and when I make a promise, that's when I'm stubbornest."

"Well, I appreciate the gesture, Mr. Voet. And I know my wife does as well. Don't you, honey?"

"Of course," Joanna said. Her voice was ice.

"That's all I needed to say. Thanks for your time."

"Oh, Mr. Voet?" Daniels said.

"Yeah?"

"I'm setting up a citizen's advisory council on veteran's issues. If you'd like to be included . . ."

"Me? In a hot minute."

"Very well, then. Consider yourself a member. We'll be in touch. I'm pretty sure we have your contact information at the office."

Voet laughed, ran the back of his hand across his lips. "Yeah, I just bet you do."

"Thanks, Mr. Voet," Daniels said.

Voet swiveled around. Once again, Kovash got out of his way as he clomped out of the room and back to the elevator. When the elevator doors were closed behind him, Daniels said, "And that, my friends, is how you win a viewer for life."

Everyone laughed. Greg's was a little forced, because he couldn't tell if the whole thing was a brilliant display of personal, one-on-one politics, or a shameless hustle. In the end, he figured, it was a little of both, and the line between them was probably considerably less distinct than he cared to know.

Finally, Daniels seemed to notice that he had been standing in the doorway. "Are you here to atone for something, too? This seems to be the time for it."

"I'm actually here to make Mr. Kovash open his mouth," Greg said.

"The rest of us are usually trying to get him to close it," Joanna said. "So your job shouldn't be hard."

"Mr. Kovash?" Greg took the cap off his swab. "Say aah."

25

SARA AND NICK stood on the street in front of Collin Gardner's house, trying to figure out their next move, when Sara's smart phone alerted her to a text. She read it and summarized the salient points for Nick.

"We got the details on the wax," she said. "It *is* candle wax, like we thought. From the chemical composition and the dye used, Hodges has determined that it's from a candle made by a company called Luxu Candles, in Santa Monica, California. It's a bayberry-scented candle they make, two inches in diameter and either seven, nine, or eleven inches tall. It's a red color they call 'Vin Rose.'"

"So now all we have to do is find a house on this mountain with a partly burned candle matching that description? That couldn't take more than two or three weeks, could it?"

"Might as well start with Mr. Gardner," Sara said. "He's just begging for attention."

"Guy might go out and buy an angry dog so he can sic it on us," Nick suggested.

"I'd hate to subject a dog to that. Living with him, I mean, not eating us." Sara went back up Gardner's walkway, knocked on the door again. "Mr. Gardner!" she called. "It's us, LVPD Crime Lab!"

The door opened and Gardner stood there, his face purple with rage. "Again with you guys? Didn't I tell you to get the hell out of here? Don't tell me you've got a warrant already."

"No, sir," Sara said. "We just had one more question for you, before we do. Do you own any candles?"

Gardner blinked several times. Sara understood that the question was out of the blue, which was intentional. When people expected a question, they usually had also worked out how they would answer it. "I guess maybe some of the birthday cake kind," he said. "I have a granddaughter, and her mom brings her here for birthdays sometimes."

"That's it? None of the big fat ornamental kind?"

"I got a propane lantern and some flashlights, for when the power goes out."

"Okay, thanks."

"That's it?" Nick asked as they walked away from the door again. "Taking his word for it?"

"We can't go in and look," Sara said. "Besides, look at him. Does he really look like the candle-burning type to you?"

"Yeah, I guess not."

"But that gives me an idea."

"Yeah?"

"Let's take a walk, Nick."

"A walk?"

"It's a little too dark to go tramping through the woods looking for clues. But if people up here are candle-burning types, this is when they'll be burning them. Let's walk the neighborhoods and see if we can see any through the windows."

"I like it. It could still take a week, but it'll be faster than going door to door and asking."

"Faster, maybe. But less certain, since not everybody who uses candles lights them every night. Still, if you've got a better idea . . ."

"I'm fresh out," Nick said. "It's either that or knock off for the night, I guess."

"Then let's take a walk."

Ray was in with Hodges, peering at the display from a scanning electron microscope on a computer screen. Standard microscopes used light to view the object under consideration, but a scanning electron microscope used an electron beam. Viewed through electromagnetic lenses—or displayed on the appropriate screen—even infinitesimal details achieved amazing clarity. They were looking at one of the tiny metallic disks Ray had found at Lucia's home, which under the scope proved to be faceted and not as perfectly round as it had first appeared.

"Now we know what it looks like," Hodges said. "But I still have no idea what it is."

"Looks like a tiny flying saucer," Ray admitted.

"If it is, I don't think we have to worry about alien invasion."

Catherine walked in while they were staring at it. She, too, studied the screen for a moment. "What's that?"

"That's what we'd like to know," Hodges said. "Dr. Ray found a couple of these at the scene where the man missing his hand was abducted."

"Let me see it."

Ray glanced her way. She was looking at the same screen they were. She read his meaning before he had to ask the question. "The real thing," she said. "Not the magnification."

"Oh," Hodges said. He shut down the SEM and removed the tiny disk. Catherine pressed down on it with her fingertip, picking it up. "Too small to get any usable impressions from, so it's not like I'm blurring any, right?"

"Makes sense," Ray admitted.

"You guys really don't know what this is?"

"Should we?" Ray asked.

"I was thinking nanotechnology," Hodges replied. "But I—"

"It's body glitter."

"Excuse me?"

"Believe me, I know body glitter when I see it. Probably eighty percent of the exotic dancers in Vegas wear it."

"Oh," Hodges said. "*That* kind of body glitter."

"That kind, exactly. You would have recognized it if you'd seen more of it, but with only a few flecks it's harder to identify. In my dancing days, though, I learned that once you get a little on you, you're going to keep finding specks of it, in the strangest places, for days to come."

"If it's that common," Ray said, "then it doesn't necessarily help us narrow our search much."

"And it's not just strippers," Hodges pointed out.

"Plenty of women wear some when they're going out. And prostitutes use it, too. There must be forty or fifty strip clubs in the city, and thirty or so brothels in the state."

"And you know that prostitutes use it because . . . ?" Ray asked.

"Let's just say I have a well-rounded education. Besides, hookers are easy prey, so we've had more than our share wind up in the middle of investigations. Catherine's right, if there was more of it than just those couple of pieces you found, I'd have known it right away."

"Well, I'm sorry there wasn't enough left behind for you to make that call. I brought back what was there."

"You're right," Catherine said. "That doesn't limit your search parameters much. The stuff's commonplace these days. Even if you can get a line on the manufacturer of this particular glitter, which is probably going to be difficult with such a small sample, it wouldn't help a lot."

"It looks like field work will be required," Hodges said. "I can help with that, if you want."

"Thanks for the offer," Ray said. "I'm sure you're needed here in the lab, though. We still need an ID on those fibers I collected at the scene."

"He's right, David," Catherine added. "You're not going anywhere tonight."

"Okay, fine," Hodges said. Few adult men Ray had known pouted as frequently, or as obviously, as Hodges did. Most men held their feelings inside, to some extent, but Hodges wore his right out there on his face for everyone to see. Maybe it was healthier that way.

Then again, did he really want to hold David Hodges up as an example of sound mental health?

Ray sat at his desk, using his computer to research ownership of the city's many nude and topless clubs. Progress was difficult because so many were owned by shell companies, and he had to trace the principals of those back to the actual corporations, sometimes offshore, that owned them. Others were owned outright by locals, including characters with suspected racketeering ties, chased out of gaming but not out of the skin trade. Ray's operating assumption, based on the available evidence, was that any gang that had grown up around the business of smuggling illegal immigrants in from Mexico would be largely, if not entirely, made up of Mexican nationals and/or Hispanic Americans. Those would be the people who could function most effectively on the far side of the border—it seemed self-evident that anxious would-be border crossers would be more trusting of their own kind than of gringos.

When he worked through the layers of obfuscation, he found that most Las Vegas strip club owners were Caucasian males. Two clubs were owned by African-American males, and seven, to his surprise, were owned by three different white women, one of whom ran a chain of four clubs.

A tap at his door drew his attention away from the monitor. Hodges stood there with a printout in his hand. "You probably didn't think I'd get to your fibers so quickly."

"I don't know what your workload is tonight, but I know there are several open cases, so—"

"Well, I did. And here's the result." Hodges handed over the sheet of paper. Ray scanned it, seeing details of fabric type that were essentially meaningless to him. "It's an upholstery fiber," Hodges continued. "A unique blend of rayon, nylon, and cotton. I ran it through GC/MS and separated out the chemical structure of the dye, which you can see on the printout I gave you. I also found that it's been treated with titanium oxide, and a combination of tin and bromide."

"That's a fire retardant," Ray said, slightly distracted by perusing the details of the gas chromatography/mass spectrometry treatment Hodges described. "What's the titanium oxide do?"

"You know how Converse sneakers aren't shiny, but instead have a kind of matte finish to them?"

"I guess so."

"Same idea. It's a delustering agent, designed to keep the fabric from being too shiny. Perfect for a place where you want the bodies to stand out, not the chairs."

"Like a strip club."

"Exactly like a strip club. Fortunately for you, there's only one in town that uses this specific upholstery fiber treated in this way."

"Let me read your mind," Ray said. "Think about the name."

Hodges closed his eyes and wrinkled his brow.

"Are you thinking about it?"

"Yes."

"And nothing else?"

"Yes! Just the name. Come on, Ray, this is—"

"Cougars."

"—silly, you can't—what?"

"Cougars."

Hodges's mouth dropped open. "That's right. How did you—?"

Ray tapped his computer screen. "I've been looking for strip clubs in town owned by someone with a Hispanic surname. I've only come up with a couple. One is owned by Oswaldo Carrizoza, and an informant told me to look for someone called Oz or Ozzie. Do you know the place?"

"Only by reputation," Hodges said. "They specialize in dancers over thirty."

"That's old, for exotic dancers."

"Hence the name. I gather the audience is mostly younger men, embracing their older woman fetish."

"I'm hardly a younger man, but I guess I've got to pay the place a visit."

"I could go along," Hodges volunteered. "In case you need backup."

"I remember when you couldn't stand the idea of going into the field."

"People can't change?"

"I think I'll be fine," Ray said. "Sam Vega's working on another angle, and I'm sure he'll be able to meet me there."

"Well, just in case, keep me in mind," Hodges said.

"Catherine wants you here. But I'll remember the offer. Thank you."

"Sure." Hodges spun around and started back toward the trace lab. "Sure, I do all the hard stuff, but am I appreciated? I am not."

"You're appreciated, David!" Ray called after him. "Trust me, you're appreciated." He reached for the phone to call Vega and muttered, "But you're not going to any strip clubs tonight."

26

"ABSOLUTELY NOT!"

Officer Fabrizio was surprised by the vehemence of Justine Marie Taylor's reaction. His partner, Klein, had informed her that she would be under police protection, and her response almost blew them both out of their shoes. She was not a large woman, but she could really belt it out when she wanted to. They were at the BOOM headquarters, which still had yellow crime scene tape fluttering in a light breeze under the streetlamps.

"It's for your own safety, ma'am," Klein went on. He was trying to reason with a tornado, Fabrizio thought. Pointless. "Especially since the attack on Mr. Watson, we—"

"Officer, I have a registered, legal SIG Sauer P290 nine-mil in my purse and I know how to use it. I must have told Alec a thousand times that he was a fool for not carrying. I, however, am no fool."

"Ms. Taylor," Klein bravely continued, "Mr. Watson was shot a dozen times with an automatic weapon. Probably something like an AK-47. Your SIG is a good defense against muggers and carjackers, but if someone with an automatic rifle wants to get to you, they can do it from a considerably greater range than you're likely to be able to shoot the nine."

"There's something you don't understand, young man," Taylor said. "This movement that I'm part of is all about personal responsibility. I have nothing against the police force fighting crime, protecting the public safety. Those are activities that a private force can't do as efficiently or as cost-effectively. But when it comes to defending myself, I am entirely capable, I assure you."

Fabrizio had to give it to his partner; he didn't give up easily. Klein was a dark-haired guy with a lean, compact build, more muscular than he seemed at first glance. He could have been constructed of tightly wound steel bands, and when he unleashed his stored energy it was a sight to see. Fabrizio, by contrast, was laid back; not lazy, exactly, but he seemed to cycle at several hundred RPMs less than Klein did.

"I'm sure you're right, Ms. Taylor," Klein said. "But I'm also sure of something else. We've been ordered to stick to you like white on rice, and that's what we're going to do. You don't have to like it. I'm just telling you so you're not alarmed every time you see a squad car in your rearview."

"And I'm telling you, officer, that it's an abuse of taxpayer money. Which makes it *my* money. Which means I'll be calling your captain, your chief, the

mayor, and the governor if I have to. I will not
stand for this."

"I'm afraid the choice isn't yours, ma'am," Fabrizio said. Might as well take some of the heat off
his partner. "We have our orders. As long as there's
a feud going on between these various groups—and
especially now that the feud has drawn real blood—
the danger not just to you, but to any member of
the general public who happens to get caught in the
crossfire, is very real. We're not taking any chances,
so as my partner says, we'll be there, whether you
need us or not."

"We'll see about that."

"Yes, ma'am, we will."

She shot them each a look that was at once dis-
missive and contemptuous. It made Fabrizio wish
that she, not Watson, had been the killer's target
earlier, because it made him feel about two feet tall
and seven years old. But, paradoxically, it also made
him respect her strength. Lady had as much back-
bone as any cop he had ever known, and then
some. He was pretty sure that she was right—if her
life was threatened, she'd have that 9mm in play
before her attacker knew what was happening, and
by the time he and Klein were out of their vehicle,
the action would be over.

If there were a sports book in town that would
take the bet, he would put his whole retirement
fund on her for the win.

For a big guy, Brass could move like a ghost. He had
a habit of appearing and disappearing at will. Catherine, concentrating on an autopsy report, didn't

notice him standing in the doorway of her office until he spoke. "Catherine."

She lowered the report to the desktop. He looked pale, like all his blood had gone to his feet. His arms, more likely; when someone was afraid, their feet really did turn cold, sometimes dropping as much as fifteen degrees in minutes. But the palms and underarms sweated, as if compensating for that temperature fluctuation. "What's wrong, Jim?"

"I don't know if you know Joe Hewitt and Hale Boren," Brass said.

"I think I've met Boren. He's a patrol officer, right?"

Brass leaned against the doorjamb, but out of what looked more like exhaustion than his more typical casual demeanor. "Yeah, they both are, partners out of the South Central Command. I just heard from their commander. Hewitt's been killed in the line of duty. Boren is in critical condition at Desert Palm."

"Oh, God," Catherine said. "How?"

"They made a traffic stop. Vehicle ran a red light at high speed. They pursued for a few blocks, called in the license plate, and then the vehicle stopped. They approached it."

"And?"

"The vehicle was a new Mercedes sport-utility. High end. South Carolina tags."

"Not—"

"The vehicle is the same one Lou and I saw the Kirklands leaving the Orpheus parking garage in. No way to know if they changed cars or not. Someone opened up on the two officers with an automatic weapon. First responders found brass at the scene, looks like the same size rounds that did Watson."

"Didn't they know about the BOLO?"

"You know how it is. In the moment, your adrenaline's racing because you just saw this car rocket through a stoplight. You call in the plate without thinking that it sounds kind of familiar. By the time dispatch tried to warn them, they were already out of their vehicle."

"And then it was too late."

"Sounds like it."

"We've got to find those guys," Catherine said.

"We're working on it."

"I know, Jim. It's just . . . it's infuriating."

"Tell me about it. Hewitt was supposed to be married next month. Hale's got two kids, five and eight. If he doesn't pull through . . ."

"Why?" Catherine asked.

"Sorry?"

"What are these two idiots trying to protect? Their diamond-selling scam? Their little boys' club? Running around with guns, trying to frighten people into thinking the federal government and local law enforcement are somehow in cahoots to stomp all over their rights? It just doesn't make any sense."

"You nailed it, Cath. It's about scaring people. If you scare enough people bad enough, you can make them buy whatever you're selling."

"I know we're the good guys, Jim. But when I hear about things like this, I can't help wanting to take off my badge and . . . that's not very ladylike, is it?"

"It's human," Brass said. "And believe me, you wouldn't be alone."

27

Cougars was a splash of pink and purple neon on an otherwise dark, drab Las Vegas industrial block, miles from the Strip. It looked, from the outside, as if Oswaldo Carrizoza had simply leased or purchased a small industrial building, covered the walls with a coat of paint, and installed enough neon to be visible from deep space.

The largest sign, thirty feet above the road on a pedestal, showed the outline of a cougar, the big cat, but subtly altered so that its typical sinewy grace also suggested feminine sexuality. Ray was not a devotee of strip clubs, and the sign didn't necessarily entice him, but he respected the artist's abilities just the same.

Sam Vega approached as Ray got out of his car, wincing a little at the necessary bending and twisting involved. Ray got his cane on the ground as Vega reached him. "You okay, Ray?"

"Fine," Ray said. "Just a little more tender some days than others, that's all."

"Good, glad to hear it."

"Have you been here long?"

"I just beat you."

"Ready to brave it?"

"As I'll ever be."

Ray could feel the bass thumping through the walls before he even reached the door. Vega got to it first, pulling it wide, and the music blasted out like floodwaters bursting through a sandbank. "I hope we're not deaf by the time we get out!" Ray shouted.

A bouncer met them inside, the sleeves of his black shirt rolled back to reveal tattooed arms corded with muscle. His hair was spiked and oily, his eyes small and dull. "Twenty bucks cover, guys!" he said.

"Not for us!" Vega showed his badge, and Ray revealed his. "We're looking for Oswaldo Carrizoza!"

The bouncer offered a shrug. "Hey, I just work the door, I don't know anybody's name!"

"Somebody's got to sign your paychecks!"

"Direct deposit!"

He didn't block their way, but it didn't look like he planned to be helpful, either. They went past him, through another doorway, and into the club's main stage area.

Here, counter-intuitively, the music was not as loud. Ray supposed it made sense—blast it toward the parking lot to let people know the party they were missing if they weren't inside yet, but keep it softer where the dancers had to negotiate financial arrangements. The inside smelled like possibly toxic doses of perfume and body spray, and though the stage was spotlit, there were blinking lights and flashing lights and moving lights all over the place. Someone prone to seizures might never make it out. At the back of the room, beyond the main stage, stood a bar. Lights glowed under glass shelves holding hundreds of bottles, and there were two TV sets mounted above the mirror, incongruously showing figure skating on a sports channel.

Tables surrounded the main stage. In two corners there were smaller stages, unoccupied at the moment. A staircase curved up to a VIP lounge. The men's restroom was indicated by glowing neon, but if there was a women's room, it was not similarly marked. Between the main stage and the bar was a hallway, dark except for shimmering lights clinging to the walls and ceiling. That probably led back to the offices and dressing room.

The main stage was set against a side wall. Mirrors curved around part of it, and there were mirrored panels in the ceiling as well. A woman, nude except for plastic spike-heeled shoes and a fine silver chain around her hips, writhed on the stage, one arm reaching around behind her head to maintain contact with a gold pole, as if it was her only lifeline. Ray could only take the club's word for it that she was a cougar; she didn't look older than twenty-five or twenty-six to him.

He did notice the glitter dusting her body, gleaming every time she moved into the spotlight.

"You gotta pick a table," a waitress told them. She wore a tight T-shirt tucked into a belted skirt that almost covered the tops of her thighs. "There's a two-drink minimum, but I can't take your order until you're sitting down."

"We don't want to drink," Vega told her. He flashed his badge, but in a discreet way, not calling attention to it. "We're here to see Oswaldo."

She gave a subtle nod toward the hallway Ray had noted. "He's usually in his office, if he's not out here pawing the hired help."

"He doesn't paw in his office?" Ray asked.

"He likes an audience."

"Thanks," Vega said. He headed in that direction, but before they had made it halfway there, a half-naked woman lurched toward them, as if she had just strapped on her high heels and hadn't quite learned to walk in them yet. She had masses of red hair, nothing on her upper torso but a sheer strip of metallic cloth, and a crimson G-string below. She, unlike the one on stage, was definitely cougar material; Ray guessed forty-two or forty-three, at a minimum, even though she snapped her gum like a high school girl.

"Where you going?" she asked. "Don't you want a dance? I want to dance for you. Both of you at once, if that's how you like it. I don't see many real men in here. Lots of little boys, if you get my meaning."

"We're kind of in a hurry," Vega said.

"I can be fast. Real fast."

"Not just now, thanks."

Ray felt a hand on his leg. He looked down to see a man sitting at one of the tables with two empty beer bottles in front of him. From the looks of him, those had only been the most recent two out of considerably more. "Hey, dude, when a nice lady wants to dance for you, the polite thing is to let her."

Ray resisted the impulse to bring his cane down hard on the man's arm. Instead, he pried the fingers off his pants. "When a man is on official police business," he explained, "the sensible thing to do is to keep your hands to yourself and leave him alone."

"Oh! Oh, I'm, I'm sorry, dude, I'm sorry."

"Not a problem, friend," Ray said. "Enjoy yourself."

The man waved his hand in the general direction of the stage. "How could I not?"

The way finally clear, Ray and Vega made it into the hallway. They met another stripper on her way out, this one dressed in a fetishist's idea of a Catholic girl's school uniform, but she didn't impede their progress. Only when they burst through a door marked NO ADMITTANCE did they encounter an obstacle. Two of them, in fact, with dark hair and burning eyes and fine silk shirts open to the chest to reveal muscle-bound physiques. They shot to their feet, manifesting guns. "You can't read?" one said. "The girls are the other way."

"We're not here for the ladies," Ray said.

"Where's Carrizoza?" Vega asked. He showed his badge. Ray did likewise. "LVPD." Vega added, in case the message wasn't clear.

A third man rose from a low-slung black leather couch. He was the only one wearing a jacket, and he had a cigar burning in his left hand. He was older than the first two, fifty at least, his sleek black hair shot through with silver strands. "I am Oswaldo Carrizoza," he said. "Put those away, you idiots."

His thugs obeyed. Ray breathed a little easier once the hardware was gone.

"Welcome to my establishment. I trust it's to your liking?"

"It lacks a certain *je ne sais quoi*," Ray said. "Oh, wait, *class*, that's the word."

"Hey, this is one of the finest off-Strip gentleman's clubs in the city," Carrizoza said. "Unless maybe girls aren't your thing."

"I like women just fine," Ray said. "But I prefer conversations that don't include a price list."

"We provide a service. Everything here is on the up-and-up. You might be surprised at our clientele. Cops, DAs, judges, athletes."

"I'm sure you have friends in important places," Ray said. "That's not pertinent to the conversation we came here to have."

"Which is?"

"It's come to our attention that somebody's shaking down undocumented aliens," Vega said. "It's also come to our attention that it might be you."

"Because I'm Latino and I own a strip club? That's a stretch, even for cops."

"Because evidence was found at the scene of an abduction connecting this club to that scene," Vega said. "And because a confidential informant pointed us in your direction as soon as we started asking around."

"If you're convinced, by all means, arrest me," Carrizoza said. "Of course, I'll be out an hour after I'm booked. As you said, I have powerful friends, and plenty of resources at my disposal. But if you want to waste everybody's time, then be my guest."

"We're not here to waste time," Ray said. "We thought we'd give you a warning. We're on to you.

If you lay a *hand* on one more person—" He had chosen the word *hand* intentionally, hoping to elicit some sort of reaction, but none came. Carrizoza stood with his arms crossed over his chest, the look on his face as calm as if he were watching a not particularly exciting chess game.

"Frankly," Carrizoza said, "I'm surprised that you would even bother yourselves over some illegals. Wouldn't you rather be rid of them?"

"Immigration status has nothing to do with it. Assault, kidnapping, and murder are crimes, whoever the victims are, and we don't allow them in this city," Vega said. "Am I clear on that?"

"Crystal clear," Carrizoza replied. "If we're done, Erwin will show you the way out."

"We can find our own way."

"Nonsense, I insist."

Ray hadn't expected the man to confess. He had wanted a look at him, though, and he had wanted to issue his warning, to at least try to make Carrizoza put his activities on hold while Ray continued gathering evidence. "Fine," he said. He extended a hand, offering the bruiser named Erwin the opportunity to lead.

Erwin was the taller of the pair by a couple of inches, and Ray estimated his weight at somewhere more than 270 pounds. He was one of those guys who looked like he could barely clap his hands, because the muscles of his arms and chest would get in his way. He had a zigzag pattern shaved into his scalp, and what looked like a fairly fresh scrape under his left eye. "Paper cut?" Ray asked.

Erwin grunted something unintelligible and

opened the door. Ray figured Carrizoza didn't keep him around for his scintillating conversation. When Erwin released the door, Ray noted a damp film where the man had clutched it. Apparently the thug suffered from palmar hyperhidrosis, more commonly known as sweaty palms. The affliction was not uncommon, and it was worse when the subject was under some sort of severe stress. Probably not a good sign for hired muscle—overbearing stress might cause him to pull a gun too readily, and assuming he could hang onto it, he could do some damage. Ray greatly preferred thugs to be relaxed and easygoing, if he had to deal with them at all.

Passing through the club, they were blocked by a dancer draped over a customer's chair, back arched, her exposed rear and legs extending into the pathway between tables. Erwin laid a meaty paw on the curve of her back, and she straightened with a giggle. "Oh, it's you, Erwin," she said, moving aside to let the big man pass.

She was starting to turn her attention back to the seated customer when Ray reached her. "Excuse me, miss," he said.

As if she smelled money, she swiveled toward him, giving him a slyly seductive smile and a sensual shimmy. "Something I can do for you? You want a private dance? I'm very good in private."

"I'll just bet you are," Ray said. "But actually, I was wondering if I could scrape off a little of your body glitter. It's got nothing to do with you, I'm just trying to have a basis for comparison back at the crime lab."

"Crime lab? Sounds sexy."

"Appearances can be deceiving."

"Still, it's like, I'll be evidence or something. Scrape away. But when you come back and you're off duty, you have to let me dance for you."

"It's a deal," Ray said, knowing that when he was off duty, no force on Earth could drag him back through that front door.

The dancer squeezed her arms together to pop substantial breasts out even more. "Where do you want to scrape from?"

"Your back, if that's all right."

She let out a sigh. "You are just no fun."

"You might be surprised."

"So show me."

"Not just now." Since she wasn't turning, he moved around her, tore two clean sheets of paper from his notepad, and used one to scrape glitter from the center of her back onto the other. That one he sealed with a druggist fold.

"Thank you," he said. "What's your name? Your real one, not your stage name. For evidentiary purposes."

She whispered it to him, and he jotted it down in the book. "Now that you know that, are you going to stalk me?" She sounded hopeful.

"You never know, do you?"

Vega was waiting with Erwin, a dozen paces ahead. They had made it that far before realizing that Ray had stopped. Most of the patrons sitting nearby were watching Ray instead of the stage, and Vega and Erwin's gazes were locked on him. "What was that about?" Vega asked when Ray caught up.

"I needed a glitter sample, to match with what

we already have," Ray said. He didn't finish his thought until they were out in the parking lot, and Erwin had closed the door. "And I wanted it from her, from the spot on her back that Erwin touched, in case I could get some touch DNA off it. His hands are sweating rivers. The sample's minuscule, but it's still possible."

"You are an evil genius," Vega said. "I saw you writing in your notebook, thought maybe you were getting her number."

"She thought the same thing," Ray admitted. "I guess I'll have to disappoint the both of you."

Out in the city, Brass assured Catherine, every cop on duty was looking for the Kirklands. There were helicopters in the air, cruisers at major intersections and freeway on-ramps. Las Vegas-McCarran International Airport swarmed with uniforms, as did bus and train stations. The father and son scam artists— and possibly murderers—would not, Brass swore, make it out of Las Vegas.

That wasn't good enough.

They were obviously plenty dangerous *in* Las Vegas. They had killed Alec Watson, who hadn't been Catherine's favorite person in the world, but at least had hoped to ratchet down the rhetoric embraced by his fellow activists. Worse, they'd killed one cop and injured another—men whose only transgression had been enforcing society's laws.

Sitting at her desk, she felt powerless. She hated that. She wanted something she could examine, put under a microscope, test with chemicals. Some reagent that would turn red if the Kirklands were within a five-mile radius. This kind of police work was outside her area of expertise. This was grunt work, relying more on sheer numbers of officers in the street than a fancy education and costly instrumentation.

She didn't know enough about the suspects to even speculate on where they might go. They were from Georgia, originally. Nevada was a long way from the deep South. They did have local allies, though, and—

"Archie!" she shouted before she had even left her desk. "Archie!"

Archie Johnson wasn't the only tech geek in the lab, but he was the best. Catherine stopped shouting and hurried to his lab, where she found him hunched over a monitor.

"Whatever you're doing, stop," she said. "This is priority number one, as of right now."

"What is, Catherine?"

"I don't know if you've heard about these Free Citizen people putting a lien on my house—"

"Just rumors, nothing concrete."

"—well, it's bogus. The point is, apparently this is a regular stunt for them."

"Okay."

"And sometimes it works. They actually manage to seize property, because the real owners don't have the knowledge or the wherewithal to fight back."

A trace of a smile played about his lips. "So you want me to find those properties."

"That's right. Any property the Free Citizens or their members own here in town. The Kirklands are in the wind. I think they've gone to ground someplace, and I'm guessing it's with supporters."

"Makes sense," Archie said. "Safer than a hotel, when you're on the lam."

"Exactly."

"It could take a while."

"We don't have a while, Archie. We need this now. Sooner."

"I'm on it," he said. With the slightest wiggle of his shoulders, he indicated that he was not to be disturbed. Catherine left him with his computer. If anyone could pull the information together quickly, he was the one.

With so much at stake, it was hard to put her trust in anyone. But she was part of a team, and trust, as much as anything else, was the key to teamwork. She glanced back once, then left Archie to do his job.

28

IN THE GENTLE night breeze, dry burned branches clattered together like the bones of skeletons on the march. The streets were dark; those families that had been able to return had done so, but others had gone back down the mountain for the night. Empty homes, and the shells of structures that had not survived, loomed against scorched hills, black on black. Here and there, a light burned in a window.

Sara and Nick walked quietly, side by side, studying the houses and the windows. Sara wondered about the people inside. The fact that they lived on a mountain separated them from most. The nation had changed; over these past few years the population had shifted to one that predominantly lived in urban areas.

That left people like these—people who chose to live away from cities, closer to the land—pioneers, of a sort. They clung to old ways, perhaps, not pre-industrial but not quite contemporary, either, in spite of their satellite dishes and cell phone towers. She thought that at their cores, they might have more in common with the mountain's earliest inhabitants than with the people crowding Las Vegas.

More in common with her, as well. Once she had escaped—and that's how she thought of it, as a form of liberation from the cage she had grown up in—from her childhood home, she had lived in cities. San Francisco, Cambridge, Las Vegas. She thought it was her decision to do so, only later coming to realize that it was less conscious choice than reaction. She felt safest surrounded by faceless masses. But when it came to interacting with people one-on-one, she was out of her depths. It was easier to look at the lifeless face of a murder victim than to make small talk at the mailbox with an upstairs neighbor.

When she had left Las Vegas, fleeing, once again, she accepted, she took to the jungles of Costa Rica. There she could be alone with the animals and plants. They asked little and gave much in return.

It took Grissom to draw her out of that, to make her feel that she had the strength, once again, to face city life. Looking at these homes, though, surrounded by tall trees, cut off from the scars a city left on the land, an uncomfortable tightness filled her chest. She recognized it as envy, and more—as the urge to shake off the bonds of city life one more time. Even the campers down the hill, with their tents and tarps and fire ring, were living a life she would more willingly embrace than the miles and miles of concrete, the chuff and chatter of millions of souls, the fumes of their automobiles and the profligacy of their water use, the mess they made of their own lives and the devastation they visited upon others.

If she did walk away from Las Vegas, she knew it would be the last time. She wouldn't return again. She couldn't. If she turned her back on what people liked to call "civilization," she would do so for keeps. Grissom could join her in the woods or in the jungle, but except for his, she would be okay if she never saw another human face. She wouldn't even take a mirror.

"It's peaceful up here," Nick said, as if reading her mind. He was like that, extraordinarily perceptive, even when he didn't recognize it in himself. He carried a field kit, she only a flashlight. "In the dark, if it wasn't for the smell, you wouldn't even know there had been a fire."

"The smell and the sound," Sara countered. "A living forest makes a shushing noise in even the slightest breeze, like it's reminding you to slow down, step lightly, to be one with the trees. This one, though . . . it sounds dead. Brittle and broken."

"It'll come back, though."

"Oh, sure. Fire's a natural part of a forest's life. Fire's good for it, in the long run. If it weren't for all these people and houses, a big fire would be win-win."

"It releases a lot of carbon into the atmosphere, though. The trees store it, but fire lets it out."

Sara nodded. "That's true. But again, if it weren't for all the people—not just on the mountain, but everywhere—that much carbon wouldn't be a problem. Face it, Nick, nature has its systems. We're the ones who get in the way."

"If it wasn't for people causing problems, we'd be unemployed."

"I don't know about that. If people stopped hurting each other, stopped committing crimes tomorrow, Nicky, wouldn't you be okay as . . . I don't know, a cobbler? Maybe a baker? Nick's Cupcakes, I can see it now."

"I could find something, I guess."

"I'm sure you could."

"Not gonna happen, though."

"You're right." Sadness threatened to overwhelm her as she said it, to wrap over her face like a soaked blanket, smothering her. She saw it coming, though, and determined to fight it off. "You're right, that's not likely to happen."

"Hey, Sara." Nick's tone had changed, and he touched her left arm. "Take a look."

She followed his pointing hand, and saw a window with a three-pronged candelabrum in it, points of light flickering above. "Candles."

"That's right."

"Let's pay a visit. You know whose place that is?"

She couldn't see much of it in the dark. A covered walkway angled toward the front door, and the place beyond looked like a glorified cabin, knotty pine walls with a base of river rocks, rounded and smooth. It was two stories tall. Whether it had survived the fire intact, she was unable to determine. "I have no idea."

"Let's find out."

Something seemed strange to Sara, and the closer they came to the house, the stranger it appeared. Instead of approaching the door, she stepped into the yard—a dirt patch covered in pine needles, still muddy from water sprayed to hold the fire back—and walked to the window. She returned to Nick's side, shaking her head. "It's electric," she said. "The 'candles' are those flickering light bulbs."

"They might have real candles, too," Nick suggested.

"Any house might have some candles in it. Most probably have at least one or two. But anyone who would put an electric candle in a window is probably the least likely to be a big user of real candles—it's a whole different mindset."

"You're right, Sara. Guess I'm grasping at straws."

"When you've got so little to go on, straws start to look pretty good."

They continued down the street. "We need something more substantial," Nick said as they approached the next property. "One partial footprint and a few half-burned matches aren't much of a case."

"The fire didn't help, and neither did the firefighting effort. But those things and the chemical composition of the wax will seal a case, once we've got a suspect," Sara reminded him.

She glanced at Nick's profile as he nodded his agreement. From there, her gaze traveled past him, to a house set back in the trees, well off the road.

From a downstairs window came a warm but unsteady golden glow.

"Nick, that looks like candlelight." She pointed out the house.

"Yeah, it does."

"It's too irregular to be another electric," she said.

They crossed the street and started up an unpaved driveway. The fire had not come near the house, and the pines were gathered thickly around it, shielding most of it from the road. The house was built against the hill, with stilts supporting a front porch. Firewood was stacked between the stilts. They were lucky that hadn't ignited, Sara thought. Like the last house, it was a two-story, cabin-style job. Next to the house was an open carport, offering shelter to a Honda Insight hybrid.

"Now this looks like a candle lover's place," Nick said, climbing the wooden steps to the porch and front door. "Bet they've got granola in the pantry, too."

"They just might."

Sara looked at her watch as she knocked on the door. Almost ten. Late to go visiting, but she couldn't worry about manners. If the arsonist lived here, he or she had certainly not taken etiquette into account.

She and Nick waited almost a minute. She was about to knock again when a male voice called through the door. "Who's there?"

"Las Vegas Crime Lab," she said. "We'd like to ask you a few questions."

"Just a moment!"

They heard rustling, rushing footsteps, the flush of a toilet. Nick and Sara locked gazes. Nick's right eyebrow elevated, his expression bemused and quizzical at the same time. "Flushing a stash?" he asked.

"Could be."

When the door opened, the lingering aroma of pot, sweet and woody, confirmed his suspicion. Another smell almost overpowered it—sandalwood, Sara thought. Incense, burned to disguise the marijuana smell. She was reminded of college days. "Definitely," Nick said softly.

A man stood in the doorway, effectively blocking it. He was in his fifties, Sara guessed, his hair gray and curly. He wore wire-rim glasses with thick lenses, making his eyes appear small and far away. A black long-sleeved T-shirt did little to hide a pronounced paunch.

Behind him was a woman of about the same age, her hair long and straight, tucked behind her right ear but loose over the left. She had on a brown corduroy shirt with a denim collar, blue jeans, and sandals. The man's expression was curious but without guile; hers was closed-off and suspicious.

"Is there something we can do for you?" the man asked. "You're with the sheriff's department?"

"We're with the crime lab," Sara said again.

"You're the ones who are here about the fire?" the woman asked.

"That's right, ma'am," Nick said.

"We know nothing about that except it was a tragedy. We're thankful our home was spared."

"I'm sure you are, ma'am," Sara said. "Do you mind if we ask you a couple of questions?"

"It's late," the man said.

"But not too late for some weed," Nick said. "We're not here about drug use, sir. We really just have some questions about your candles."

"Candles?"

Sara nodded her head toward the front room. "There is a candle burning in there, right?"

"It's not a crime to like candles, is it? Is that the latest assault on our civil liberties?"

"Not at all. No one's accusing you of any crimes."

"Your friend just did," the woman said.

"Let's back up a minute, here," Nick offered. "I'm Assistant Supervisor Nick Stokes with the Crime Lab. This is Sara Sidle. And you are . . . ?

"I'm Arnold Cox. Arnie," the man said. "My wife, Cynthia."

"If you don't mind, we'd like to take a small sample of that candle," Sara said. "And any other candles on the premises. We'll be careful."

Arnold Cox swallowed hard and tilted his chin up, displaying resistance Sara had not expected. "Do you have a search warrant?"

"No, but—"

"Then absolutely not. That's a gross invasion of our right to privacy."

"Invading your privacy is not our intent, Mr. Cox," Nick said. "Solving a multiple murder is."

"Well, I can assure you, we've got nothing to do with—"

Cynthia Cox's protest was cut off by the slamming of an upstairs door. She whirled around, covered the space to the stairs in two quick steps, and started up. "Kevin?"

More noise came from upstairs, shuffling and pounding, then a loud squeal. Arnold joined Cynthia on the staircase, both of them rushing up and calling Kevin's name.

"That noise was a window," Nick said.

"Come on." Sara remembered Kevin Cox, the kid who was always on the periphery of things. She went down the steps three at a time, Nick right be-hind her. They raced around the house, hearing a loud crash and thump just before they made the corner.

"Kevin Cox!" Nick shouted. "Stop!"

His cry was answered only by further crashing. Kevin had gone out his window and torn off into the forest. Sara and Nick clicked on flashlights and beamed them behind the house, but he was gone.

"You think he's our guy?" Sara asked.

"Maybe he's the one who's been smoking dope, and he's paranoid about it," Nick said. "But jumping out the window seems a little extreme for a pot-head. And a little physical, too, unless someone's out there waving a bag of chips at him."

"I think he heard us," Sara said. She went into the trees after him, shining her light to illuminate her path. "As soon as you mentioned murder, he took off."

"Well, he knows these woods better than we do." The sound of Kevin's passing had almost faded to nothing, replaced by the buzz of cicadas and the dry click of burned branches in the breeze. "But he doesn't know how much tracking experience we have."

Most of Sara's tracking, prior to this case, had been in urban settings. It was easy to follow bloody sneaker prints down a sidewalk. Trailing someone through a dark, blackened forest was another mat-ter altogether.

Except that, as before, when they were following the path of the campers up the slope, it turned out to be easier and more natural than she thought. The insides of scorched branches snapped by his passing gleamed white in the flashlight's beam, set off from their surroundings as if spotlit. Footprints left a distinct trail through the thick coating of ash. Although he had a decent head start, he wasn't carrying a light, and his progress was noisy and uneven.

Cynthia and Arnold Cox followed, calling out Kevin's name. They drowned out some of his flight, but not enough to make Sara turn back and warn them off.

On the bright side, she didn't think he was headed toward a vehicle. If he was, they would almost certainly lose him. But in the direction he had fled, there were no roads for miles and miles.

After a brief time, Kevin's noises grew louder, the ragged gasps of his breathing audible over the splinter and shake of his forward progress, and the shouts of his parents grew dimmer and distant. "We've got him," Nick said.

"Not yet," Sara corrected. "Soon, maybe."

"Oh, he's ours now."

As it happened, Nick was right. In another couple of minutes, they came upon Kevin Cox beside a burned tree trunk. He was bent forward at the waist, hands on his knees, breathing hard. Pink spots blossomed on his cheeks, and his mouth was open, his long hair hanging in his face.

"Kevin Cox," Nick said. He saw them but couldn't gather the energy to run again. "You're under arrest, for arson and murder."

Kevin tried to reply, but his words were lost in labored panting. Nick took handcuffs from his belt, straightened Kevin, drew his arms behind his back and snapped a bracelet over each wrist. Sara read Kevin his Miranda rights.

When that was done, Nick released Kevin again. The young man sagged against the tree. His face was streaked with ash.

Sara shined her light on Kevin's footprints in the ash. "Nick, look. Those are our prints."

Nick eyeballed the markings, then grabbed Kevin's right foot, lifted it off the ground. "No question."

"We'll still have to check the candle. But that'll wrap it up. No jury's going to think the prints and the candle both are a coincidence."

"What are you talking about?" Kevin asked when he was able to speak. "That fire?"

"That's right, Kevin," Sara said. "You started it, didn't you?"

"Sure."

"Why?"

Kevin offered only a shrug. She couldn't push— minors had to be accompanied by parents and/or counsel before being questioned, and she suspected he was not yet eighteen. But anything he put forward on his own might point them toward more evidence.

"You must have had some reason. You went to great pains, covering the matches in wax, bundling them together."

"I was bored, I guess."

"Bored?"

"Dude," he said, though he was still addressing Sara. "I live on a mountain. All my folks do is get high and listen to old music. When they're not high, they argue, and I can't stand being in the house. But there's nothing outside except trees and squirrels and shit. I got bored, I started a fire. End of story."

"Except it's not," Sara reminded him. "There's more to it than you're saying, right? What's going on?" She thought about what he had said. "Your parents?"

"Yeah, blame them," Kevin said. "That's what Freud would say, right?"

"I'm not blaming anyone," Sara argued. "I'm just trying to understand. Lots of people get bored. You started a fire that cost the taxpayers hundreds of thousands of dollars. When all the property damage is added up, it'll almost certainly go over a million. Worse, you killed six firefighters, brave men and women who were only trying to limit the damage you caused. It's going to take the people up here years to rebuild their homes and their lives, those that can be rebuilt. That doesn't come from just being bored. But it could be a cry for help."

He started to shrug again, thought better of it, and stopped mid-motion. But he didn't replace it with anything else, so he stood there awkwardly, one shoulder raised, handcuff chain jingling softly.

"Your folks get high a lot?"

"Depends. Is every day a lot? Or does it have to be hourly?"

"It bothers you."

"Whatever. It is what it is."

"But you know that not every family is that way. What are they like when they're high?"

"Ever watched rocks?"

"What does that mean?"

Kevin reached down and lifted a pebble from the ground, held it out on his palm. "Watch this for a couple of hours. Maybe all day. Let me know if it does anything interesting."

"I think I get the idea," Sara said. His must have been a miserable existence . . . on this mountain with few people his own age around, in a house with parents who, when they were using—which was constantly—paid him not the slightest attention. In the midst of his own family, he was at his most solitary. No wonder he had acted out. "I'm sorry, Kevin. I know it's been rough."

Kevin gave a snicker, but his eyes were moist. "Hey, at least they got off the couch to watch the flames. We had to stay in a motel, and they were afraid to smoke. We watched TV, played some cards. It was pretty cool."

"Maybe this will be a wake-up call for them," Nick said. "Things will be different now." Nick took his arm, led him away from the tree. "Come on, man. Let's get going."

He started walking Kevin up the hill. Cynthia and Arnold Cox were coming, without lights, threading their way noisily through the darkness. In the near distance Sara heard the plaintive hooting of an owl; a bird sound, at last. The forest would recover. By the time Kevin got out of prison, it would be green and vibrant again.

Sara let Nick and Kevin get away from her. She got out her cell phone, which surprisingly had a decent signal. Time to call Juan Castillo, to tell him what they'd learned.

She didn't know if Castillo had anyone in mind for the firestarter, but believed he would be surprised by their suspect. She was. She had wanted there to be a motive, something that made sense, greed or lust or passion. But the motive was more tragic than those. It was loneliness. It was a message sent to parents who couldn't be bothered to acknowledge their own son's existence.

If anything could have made Sara sadder, she didn't know what it would be.

29

"HERE'S YOUR DNA result," David Hodges said, handing Ray a manila file folder. "Don't say I never gave you anything."

"What happened to Carrie?"

"She's off duty. Guess who's on night shift DNA? Like I don't have anything else to do."

Hodges was still on the testy side, and had been since Wendy Simms had left the lab. Ray kept hoping he would get over it. Then again, he was Hodges. He had been testy the first time Ray had met him, and no doubt long before that. "Thanks, David," he said.

"In case it's too much reading for you, the touch DNA off that stripper you fondled—"

"I didn't fondle her."

"—whatever, is a match for the epithelial cells you brought in from that abduction scene. And under the fingernails of the severed hand found earlier. Which means . . ."

"Which means that Ruben Solis was taken by the same crew who've been cutting off hands, and Erwin was one of the people who took Ruben Solis. Or at the very least, he was at the Solis house. And given the specifics of how we found Erwin . . ."

"Far more likely that he was one of the snatchers."

"Correct." Ray flipped open the file, scanning it quickly. Hodges had summed up the important points, though. "This should be enough to get me a warrant."

"If you're going back to that strip club . . ."

"I think you're needed here at the lab, David. But thanks again for offering."

"Verbal thanks. All I ever get," Hodges mumbled. He walked away, still grumbling to himself, but Ray ignored him, already reaching for the phone to try to arrange that warrant.

Before he and Sam Vega could make it back to Cougars, though, Ray received a call about the Friends of the East Side Community Center. He listened, asked a couple of pointed questions, and put his phone away. "Change of plans," he said.

Vega, behind the wheel, slowed the car. "What's up?"

"Mickey Ritz's been snatched."

"Who?"

"He runs the Friends of the East Side Community Center. He's the one who told me I was looking for someone called Oz or Ozzie."

"Oswaldo Carrizoza."

"Precisely. He was worried about the possibility that someone might overhear our conversation."

"Sounds like he had good reason."

"So it appears."

"You think we should head over there?"

"I do," Ray said. "He lives at the community center. We may be too late to help Ruben Solis, but I'd rather not be too late for Mickey Ritz."

"Tell me where to go."

Ray did. In less than twenty minutes, they had pulled up outside the community center. There was already a cruiser parked in front, and a uniformed cop was doing his best to keep neighbors and onlookers off the property.

Ray and Vega flashed their badges and went inside. The first person Ray saw was the white woman who had been helping out with the cooking earlier. She was standing in the hallway, near the door. "You're a detective, right?" she asked.

"I'm with the Crime Lab," Ray corrected. "Sam Vega here is a detective."

"I want to know what's being done to help Mickey," she declared. "These officers here don't seem to know anything at all."

"They're patrol officers," Vega said. "Not part of the investigation. And even if they did know anything, they wouldn't be at liberty to tell you."

"But you? You're part of the investigation?"

"We just got here, ma'am. The investigation begins now." Vega flipped open a notebook with a wire spiral at the top. "Do you mind telling me your name?"

She gave it to him. Her eyes wouldn't be still, but darted this way and that, as if afraid the attackers might return from any direction. "Were you here when Mr. Ritz was abducted?" Vega asked.

"Yeah, I was. He lives here, you know."

"His apartment is off his office," Ray said. "He told me."

"Yeah, well, he likes to be on the scene in case there's some kind of emergency. So he can open the doors, get the community whatever support he can on a moment's notice. And sometimes, if there's someone in the neighborhood who doesn't have a place to stay, he'll let them sleep on the premises. So he likes to have a couple of staff people on hand at night."

"And you're one of those people?"

"Honey, nobody's been with Mickey as long as I have. I used to be married to him, way back when. We were just kids, really, then. Married too young, what a mistake. But he was quite a guy. Still is, for that matter. Just not someone I could stay married to, now or then."

The name she had given wasn't Ritz. But she might not have taken his name. She might have given it up after their divorce, might even have remarried.

"So what happened tonight?"

"I was going to bunk in one of the community rooms. I think you saw it, the one with the TVs and the board games? One of the sofas there is a hideaway bed. There was a family, temporarily homeless because of a fire at their apartment complex, using another room, and Mickey wanted me around as backup. If someone needed something that we didn't have handy, one of us would have to go out for it, and there has to be someone employed by the center on the premises at all times, if there are guests here."

"Was anyone else here?"

"Candy hadn't gone home yet. She was making the bed up with me, then she was going to take off."

"Candy's another employee?" Vega asked.

"Volunteer. There are only four paid employees, rest of the staff are volunteers."

"That's a noble thing," Ray said.

The woman shrugged, wiped an errant lock of hair away from her face. "I guess. Anyway, somebody knocked on the door. I had my hands full with the bed, so Candy went to see who it was. Next thing I know, she screams, just a little scream, you know? Like, cut off."

"Go on," Vega urged.

"These three dudes came inside. They had guns. Candy was holding her neck, I guess one of the guys punched her or something. They waved the iron at me and told me to keep quiet. I told them I wouldn't make a peep. By then, Mickey was coming out of his office. They pointed their guns at him, told him he was going for a ride. He said no, and one of the guys shoved his piece against Candy's chest. He would start with her, he said, then he was going to shoot me, if Mickey didn't go easy. At that point, Mickey gave in. He told them not to hurt us, we had nothing to do with anything. The men agreed, and they left with Mickey."

"Is Candy still here?" Ray asked.

"I keep a flask of something out in the car, for emergencies. Not while I'm driving, you know," she added quickly. "I gave her a couple snorts and that calmed her down a little."

"We generally like crime witnesses to be sober when we talk to them," Vega pointed out.

"Listen, I hadn't of medicated her some, she wouldn't be talking to anyone. She was a wreck."

"Can you describe the men?" Ray asked.

"I can describe their guns. Big and mean looking. The guys, I hardly noticed. Latino, I think, or something else. Dark skin, but not African-American." She nodded toward Vega, then Ray. "More like you than you."

"Surely you see plenty of Latinos on the job here," Vega said.

"Yeah, but like I said, once I saw the guns, I stopped looking anyplace but at those. When you think one might be used on you . . . it gets your attention, let's say."

"Understandable," Ray said. "Did they say anything else, before they left?"

"Not to me. I had Candy, and I was trying to calm her down, and they talked to Mickey for maybe a minute. Then they were all gone and I was dialing 911."

"You did the right thing, ma'am," Vega said. "Did the other family see anything? The folks who are staying here?"

"They've been sleeping in a car for a week, four of them. They were probably out the second their heads hit the pillow. Didn't wake up until that car came tearing in with its siren going."

"All right, ma'am," Ray said. "Where can we find Candy?"

"She's in the kitchen. Still got my flask, too. If there's anything left in it, I could use a taste."

"We'll mention it," Vega said. "Thanks for your help."

Ray showed him the way to the kitchen. Candy had indeed polished off the flask. Ray wished she hadn't done that. She had also scrubbed her face and neck red with a kitchen sponge, probably eliminating any trace evidence that might have been left on her skin. She had a bruise on her throat that would be ugly by morning. Her speech was slurred, and when Vega introduced himself as a detective, she fell against him, clinging to him like a teenybopper to a pop star. For all Ray knew, she had done the same to the other woman, and to the uniforms who had responded to the 911 call. So much for trace from her clothing.

They questioned her, but her answers were barely coherent. She claimed that the men were white, then black, then admitted she couldn't remember. She said there were two, then four. Once she sobered up, she might be more helpful, but that was anybody's guess.

Back in the car after they gave up on Candy, Vega said, "I think we have a pretty good idea who to look at, even without her."

"Carrizoza's goons," Ray said.

"Right." Vega pulled away from the community center, heading down the street at ten miles above the speed limit and climbing. "Before I got the warrant, I did a quick records check for any other businesses he owned. I figured, you know, if he was snatching people up, cutting their hands off, a strip club might not be the best place for that. Lots of people around, and the music's pretty loud, but someone might still hear screams or power tools from a back room."

"Did you come up with anything?"

"A few places. He has a couple of restaurants, an apartment building. Real diversified businessman, right? But get this—one of his businesses is called Ozzie's Auto Parts. New and used, mostly used."

"Car parts?"

"Turns out the department's auto theft task force has had their eye on the place for a while now. They think it's a chop shop."

Ray squirmed a little at the phrasing, though he did his best to hide it. The hard part about being a CSI was seeing close up the depths to which human beings could sink. As a doctor, he had seen plenty of injury and death, but the causes had always been a few steps removed, and thus more abstract. "An unfortunate nomenclature," he said.

"If they do their chopping there, chances are that's where they've got Ritz."

"They didn't kill him outright," Ray said. "Which implies that he's got something they want."

"We think they know he was talking about Carrizoza to someone, and that's what got him in trouble. Then we showed up at the club. Carrizoza might think Ritz was talking to you or me, but if he doesn't know that for sure, he'll want to find out."

"They're going to torture Ritz?"

"They might not need to. Most people, the threat of it is more than enough. Thing is, once he's told them what they want to know, then he's dead. We just have to hope Ritz knows that, and holds out as long as he can."

Ritz had seemed plenty tough, during his brief meeting with Ray. But predicting how someone would stand up to torture, even something as brutally direct as having a hand cut off, was not an area of human psychology Ray considered himself proficient in.

Vega was right, though. Once Mickey Ritz talked, they'd have no reason to let him live. "Faster, Sam," he said softly.

Vega floored it.

30

"DROP WHAT YOU'RE doing, Greg," Catherine said.

Greg didn't take her instructions literally. He was in the ballistics lab, test-firing an AK-47 confiscated at the Free Citizens compound to compare the rifling marks from their barrels with those on the rounds found at Alec Watson's office. Those particular firearms had been in the lab before the cops were shot, so they weren't suspect in that case. But so far, it was only a supposition that the same gun had been used on Watson and the cops, and no brass had been found at the police murder scene.

Instead of dropping the gun, he removed the magazine and put it down carefully on a work-bench. "What's up?" he asked, peeling off goggles and ear protectors.

"We've had units out looking at the likeliest properties taken over by Free Citizens, either as individuals or the organization," she said.

"Right." He already knew that. Catherine started walking, and he hurried to keep pace with her.

"A chopper did a flyover of a few bigger scores they've made—a ranch outside of town, some desert acreage—and when they passed over the Empire Resort and Casino—"

"Isn't that the place that went under before it was finished?"

"The builders declared bankruptcy. They were probably glad to wash their hands of it when the Free Citizens placed a lien against it. So yes, it's unfinished, and there's every likelihood that it always will be. Anyway, the chopper pilot saw a recent model Mercedes SUV parked there, along with a couple of other vehicles."

"The Kirklands?"

"That's what we're guessing. Brass and Lou are already on their way, but I want to be in on this arrest. If there's evidence on those creeps, I want to get it before they're booked and it's compromised forever."

"Works for me," Greg said. "You want me to drive?"

"No. I'll drive." Catherine was silent for a moment, walking fast. "Never mind, you can drive." She was distracted, Greg guessed. He would drive. It would be safer all the way around.

Catherine didn't know why she had reacted that way to Greg's suggestion that he could drive. She supposed it had to do with her unwillingness to let go, to simply let her team do their work without riding herd on them. Maybe it had to do with being the single mother of a teenage girl—a task requiring constant attention. Then again, it could have been a reaction to having to take over from Gil Grissom, who had often seemed almost preternaturally capable. She didn't think she could ever follow in his footsteps; instead, she had to carve her own path. If that meant overcompensating sometimes, well, she would just have to overcompensate.

For the most part, she was comfortable with her leadership style. It was only at times like this, moments of real crisis, that she found herself second-guessing, wondering if she had made the right call. And sometimes that second-guessing came across wrong. She didn't mind Greg's driving, it had simply been one decision too many, when she had more important things on her mind.

Nick had reported in, letting her know that an arrest had been made in the forest fire. The suspect was a seventeen-year-old kid who claimed to have started it out of boredom, just for something to do. Nick and Sara were on their way down the hill, and the kid was in the custody of state police, with Juan Castillo overseeing his booking.

That was one thing off her plate. But that still left the attacks on Daniels, the shooting of two cops, the murder of Alec Watson, and the invasion of her own personal life.

Who's going to drive?

The last thing she wanted to think about.

Las Vegas already had one casino with an ancient Roman theme, which Catherine thought sufficient for any given city. More than sufficient, for that matter. But the Empire Resort and Casino had promised to far outdo the existing outfit in tastelessness, and from what she had seen, it was well on its way to succeeding in that goal. The main building was to be an oversized replica of Rome's famous Colosseum—never mind that until it had become famous simply for its architectural splendor, and for the fact that it had survived the centuries while Rome evolved around it, its main claim to fame had been the sheer amount of blood spilled within its curved walls. The promoters had implied that with its private areas, its members-only dining room and bars and pool, it would be the closest thing possible to storied Roman orgies. High rollers would, of course, have access to those areas; the general public would have to pay richly to join the private club. Many would no doubt be denied membership even if they raised the price, since the point of a private club was its exclusivity—not who could belong, but who could be kept out.

And yet, despite these appeals to the worst in humanity, the builders had gone belly-up before they got the doors open. Construction costs had skyrocketed, then credit became tight, land values plummeted. The economy of Las Vegas had suffered, and though it had hit the working poor and middle classes hardest, even people like those behind the Empire—entrepreneurs hoping to get rich on borrowed money—had been impacted. The last Catherine had heard of the Empire's main "visionary," he had moved back to Pittsburgh, where he'd come from originally, to run a branch of his family's regional chain of hardware stores.

The empty, half-finished structure sat on the desert at the edge of town, like an open sore on someone's jawline. Once there had been billboards and banners promoting the project, but those had mostly been taken down or painted over. A few banners still fluttered in the night breeze, as forlorn as orphans or abandoned pets. So die the dreams of the boosters and boom-followers, Catherine found herself thinking. The history of the West followed the same pattern, over and over—boosters moving into a place, promising to make the desert bloom, swearing that the land would provide the kind of greenery that could be put in a bank. Whether it was crops or cattle, oil or uranium—or casinos—the boosters made promises that could be kept only in the short term, if at all. The gaming industry had proven more resistant than most, but over the decades of Las Vegas's existence, casinos had gone under with distressing regularity. New ones were built in the ashes of the old. The fact that those ashes existed should have been a warning to the promoters.

Police vehicles were parked in no particular formation in the parking lot, along with a SWAT bus. Two helicopters chattered overhead. If anyone was hiding inside, they knew they weren't alone. Greg and Catherine showed their badges to a cop at the top of the paved driveway and were waved inside. They found Brass and Vartann standing with a clutch of other cops and a SWAT commander, in the parking lot. The Mercedes SUV from the Orpheus parking garage was there, along with a pickup truck, an old Chevy Nova, and a recent model Ford Mustang.

A disturbingly authentic Colosseum loomed over it all, moonlight shining through its unfinished walls.

"Any sign of them?" Catherine asked, approaching the gathered men.

"Not yet," Vartann replied. "Unless they've gone for a nighttime hike in the desert, they're somewhere inside. We're trying to get the blueprints brought up here so we can get a sense of the layout before we go in."

"I guess the element of surprise isn't really an issue."

"Not at this point," Brass said. "If I were them, I'd surrender. But I guess rationality isn't highly valued in their circles."

"Apparently not," Catherine agreed.

A squad car rolled down the gentle slope of the driveway and came to a stop nearby. The uni who got out of the front passenger seat carried a long cardboard tube. "Here they are," the SWAT commander said, putting his hand out for the tube. Catherine had met him a couple of times before. His name, Saenz, was lettered on the chest of his Kevlar vest. He was one of those men who had probably played football in school and looked like he still could—thick-necked, with a strong, assertive jaw, a mouth that looked somehow too small, and a nose that some previous confrontation had left skewed slightly to the left. His eyes were the only thing out of character; they were large and liquid, soulful eyes, she would have said, not the calculating ones she would have expected on someone in his position. When he was on the scene, it was an indication that violence was imminent. "Let's have a quick look and put together an entry plan."

The SWAT commander unrolled the blueprints on the hood of the car as other cops illuminated them with flashlights. He was pointing out the various entrances when the unmistakable crack of a rifle sounded in the distance. Almost simultaneously, the cruiser's windshield shattered.

"Down!" Brass shouted. "Looks like they've moved up the timeline on our assault!"

Another shot rang out, echoing in the still night. This one found a human target, and a cop went down, blood spurting from his leg.

Catherine hunkered behind the cruiser with Greg, Lou, Brass, and Saenz. "They've hit one of our boys," the SWAT officer said. "We're going in, Jim. We're hitting them hard and fast."

"I'm right there with you," Brass said. "Let's wrap this up before they kill any more cops."

31

RAY AND VEGA were the first ones at Ozzie's Auto Parts, but shortly after they stopped in front of the main building, two squad cars pulled up and four uniformed cops piled out. The five men and one woman fanned out around the front, Ray and Vega heading for the front door, Ray with his field kit in the hand that didn't hold a cane.

The place didn't exactly inspire confidence. A sign announcing the business name hung above a sagging overhang that shielded the doorway from Las Vegas's occasional rains. The walls were streaked and stained, as if the rust that attacked the steel of the parts they replaced had migrated onto the adobe. Two garage bays were closed off by huge steel doors, painted white many years earlier, and since then coated with soot and exhaust and graffiti until they were multicolored blurs, almost black above the reach of taggers.

The door was steel and glass, much of it covered

by decals from auto part suppliers, signs announcing special offers, and the business hours. Although the place was open, according to the sign, the door was locked.

Sam Vega pounded on the glass. "LVPD!" he called. "Open up!"

When nobody responded after a minute, Vega turned toward one of the uniformed officers. "Open it, Mitch," he said.

"Yes, sir," the cop replied. He returned to his car and got a small handheld battering ram from the trunk. Vega and Ray stepped back from the doorway, and Mitch drove the ram into the steel frame of the door, just above the lock. With the fourth strike, the jamb cracked and the door swung open, its glass shattered.

The cop moved out of the way and Vega pushed through the broken doorway. He announced himself again, and went inside. The female cop followed him in, service weapon in her hand, and Ray went after her. The other three remained outside, on the watch for anyone trying to leave the premises.

They entered a sales area, with parts arranged neatly on display fixtures, a high retail counter, and behind that, tall shelves packed with cardboard cartons. The lights were on but nobody was in sight. Vega flipped up a hinged section of the counter and went behind it. A doorway at the back of the shelving area led to a lighted hallway, beyond which frantic activity could be heard.

"The place is surrounded!" Vega announced. "We have a warrant to search these premises."

Still, no one responded or interacted with them.

Vega and the uniformed officer, with Ray still close behind, hurried down the hall and into a garage bay. There was a BMW up on an elevated rack, half a dozen workmen in grease-stained jumpsuits around it. They had stopped work and stood in poses of tense anticipation, watching the newcomers.

Auto parts were stacked against a wall—bumpers, fenders, wheels, axles, hoods and more. Hanging fluorescent fixtures lit the room. The place had the air of a medieval torture chamber, with heavy chains and sharp-edged tools everywhere, the smell of burnt steel hanging in the air.

A man in a stained blue work shirt stared at the cops. He held a clipboard and wore a perplexed expression. His dark hair was thinning, showing patches of pale pink scalp underneath. "You shouldn't be in here."

"You didn't exactly answer when we knocked." Vega said.

"We're closed."

"Closed doesn't apply to us."

"There's nothing I can do for you. The owner—"

"We know who the owner is," Vega told him. "We'll be dealing with him separately."

"What do you want?"

Vega slapped the warrant onto the man's clipboard. "We're looking around," he said. "And nobody's going to get in our way."

Ray drifted over to a workbench. He was used to mechanics who knew the value of their tools, who cared for them like they were their own children. But many of these tools were coated with rust and metal filings, blades chipped, drill bits worn and dull, only a few were clean and bright and cared for.

At a glance, he would not have guessed these were people who relied on their tools for their living.

One of the tools that was in reasonably good repair was a handheld circular saw, lying on its side with its blade up. The blade looked sharp and clean. But the casing didn't, it was caked and flecked with brown. Like rust, except that rust had not settled on the saw itself.

Ray set his case on the floor and opened it. A little luminol spray could quickly confirm his suspicion, but there was no way he would be allowed— or willing—to turn the lights off, to see if it would fluoresce. Instead, he took out a bottle of Hemastix and a small container of distilled water.

"What's he doing?" the man with the clipboard demanded.

"Never mind him," Vega said. "Everybody just stand where you are and we'll be done here as fast as we can."

With his usual care and precision, Ray took a three-inch plastic strip from the first bottle and dampened the little yellow pad at its end with some of the distilled water. He went back into the field kit for a control sample of known blood on cotton gauze, and he rubbed that against the moist pad. Almost immediately, the pad turned dark green. Although he knew what that meant, it only took an extra second to hold it up to the color chart printed on the side of the Hemastix bottle. The green color was a confirmation of the presence of blood. The

Hemastix solution was still good. He put the used stick and the bloody gauze into separate envelopes and tucked them into the kit. Then he moistened another stick, and swabbed at the brown flakes on the saw casing.

Again, the yellow turned dark green.

The solution didn't identify the source of the blood. It could have come from a butchered cow, or from a worker who had failed to exercise care when using the saw.

But it could also have come from using it to sever someone's hand. Comparing its tooth pattern to the toolmarks found on the wrists would be the only way to confirm that. It was, he thought, enough to take some people in, and maybe under questioning one of them would crack.

"Sam, arrest these men," he said. "There's blood on this saw."

"You heard the man," Sam said. "You're all under arrest. On your knees, now, hands behind your heads."

Ray was making notes on the envelope his Hemastix sample would go into, and he almost missed what happened next. If the man hadn't dropped a wrench, he wouldn't have seen it at all. The man did, though, and the clatter of the tool on the concrete floor snapped Ray's head around. He saw the man rushing toward a rear door, hand snaking inside his work suit.

When it came out again, it held a gun.

The man had his hand on the doorknob, but he was looking back into the garage bay, his eyes wide with fear. Sam had drawn his own weapon, and the uniformed cop had hers raised. "Sir, stop!" she commanded. "Drop that weapon!"

The man yanked open the door. At the same time, he jerked the trigger of his gun. The shot was loud in the small space, echoing off concrete walls and floor, but his shot went wild.

The patrol officer's didn't.

The man was barely through the door when her first round caught him on the shoulder. The impact drove him to the pavement outside.

Ray crouched by his field kit. In this small space, even a few shots fired could turn into real trouble. Ricochets off concrete or steel could do just as much damage as direct hits.

As if the two shots had turned off some kind of governor, weapons appeared in the hands of other workers. Vega and the uniformed cop called out warnings and took what little cover they could find. Ray could make for the door, but sticking his head up would likely result in getting himself shot, and he couldn't move fast enough to dodge trouble.

The scene was frozen like that, a moment suspended in time and space, until the sound of rushing feet and the tinkle of falling glass came from the front. "Police!" Mitch shouted. "I heard shots fired!"

At that, the tableau thawed. The men in work clothes opened fire and charged the back door. Vega and the two unis returned that fire. A spray of blood erupted from one man's thigh, and another crumpled to the ground just outside, almost on top of the first man shot. A sudden flurry of smoke and muzzle flashes, the deafening roar and high-pitched whine of bullets flying, the bitter tang of gunfire, gave the distinct impression of a war zone.

The battle was over as suddenly as it had started. The man with the clipboard, who had never drawn, threw himself onto the oil-soaked floor, hands splayed out ahead of him. Two other men in work clothes threw their guns down and dropped to their knees, folding their fingers together behind their heads. The cops moved swiftly to them and hand-cuffed their wrists, then went to those who had fallen, kicked their weapons clear, and did the same to them. The female officer called in a request for backup officers and a medical bus for the wounded.

Ray followed Vega out the back door. A tall fence encircled the property, topped by coiled razor wire. The hulks of old automobiles sat quietly rusting away on the pavement. There was a back gate, but it was closed and chained shut, the chain held fast by a large steel padlock.

If the men weren't heading for that—and it would not have offered a quick escape route, unless someone had a key on him—where were they going?

Then he saw, behind a stack of car carcasses, the straight lines of another structure, low and flat-roofed. "Sam," he said, "there's a building back there."

"So there is," Vega said. "You can barely see it from here." He beckoned one of the uniformed cops. "Mitch? Come back here with me."

"Right," the cop said.

Vega and Mitch approached the outbuilding with weapons drawn, Vega once again calling out a warning.

In return, Ray heard a muffled cry, and then a louder sound, an angry voice and a thumping noise.

"Someone's in there."

Vega nodded. "You're surrounded!" he shouted toward the building. It was bigger than a shed, but not much. There was a single-car garage-sized door, and beside that a regular wooden door with a flaking metal knob. "Come out with your hands on your heads!"

The knob turned and three men filed out, hands locked behind their heads. They wore jumpsuits, but these were spattered with fresher, red liquid instead of grease. Unis handcuffed them, taking them out into the open concrete area.

Vega and Ray entered the smaller building. Ray scented blood before he passed through the door.

Inside, Mickey Ritz sat in a straight-backed steel chair. His hands were bound behind his back, and a length of chain was wrapped around him. A dirty rag had been stuffed into his mouth. Fresh scrapes glistened on his cheeks, and his right eye was swollen, almost shut. Blood had dribbled from his mouth, caking at the corners and streaking down to his chin. His eyes were wild with fright.

"Mickey," Ray said. "It's me, Ray Langston. The police are here. You're safe now."

Ritz had not seemed to recognize him at first. When he started talking, the bound man struggled against his tethers. But then Ray's words sank in. He went still, his eyes settled, and he started trying to speak against the gag. Ray yanked it from his mouth. It was wet with blood.

"Are you all right, Mickey? Paramedics are on the way."

"They . . . they worked me over pretty good," Ritz said. "Wanted me to tell them . . . tell them who I mentioned Ozzie to."

"You give them my name?"

Ritz spat blood onto the grimy floor. The shed, Ray decided, was where they did their dismemberment. A steel workbench had old, dried blood all over the surface and coating the legs. Contented flies buzzed around it. If the garage had vaguely resembled a torture chamber, this place, lit only by a single bare bulb hanging from the rafters on its cord, could have been nothing else. Here there were chains of various sizes and more tools—saws, screwdrivers, iron bars and pipes, knives, even a machete—all apparently caked in blood. The stink was horrific.

What was worse was something that, in another context, would have brought Ray a sense of satisfaction. On a workbench he found human shapes made of wire and hardware scraps. They weren't set into a scene yet, but he had seen enough of Ruben's work to recognize it. He picked up one of the wire men, and he was holding it when Ritz answered the question Ray almost forgot he had asked.

"I gave 'em nothing," Ritz said. "Bastards threatened to cut off both my hands. I told 'em where to stick it."

Ray had Ritz pegged as tough. But this went above and beyond. He believed Ritz—even sitting there, lashed to the chair, the man looked strong and defiant.

Ray guessed a guy who ran a community center for those society neglected or forgot or didn't want to acknowledge in the first place had to have a core of steel. He knelt behind the man and worked loose the ropes that bound his hands. "Thanks," Ray said. "A lot of people would've cracked. Most people."

"These are the bastards who took Ruben, right?"

"We think so, yes."

"I think so too. I wasn't going to give them the time of day."

Ray got the ropes loose, and started to unwind the chains from Ritz's chest and arms. "Ray," Vega called. He was on the far side of the workbench, standing by an open door.

"I got this," a uni said, lifting the chain from Ray's hands.

"Easy with it," Ray said. "He's been through a lot."

"Just get the damn thing off me," Ritz said. "I can take a few more bruises if it'll cut me loose."

Ray left him and the officer to negotiate the chain, and joined Vega. The door was iron, about twenty inches square. Inside it was a small chamber carpeted with ash.

"An incinerator," Ray said.

"I figure this is where the bodies went. After they lost their hands."

"That ash will tell the tale," Ray said. "If those are cremains, it'll be easy enough to figure out. Harder to determine who all went in there."

"We'll look around more," Vega offered. "Maybe we'll find something else."

"All the blood in here," Ray said. "We'll have to try to isolate individual samples. If we can, that'll help ID the victims."

"That's a big job."

Ray looked outside at the sunshine. "Day shift can tackle it."

"Works for me."

Ray closed the door gently, to keep the ash from being contaminated any further. He was pleased to find Ritz alive, but that pleasure was cut by the fact that Ruben wasn't on the premises. His belief was that Ruben had gone into the incinerator, like who knew how many others.

He owed it to Lucia to stop by, tell her that he had found the gang, but not Ruben. He couldn't definitively tell her that her brother was dead, but he had to let her know that the prospect was grim.

It would break her heart. But, like in Mickey Ritz, he sensed in her an inner strength. She would survive.

When he left the dark, stinking shed, Vega was waiting outside, just putting away his phone. Ritz was standing with a couple of uniformed officers, near the back door to the garage bay.

"Carrizoza's been picked up at Cougars," Vega said. "He's already lawyered up."

"No surprise."

"He'll claim plausible deniability. He owned this place, but he had no idea what went on here, that kind of thing."

"He can try," Ray said. "But if we find the slightest trace of him on these premises, that goes out the window. As it is, we already have his sweaty-palmed henchman putting the snatch on Ruben Solis. I'll bet Erwin's DNA is all over this place, too. He drips it off his hands everywhere he goes."

"That's action I'll have to pass on," Vega said. "I

don't bet against sure things, and I'm sure you're right."

Ray glanced to the east, where the sun had added a golden tinge to the sky. "Thanks, Sam," he said. His voice was soft, his manner gentle.

"For what?"

"For being there tonight," Ray said. "Or last night, I guess. Every case is important, but this one—it got to me. I appreciate the help."

"It's the job," Vega said.

"I know it's the job. But you're good at it, and your input was invaluable."

Vega shrugged. "You're welcome."

Ray wished he could explain better. Ruben Solis was in this country illegally, and Ray couldn't overlook that. But that crime had made him vulnerable to a crime that was far, far worse, in Ray's eyes. A lot of countries wouldn't have wanted any effort put into figuring out what had happened to him. A lot of Americans, for that matter, and Ray saw their point of view, understood what they felt.

A victim was a victim, though. Ray's task was to do whatever was within his power to help crime victims, and to prevent others from being victimized. He hadn't been in time to save Ruben, but— and he allowed himself the slightest, grim smile at the image—but Ruben had given him a hand shutting down the ring, and that would no doubt help others, down the road.

The smile only lasted an instant, and then it was gone, and Ray was limping toward the door, where Sam Vega and a blood-drenched, battered Mickey Ritz waited for him.

32

"WE'RE GOING IN," Saenz said. He had been huddled with his team for a couple of minutes. The gunfire from the skeletal structure of the hotel-in-progress had stopped. "We think the shots came from the fourth floor, but that place is wide open and they could be anywhere."

"I'm going with you," Brass declared.

"Me too," Vartann said.

"You wearing body armor?" Saenz asked.

Both detectives answered in the affirmative. "Wish you'd put on helmets," Saenz said. "This is still a construction site, officially. Hardhats required, even if there weren't bullets flying."

"We'll let your people take the lead," Brass volunteered. "We'll hang back. But I want the Kirklands alive, if at all possible. And that's a big place, you'll need every eye you can get in there."

"We'll go too," Catherine said.

Brass whirled on her. "Absolutely not, Catherine."

"We're armed and qualified, Jim."

"You're CSIs, not cops. I want you out here and under cover, not inside there."

She wanted to argue, but tamped down her thoughts. "You're the boss," she said. "Is that an order?"

"Call it whatever you want. Discussion's over, Catherine. You and Greg stay out of that building."

"Fine. But if there's trouble, we're coming in."

Brass agreed, as Catherine had known he would. He worried about her safety—about every cop's safety, and that of the CSIs who worked alongside them. But stubborn as he was, she could outdo him every time, and he knew it.

Saenz and his assault team made a quick, final check of their armor and gear and rushed toward the Empire's dark interior, holding shields up to defend against any potential gunshots. None came. Vartann gave Catherine's hand a quick squeeze. She inhaled his scent, but before she could speak, he and Brass dashed off after the SWAT officers, the other uniformed cops accompanying them. She and Greg stayed behind the squad car, watching them go.

Catherine watched the men as long as she could see them. Greg sat with his back against the car, studying the blueprints with a penlight. "Find anything?" she asked, crouching beside him.

"This place is strange. It's got an open central area where sporting events were supposed to take place."

"The modern-day equivalent of gladiatorial combat."

"I guess. Check out how the hotel wraps around it. Some of the rooms would look out toward the parking lot and the city and others would face onto the central sports field."

"Those were probably the more expensive ones. Or would have been."

"It's just a strange place for a last stand, if that's what they have in mind," Greg said. "I would have expected camera crews, an organized presence of some kind, so they could show the world how the evil law enforcement agencies are mistreating them. They'd want it to be front page news."

"Maybe they just didn't expect to be found so quickly."

"Could be," he said. He used the light's thin beam to direct her attention to the blueprint. "And look at this. There aren't many ways in or out."

"That's typical of casinos. Once you're in the door, they don't make it easy to find an exit. Or a clock."

"Right," Greg said. "But the construction work was being done from bottom to top. Look at the building."

Catherine rose high enough to see through the car's windows. The upper levels were wide open, and she could see sky through them, lightening slightly in the east. The lower floors were a solid block of shadow.

"So what you're saying is, once our guys are inside, they might not be able to find their way back out in a hurry, if they need to."

"That's how it looks to me. But I don't know why they'd need to."

"Unless—" Catherine didn't finish her thought.

The metallic *chunk* of car doors closing softly traveled across the parking lot. She yanked her phone open and speed-dialed Vartann, noting as she did that she had less than a full bar of service out here.

When he answered, she could barely understand him over the static and moments of sudden silence. "Lou," she said urgently, "get everyone out! It's a trap!"

He said something back, but she couldn't tell what, or even if he had understood her.

"I'll go get them," Greg said.

"No. The radio, in the SWAT bus. They'll all be on the same frequency. Get them out, now!"

"Okay," Greg said. "But what are you—"

She didn't wait for the end of his question. The engine of the Mercedes SUV had started. It purred like a contented cat, not far away. She supposed its occupants were waiting for the concluding act of their little drama before driving away. That distraction would also make it easier for them to get past the lone officer posted at the end of the driveway, though they would have no compunction about shooting him, if need be.

The SUV was about twenty-five yards from the police cars, and facing away. She raced across the pavement. When she came to a stop, weapon drawn, she was just feet behind the Mercedes. Six people were inside. Only three had left the Orpheus in it, so those who had come in the Nova and the Mustang were abandoning those cars and leaving with the Kirklands.

So far, no one had seen her. She meant to change that.

The driver shifted gears. Catherine hoped Greg was having luck with the radio, but didn't dare look.

Instead, Catherine approached the vehicle, pointed her gun at the elder Kirkland's head, and tapped on the glass with the barrel. He sat behind the wheel. Six surprised faces swiveled toward her, an effect she might have found comedic under other circumstances.

"Cut the engine," she said.

Immediately, weapons were pointed her way, through the windows. She had known that would happen, had to stand her ground. Reinforcements, she hoped, would not be far behind. "You can shoot me," she said. "But not before I kill your leader."

"I'm nobody's leader," Steven Kirkland said. He thumbed the window button and it slid down. Offering her, she realized, an easier shot, if she needed to take it. "This is an organization of equals."

"But some are more equal than others, right? I've heard that song before."

"Lady." Troy Kirkland brandished a revolver from the seat beside his father. The rest, all men, were crammed into the backseat. "There's no way you get out of this alive, unless you drop that piece and run, right now. I'll give you 'til a count of three, then I blow your head off."

"I'm an officer of the Las Vegas Police Department, and I'm placing you all under arrest," Catherine said. Her calmness surprised even her. It was as if she had always known this moment was coming, and was utterly prepared for it. She didn't want it to end badly—she had a daughter who depended on her, and she had lost too many loved ones not to think that her death wouldn't hurt people—but she found that she wasn't afraid of it, either. She was, almost startlingly, at peace. "Come on, guys. Let's not make this any harder than it has to be. It's been a long night."

Troy Kirkland turned his head back toward the Empire construction, and that was the only warning Catherine had. She braced herself for almost anything—but when it came, the explosion caught her off-guard. A blinding fireball shot up through the center of the building, and the roar and the concussive wave hit at about the same time. Moving by instinct, but helped along by the sudden rush of nearly physical force, she flattened herself on the ground.

At the same instant, Troy Kirkland fired, and Steven Kirkland stomped on the accelerator. Troy's round sailed above Catherine. She didn't lose her grip on her weapon, and as the Mercedes started pulling away, she went up on her elbows, steadied the gun, and fired. With five shots, she took out three tires. The SUV lurched and skidded as its tires shredded against the blacktop and its rims kicked up sparks.

Heat billowed across Catherine. She couldn't allow herself to wonder about Lou and Brass and the others, didn't dare rip her focus away from the SUV.

The vehicle's doors swung open. One of the people in the backseat jumped out first. He pointed his gun in Catherine's general vicinity and squeezed off a shot, even as he started running in the other direction. Catherine rolled to her left and the round struck the pavement a few feet away.

The Kirklands bailed out of the front seats. Catherine caught only the briefest glimpse of them; the SUV had stopped at an angle that prevented her from drawing a bead on either one. She went up on one knee, then stood, aiming over the vehicle's hood.

"Freeze!" a voice called from behind her. Greg? She risked a quick look back. Greg was running toward her, but it wasn't him. It was Vartann, another twenty paces back but gaining fast. Behind him came Jim Brass and several SWAT officers. Catherine allowed herself a moment's rush of relief, but then the Free Citizens were firing at the cops, and the police were shooting back. The man who had shot at her went down first. Another one from the backseat was hit and spun in an awkward pirouette, spraying blood. When Steven Kirkland's right knee erupted in a fountain of blood and tissue, Troy threw himself down at his father's side.

The shooting stopped. The remaining Free Citizens put their weapons on the pavement and raised their hands. Troy Kirkland held his father's head and shoulders on his lap, his legs crossed to support the old man. The first rays of the rising sun glistened on his tear-damp cheeks.

"It's over, Kirkland," Brass announced. His gravelly voice had never sounded so sweet to Catherine's ears. "You're under arrest, and so are your friends."

"You can't . . ." Troy said, his voice cracking so that he could barely force the words out. "You won't . . ."

"Won't what? Arrest you? Too late."

Troy raised the revolver he had pointed at Catherine. She tensed, ready to fire. She knew Greg and Brass and Vartann were doing the same, and no doubt the SWAT officers were as well.

As if he knew he was beaten, Troy lowered the gun again.

But when the barrel was in line with his father's skull, his hand stopped. Catherine attributed it, for an instant, to disorientation and grief. By the time she realized what he was doing and her finger started to tighten on her trigger, it was too late.

Troy Kirkland's gun boomed.

His father's head exploded, skull fragments and brain matter spraying the parking lot, mixed with a fine, bloody mist. The old man's feet drummed against the pavement for a long, ghastly moment, and then went still. Troy continued to clutch his father, holding him close, sobbing loudly. He released the revolver, which clattered to the ground beside him. When Brass grabbed his arms and twisted them behind his back, he didn't resist. His father's corpse slid from his lap onto the ground as Brass forced him to his feet.

"I don't get you," Brass said. "That was your father."

"That's exactly it," Troy said. "I loved him—loved him too much to see him surrender to you. That's one indignity he'll never suffer. I had to spare him from that. He'll be a martyr for the cause. He hated you—hated everything you stand for—and I just couldn't . . . I couldn't . . ."

His voice gave out, and whatever composure he had managed fled. He bent forward, almost double, the sobs coming furiously, only Jim's strong arms holding him up.

"At least his convictions seem to be real," Greg said softly. He had come to a stop beside Catherine. "He really believes that his father's better off dead than under arrest."

"Because he doesn't accept the authority of those arresting him," Catherine suggested. "The thing is . . ."

"What?"

"For the old man, I don't think it was ever so much about the politics or the principles as it was about scamming his followers. The movement was just a front for his criminal activity. And the son? He bought into it, just like the rest of the so-called Free Citizens. He believed it down to the depths of his soul. Now he'll have a lifetime in prison to think it over. I wouldn't want to be around when he figures out the mistake he made."

33

STEPPING THROUGH THE hospital's sliding front doors, Garrett Kovash knew the day would be another scorcher. He donned his sunglasses before he left the overhang, and stood there for a moment, at the edge of the shade, scanning the driveway and the nearby parking area. A thousand daggers of sunlight reflected off windshields and chrome, and the heat radiating off cars and pavement shimmered the air. It was not yet nine in the morning. A scorcher, and then some.

He saw nothing out of the ordinary, so he nodded toward Bryan Donavan, sitting a hundred feet away in his Nissan, and Bryan rolled slowly forward. Kovash beckoned to Dennis Daniels and Maureen Cunningham, waiting in the air conditioning just beyond the doors. Maureen was on her feet, but Dennis sat in a hospital-provided wheelchair. Just through the door, he had insisted; he would walk after that. Kovash didn't see any press around—they had intentionally leaked word that

Daniels would be released later in the afternoon, just to throw them off. But Dennis didn't take chances. He didn't want to be photographed sitting in a chair, and in case one of those vehicles in the lot hid a photographer with a telephoto lens, Dennis planned to be on his feet.

Dennis looked pale and unsteady when he got out of the chair, but he didn't have far to travel. By the time he got to the curb, Bryan had pulled to an easy stop. Kovash opened the front door and Dennis got in, sweat filming his face. He wore jeans and a polo shirt with a light windbreaker over it. Kovash thought the windbreaker was a bit much, but Dennis had been in the hospital, and he was a guy who got cold easy at the best of times.

"Where's your ride, Ms. Cunningham?" Kovash asked. "There's room in the car."

"I talked to my husband a few minutes ago," she said. "He's on his way. It'll be fine."

"If you're sure."

"Go, get Dennis home. I know Joanna is anxious to see him."

"I'm certain you're right." He opened the back door of Donavan's Maxima, paused again. "You want us to wait?"

"Brett's only a few minutes away. Go on, don't worry about me. I'll see you there in a little while."

"I'm glad to see you on your feet, ma'am." Kovash slid into the backseat and shut the door. Blessedly cool air embraced him.

As they pulled away from the hospital grounds, Kovash put a hand on Dennis's shoulder. "Are you feeling all right, sir? You look a little wiped."

"I'm fine," Dennis said. "Better than fine. I mean, you know, a little weak, I guess, but I'm ready to go. We've got a business to run."

"According to the overnights, the publicity has been drawing a lot of eyeballs," Donavan said. "People are tuning in and staying tuned."

"Well, I'm glad to hear that, but I wouldn't want to go through that experience again to keep them coming," Dennis said. "I hope I never see an explosion again, at least, unless it's on a movie screen."

Kovash realized that Dennis probably hadn't heard about the Free Citizens' incident earlier that morning. He was about to say something when Donavan made an unexpected turn, and he remembered something Maureen had said back at the hospital. "Maureen said something about seeing us there. Is she coming to your place?"

"We're making a stop at the office first," Dennis said.

"I thought we were taking you home."

"Soon enough. I wanted to make sure everyone sees that I'm alive and well. I'm sure the employees will appreciate a couple of words from me."

"You really think that's a good idea?"

Dennis laughed. "Garrett, I'm still not sure it was a good idea to get into the TV business in the first place, and every year I've become even more convinced it was the stupidest thing I ever did. You can't ask *me* if anything is a good idea, because clearly I haven't got a clue."

"The troops will appreciate it," Donavan confirmed. "We don't need to stay long."

"So this is something you discussed with Maureen?"

"Just now, while we were waiting inside. She wants to swing by on her way home."

"Does anyone else know?"

"I called Bryan, so he knows. I thought we'd surprise the gang at the office."

"What about the police?"

"I've been assured that the protests have ended, since I've been in the hospital. They might start up again, now that I'm out, but not today—they'll have no way of knowing we're headed there."

Kovash didn't like being left out of the loop. He had expected them to go straight to Dennis's home. Joanna was waiting for them. She would worry if they were late. More important still, he had driven the route to the Daniels home, but not the route to the DCN building. He hadn't had a chance to check for any surprises planted along the way.

As it turned out, that concern was misplaced. Traffic was light, and no one in the other cars spared a second glance for the metallic green Maxima. The gate guards gave Dennis the thumbs-up as the car passed through. There were only a handful of vehicles in the front lot, and Donavan was able to park close by.

"You wait here," Kovash said when the car came to a stop. "I'll go in, make sure the coast is clear, then wave you in."

"Fine," Dennis said. "I can't wait 'til I can fire you, you know."

"I'm looking forward to that myself." When that day came, it would be because whoever had been threatening Dennis had been dealt with. Kovash didn't mind the work and he liked the paycheck, but there was always work for someone like him in Las Vegas. Most of it was more interesting than sitting around hospital rooms and business offices.

He got out of the car and crossed to the front door. When he opened it, one of the employees he had met before spotted him. She was short and a little on the pudgy side, but pretty, with shoulder-length brown hair and delightful green eyes. "Garrett!" she called. "If you're here, does that mean . . . ?"

"He's right outside, coming in now," Kovash said. "Everything copacetic in here?"

"You know it. I can't wait to see him."

Kovash tore his gaze away from her and gave the big lobby area a once-over. It was quiet, except for the soft music and the murmuring voices coming from the banks of TV monitors.

He was taking too long. Dennis Daniels was not a patient guy. Kovash turned and pushed open the front door. Dennis was already out of the car, walking toward the door. Donavan stood at his car door, watching.

And another car, big and black, was racing from the front lot, its engine giving off a furious growl. Kovash noted it but didn't pay it much attention until it swerved. Then he pawed at the Colt he wore under his left arm, and screamed toward Dennis.

Too late. The car slammed into Daniels. He rolled up onto the hood, smacked the windshield with one outflung arm, then sailed off, landing in a crumpled heap on the sidewalk. Kovash got his gun out and fired two shots after the black car, and one of the gate guards got off a single shot but it was already darting between the closing gates, leaving burned rubber in its wake.

* * *

Catherine and Greg had still been in the lab, answering questions about the events at the Empire, when the call came in. Catherine took it, then explained what had happened. "I can't ask you to work the scene, Greg," she said. "We both should have been home for hours at this point. But I'm going out there. If we missed something before, I want to find out what. Somebody's still got it in for Daniels, and we need to figure out who."

"You couldn't keep me away," Greg told her.

"Even if I told you Ecklie won't authorize any overtime, because he'd just as soon let day shift handle it?"

Greg's hesitation was only momentary. "Even if."

"Let's go, then."

Daniels had already returned to the hospital, once again traveling by ambulance, so Catherine sent Greg there to collect his clothing. The initial diagnosis was a broken hip and miscellaneous cuts and bruises—injuries that, compounding his previous set, would keep him off his feet for weeks, if not longer.

At the scene, she found day shift criminalists already at work, though there wasn't much to work with. One CSI was measuring and photographing tire marks in the road where the vehicle that had struck Daniels had escaped, the scuffing at their edges consistent with a car making a fast turn. The guards reported that the car was black or dark blue, though Kovash insisted it was black and American-made, a midsized Detroit sedan. He had fired two shots at it, but his rounds were found in the side of an adobe building on the next block. One guard's slug was buried in a power pole a quarter-mile away. The reporters had left when the demonstrations ended, so there was nobody videotaping the scene, and the cameras at the gates angled out toward the street. They showed only the briefest glimpse of the car as it rocketed away.

Satisfied that the day shift team would share any pertinent information, Catherine returned to the lab. Greg was in a layout room with Daniels's clothes: blue jeans shredded at the thighs and rubbed at the hip, and a windbreaker that showed the effects of him being thrown to the ground. Only his shirt was more or less intact, though spattered with blood.

"I took paint chips off the jeans," Greg told her. He looked tired, but not ready to fall down yet. "Black. Hodges is gone, but I gave them to Kennan, a day shift trace tech."

Catherine studied the rubbed places on the jeans while Greg examined the windbreaker with a high-powered magnifying glass. "My guess is that when we do find the car, we'll find fibers from these jeans embedded in the paint."

"You think he was hit that hard?"

"Pretty hard," she said. "When he rolled up and onto the hood, the friction would have literally softened the paint, causing it to grip and hold onto those fibers."

"Well, that'll help confirm. That and the paint chips."

"Right."

"Well, look at this." Greg lifted something off the windbreaker with tweezers.

"What is it?"

He held up three blond hairs for Catherine to see.

"Where were those?"

"Right under the collar."

"Daniels doesn't have blond hair. Or hair that long."

"That other woman who was in the hospital with him does. His administrative assistant."

"Maureen Cunningham. She was released today, too."

"Maybe she hugged him before they left."

"Maybe." She took out her phone and dialed campaign headquarters. In a minute, she was talking to Bryan Donavan. "You picked Daniels up this morning, right?"

"That's right. Him and Kovash. I waited down the way while Kovash scoped the scene, and when he waved me in, I pulled up in front of the doors."

"And Daniels?"

"He waited inside until Kovash gave him the high sign. Then Maureen wheeled him out."

"In a chair?"

"Right. Once he was over the threshold, he stopped and got out and walked to the car. If anyone was watching, he wanted to be seen making the trip under his own power."

"Did Maureen or anyone else embrace him, that you saw?"

"No," Donavan said quickly. "She just stood behind the chair. Kovash talked to her for a minute, trying to make sure she had a ride coming."

"Her ride wasn't there?"

"She was going home with Brett, her husband. But he hadn't shown up yet."

"Mr. Donavan, I'm going to ask you a difficult question. Before I do, I'll remind you that I have no particular interest in the answer one way or another—the only thing I want is to find out who's been after Daniels. Do you understand that?"

He was silent for a moment. She heard him swallow. "Yes, I guess so."

"Mr. Donavan, do you have any knowledge of anything internal at the company that I should know about? Any personal issues regarding Mr. Daniels?"

"Do you have a reason to think there might be any?"

When Catherine heard his answer, she recognized his value to his employer. It was a nearly perfect political evasion.

She, however, was no politician.

"Mr. Donavan, if he's screwing around with someone, I need to know about it. We should have been told already. If the withholding of that information further endangers his life, I'll have to make that known."

Another long moment of silence from the other end. Then she heard the smack of his lips coming apart. "We all agreed to keep it quiet," he said. "We don't even talk about it amongst ourselves, very much. Just enough to do whatever damage control is necessary."

"Tell me. It's very important."

"It sounds like you already know. Dennis and Maureen. They've been at it hot and heavy for months now. It's terrifying. This kind of thing almost never ends well. Especially when one of the parties has a lot of money, and possible political ambitions."

"Did anyone talk to him about it? Let him know you knew?"

"A few of us did. He said he didn't appreciate people butting into his private life. Because Maureen is who she is, nobody wanted to push the matter too hard. She has a lot of influence with him."

"I'll just bet she does," Catherine said.

From the corner of her eye, she saw someone hand Greg a printout, then walk away. "You really should have told us about this earlier, Mr. Donavan. Somebody should have. Lives could be at stake."

"I didn't think the attacks had anything to do with this. I thought it was those protesters."

"So did most people. Which means everyone was looking in the wrong direction. You're not in law enforcement, Mr. Donavan, so I don't expect you to understand. But withholding any kind of information from an investigation can be a very dangerous thing."

"I . . . I guess you're right. I'm sorry."

Greg held a sheet of paper before her, his index finger next to the finding of the trace examiner. Catherine scanned it and nodded. "One more thing, Mr. Donavan. Do you know anyone who drives a black Buick Lucerne, recent model?"

"Ummm . . . I think that's what Brett drives. Brett Cunningham. Some kind of Buick, anyway. He got it in the last couple of years."

"That's Maureen's husband?"

"Yeah. He's not associated with the company, but—"

"But his wife is having a not-so-secret affair with Dennis Daniels. Thanks, Mr. Donavan." She hung up before he could offer any more justifications for his previous lack of assistance.

"Maureen's husband?" Greg asked.

Catherine held up a single finger, forestalling his questions. She had already punched Brass's number, and the line was ringing. He answered almost immediately.

"Jim," she said. "We need to get someone to Maureen Cunningham's residence, right away."

"Maureen who?" he asked. "Oh, Daniels's administrative assistant?"

"That's right. She and Daniels have been having an affair. Apparently it's not a big secret at the office. I think it's possible that Daniels wasn't the real target."

"What, Maureen?"

"Think about it. She was driving the second car, the night of the bombing. The bomb was on the driver's side of the road. Daniels always rode on the curb side, so he could get out quickly."

"He was hurt the worst."

"Only because the car flipped onto its side. An amateur bomber couldn't have predicted that."

"And if it detonated a few seconds too early . . ." Brass said.

"That's right. Another amateur mistake. Earl was certain this was no experienced bomber's work."

"I'm on my way," Brass said.

"Are you at home yet?"

"I'm about two minutes from the lab. I was on my way to pick up a report."

"I'll meet you in front."

She ended the call and turned to Greg.

"I'm coming, too," he said.

"Are you sure? You look like you need some sleep."

"That makes two of us, Catherine. I'm as involved in this one as you are. I want to see it through."

"No overtime."

"I know. That's okay."

"Well, no. It's not. But it's the way it is."

"Things are tough all over. Come on, we'd better get outside before Brass gets here."

34

"BRETT CUNNINGHAM DIDN'T go to the event that night, did he?" Greg asked on the way.

"No," Brass said. He was driving fast, lights and siren going. "He stayed home. But Maureen probably let him know when they were leaving. And by then she knew what route they would take."

"That's what I thought."

"And neither of them were at headquarters when that fire was set," Catherine said. En route, she had called the day shift people who were out at the DCN building, and confirmed that the wheelbase measurement as indicated by the tire marks matched the 115.6 inches of a 2008 Buick Lucerne, which was the car registered in Brett Cunningham's name. Brass had made a call of his own at the same time, asking that any available patrol units be dispatched to the Cunningham house. "But that was a nuisance fire, not a serious effort to hurt anyone."

"So you think Cunningham was just harassing Daniels," Brass said.

"He knew he couldn't get at either one of them in the hospital. Dennis and Maureen spent most of their time together in Daniels's room—which must have burned him up. But Garrett Kovash was there most of the time, and even when he wasn't, there was a cop right outside the door. Brett could be in the room with them—"

Greg interrupted. "He was there when I went by."

"—but he couldn't make a move. Not and get away with it."

"So he took his rage out on the building," Brass said. "By lighting a fire."

"That's what I think. I believe he was hoping the demonstrations would give him cover, deflect suspicion."

"It almost worked," Greg said. "Almost."

"Their place is on the next block," Brass told them. They were tearing down a wide, gently curving residential street, in a development with mature desert landscaping between the houses, which were fronted by gravel yards instead of grass ones. Las Vegas had made a concerted effort to eliminate grass lawns, which Catherine was sure this place had when it was built. "I go in first."

"Last time you went in someplace first," Catherine said, "you almost got blown up."

"I don't think I ever thanked you for that, Greg. Your warning came just in time."

"I'm just glad you were all able to get out."

"A couple of the SWAT guys had some minor

injuries. Ringing in the ears, a few scrapes from debris or from being knocked down. We were still pretty close when it went off. The Free Citizens were better bomb makers than Brett Cunningham, but not good enough to kill us once we were away from the building."

"Would have been a hell of a statement, if they had," Catherine said.

"That was the idea, I'm sure. Lure a bunch of cops into the place and bring it down on top of them. Declare open season on law enforcement. If it hadn't been for you two . . ."

"It was Greg," Catherine pointed out. "He was the one who figured it out."

"I only started to put it together," Greg argued. "You realized it was a trap."

"I owe you both a debt," Brass said. He killed the light and brought the car to a smooth halt outside a house. A black Buick Lucerne was parked in the driveway. No patrol units had arrived yet. "This is the place." He got out of the car, drawing his gun. "Stay behind me."

"Okay, Jim."

Brass went to the door and hammered on it. The windows were dark, but light glowed from deeper inside the house, showing faintly at the curtains. Brass pounded again.

"Nobody's answering."

Catherine was about to speak when she heard what at first sounded like an echo of Brass's knocking. But it was accompanied by a distant, high-pitched shriek. "There we go," Brass said. He tried the knob, which opened at his touch.

Inside, the house was mostly dark. Lights blazed upstairs, and the pounding sound continued from up there. Brass took the stairs three at a time, Catherine keeping pace right behind him, Greg at the rear.

The light came from a master bedroom, off the upper landing. Every light in the room was on. Brett Cunningham was standing in front of a door, which no doubt led to a master bath. His shirt was torn at the collar, a couple of buttons ripped off, and he had a kitchen knife in his right hand. The blade was six inches long and the edge looked keen.

"Drop that, Cunningham," Brass said, training his gun on the man. "You don't want to push me."

"You don't know what she's done," Cunningham said.

"Actually, I think we do. I know how you feel, man. But this isn't the way."

"She betrayed me!" Cunningham said. There was a wildness in his eyes Catherine hadn't seen before. She wondered what had made him snap. Had Maureen said something to him, before she and Daniels left the hospital? Told him about the affair, maybe claimed the marriage was over?

"Brett," she said, keeping her voice level. She approached him, moving slowly, working her way around Brass but careful not to come between Cunningham and Brass's gun. "I understand that you're hurting. We can work this out. It's a crappy situation, but there's a way out of it. As long as you haven't really hurt anybody yet . . ."

"That bastard Daniels. I hit him with my car."

"We know," Brass said. "Broke his hip, that's all.

He'll be okay. Nobody's dead because of you. The rest of this . . . you know, a jury's going to be sympathetic. Because of what they did."

Brett Cunningham's eyes were rimmed with red. His light hair, neatly combed the first time Catherine had seen him, looked like he'd styled it in a wind tunnel. He was unshaven, and he reeked of sweat and fear. He probably hadn't had a good night's sleep in days, if not weeks.

She took another few steps closer. "Give me the knife, Brett. We'll get Maureen out of there and we'll all talk about it. You okay in there, Maureen?"

"That maniac tried to kill me!" Maureen shouted from the other side of the door.

"We're going to straighten it out," Catherine promised. Heated rhetoric wasn't going to defuse the situation. She thought Brett was cracking, though. She took another step, put out her hand. "Come on, Brett. Just give me the knife and it'll all be over."

"It's already over," Brett said. His mouth dropped open, spittle flecking his lips, and he lunged at Catherine. She moved back but the bed was a few steps behind her, she wasn't certain where. If that blade reached her—

A gunshot rang out. She'd be hearing it for the rest of the day, and then some. Brass stood calmly where he had been, smoke drifting from the barrel of his weapon. The slug tore into Brett's upper arm and passed through, chewing into the wall behind him. He dropped to his knees, the knife flying clear, blood pattering wetly onto thick carpeting.

"Brett?" Maureen called. She yanked open the

bathroom door. "Brett, are you—oh my God, you shot him!"

"He'll be fine," Brass said. "I just winged him."

"He was trying to stab Supervisor Willows," Greg said. "The captain had to do it. If he hadn't, I would have."

Maureen went to her knees, wrapping her arms around her husband. His blood soaked them both. Catherine tugged on a poly glove and picked up the knife, holding it behind her back, out of view of the damaged couple on the floor, the wife trying to staunch the flow from her husband's arm. She looked stricken, her face as blanched as his, the tears flowing from both of them and running together and joining with his blood in a sort of impromptu communion.

All Catherine could think was, if this had happened a few months ago, it might have made all the difference for them.

35

SINCE DENNIS DANIELS wasn't leaving his hospital room any time soon, he invited the Las Vegas press corps into his hospital room. He had asked Jim Brass, Louis Vartann, Catherine Willows, and Greg Sanders to join him and his wife there. They stood beside him for a round of photographs, then moved, strobes still burned into their eyes, to the far wall so Daniels could give his statement with only Joanna at his bedside. From what Catherine had seen in the news, the swell of public opinion had moved steadily in his favor since the attacks began.

"I've asked you here today because I have a few things to say to the people of Nevada," Daniels began. Pillows behind his back propped him up, and he offered a broad smile. TV cameras were rolling and print reporters had microphones and digital recorders held out toward him. "And clearly I can't get around and speak to everybody one-on-one, as I'd prefer to do. Nor will the hospital allow me to invite every citizen of America's greatest state into my room. So I'll have to say my piece through you folks, through the media, and trust that the message will get out there. I think I've got a pretty good handle on how the media works.

"Here's the thing. I've been less than a hundred percent honest, with you and perhaps more importantly, with my wife." He reached up, and Joanna took his hand. "I made a terrible mistake, and I broke a vow that I made on the day we married. I will spend the rest of my life trying to atone for that mistake. Joanna says she'll be by my side for those days, helping me follow the right course, and together we will work on our relationship with renewed vigor. Joanna is trying to forgive me, and I pray that she can do so. I pray, also, that you can do so, because bringing you the news every day has been the greatest honor of my life, and it's an honor I hope to continue."

Catherine figured the boost in his ratings had given him the freedom to admit to the affair. The truth would have come out anyway, since the attacks were all over the news and Brett Cunningham's arrest was already fueling speculation. Putting it out there in this way—with Joanna at his side—asking for forgiveness, was probably the best way to handle the situation. He might lose a few viewers, but he might not lose enough to counterbalance the support he had gained.

"I didn't just want to talk to you about my personal problems, however," Daniels continued. "I wanted to let you know, right up front, that I will not be running for governor, after all. I know some

of you will be disappointed by this decision, and
others will be ecstatic. Here's the thing, though. I'm
going to need to spend time with my wife, and time
with my co-workers, and a political campaign is just
too demanding for the time being. That said, I
haven't lost my interest in the political process, in
how we make decisions in this country. I'll keep
bringing you the news, and commenting on it when
I feel the need.

"You've no doubt heard about the attacks on me
and on my employees, attacks that injured—but fortunately, didn't kill—other members of my staff, as
well as put me in the bed you see me in now. Other
things have been happening, these past few days,
that you might not have looked at in this particular
context, so I'd like to take a minute to tie them together for you.

"Up on Mount Charleston, we had a terribly destructive forest fire that killed six of our brave first
responders. The person who started that fire has
been apprehended, and has admitted to his crime.
Here in Las Vegas, a criminal organization—an illegal alien smuggling ring—that had branched out
into other, even more violent crimes, targeting as
victims the most vulnerable among us, has been
broken up, its leadership arrested. A vicious feud
between some domestic extremist groups resulted in
murder, including the deaths of some brave police
officers, and an attempt to kill more in a spectacular
explosion.

"The common denominator here is that the police
department and the crime lab, some of the members
of which are represented here today, worked—

worked their tails off, to be quite blunt—to stop these criminals, to preserve the public safety, and to bring the evildoers to justice. They didn't give any consideration to the wealth or social status of the victims or the perpetrators. They didn't stop to ask themselves if they would personally be rewarded in any way. They did their jobs. That's what government does, when it's at it's best. It's responsive to the people—*all* the people. It is responsive in a way that is blind to class or color, to rich or poor, to—"

"If I hear one more campaign speech this year," Brass whispered, "I'm gonna lose my lunch."

"You and me both," Catherine said. "For a guy who's not running, he sure sounds like he's running."

"Let's get out of here," Vartann added. "While no one's looking at us."

"I'm in," Greg said. He was standing nearest the door. He slipped through it, followed by Catherine, then Vartann, and finally Brass. As Vartann had speculated, not a single reporter glanced their way. Joanna Daniels saw them leaving, and with the slightest nod of her head, encouraged their decision.

"You think he's gonna run anyway?" Greg asked once they had reached the safety of the elevator.

"Not this time. But next, when people have forgotten about the affair but remember that they felt sorry for him? Without a doubt," Brass said. "Some people were born to be politicians. He's one of them."

"His wife's awfully forgiving," Catherine noted.

"Some people were born to marry people like Daniels. They know what they're in for."

"He's an okay guy," Vartann said. "I mean, he's not perfect. But he's okay."

The elevator reached the ground floor, and Brass put his arm in front of the door to hold it while the others got out. "He'd better be. One more trip to the hospital, and he'll be holding the key to the Oval Office in a few years."

"You think so?" Catherine asked. Brass was wearing his most ferocious grin; she always had a hard time knowing whether or not he was joking when he did that. More often than not, he was deadly serious, but perpetually amused by the foibles of humankind.

"If nobody attacks him in the next six years, Catherine, I predict a skiing accident in his future. A cast on his leg, some old-fashioned wooden crutches—that, and a few million bucks from close personal friends, and we'll all be dancing at his inaugural ball."

"Except him," Greg said. "It's hard to dance with a cast and crutches."

Catherine reached the hospital's front door first. It slid open and she stepped out into the oven that Las Vegas had become. "I don't know about the rest of you, but I wish he'd already been elected. After this week, I could use a night on the town."

"After this week," Vartann said, "you deserve one. Just don't use taxpayer dollars for it. I'd hate to see those demonstrators show up outside the Crime Lab next."

Catherine laughed. The day was hot, the sun as bright as the strobes of the photographers upstairs, but she worked nights and sometimes felt like she and the sun were strangers to one another, each rising while the other slept, and the sunlight and warmth felt good on her skin, healing, somehow, burning away the cares that darkness brought. "You and me both, Lou," she said, resting her hand on his shoulder and enjoying that warmth, too, and the solidity of the man she touched. The rest of her week was already looking better. "You and me both."

ABOUT THE AUTHOR

JEFF MARIOTTE is the award-winning author of more than forty novels, including *CSI: Crime Scene Investigation—Brass in Pocket, CSI: Crime Scene Investigation—Blood Quantum, CSI: Miami—Right to Die*, horror trilogy *Missing White Girl, River Runs Red,* and *Cold Black Hearts* (all as Jeffrey J. Mariotte), *The Slab*, the *Dark Vengence* teen horror quartet, and others, as well as dozens of comic books, notably *Desperadoes* and *Zombie Cop*. He's a co-owner of specialty bookstore Mysterious Galaxy in San Diego, and lives in southeastern Arizona on the Flying M Ranch. For more information, please visit www.jeffmariotte.com.